HEARTBREAK AND OTHER ORGAN FAILURES

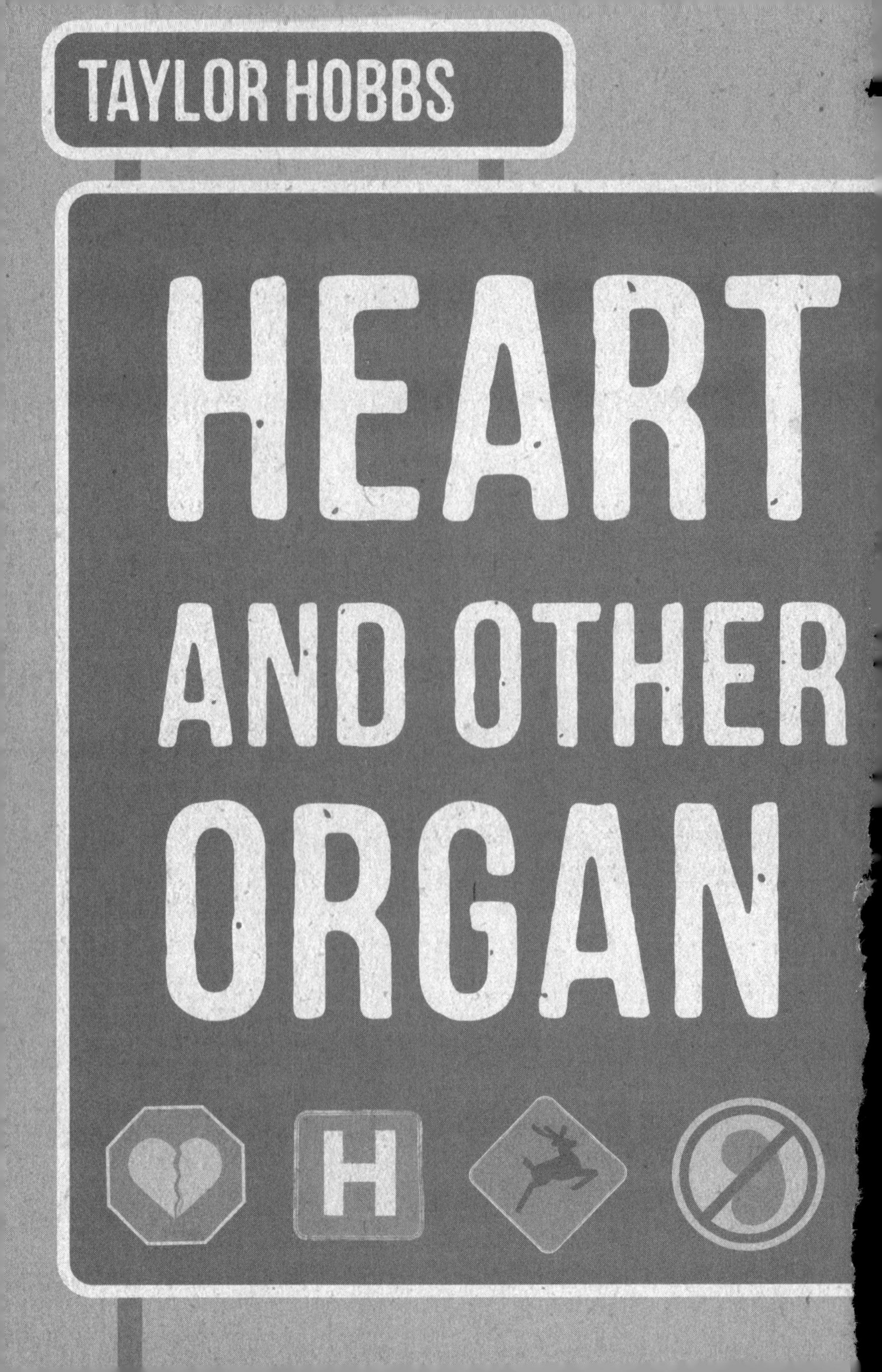
TAYLOR HOBBS
HEART
AND OTHER
ORGAN

BREAK FAILURES

A NOVEL

NORTON YOUNG READERS
AN IMPRINT OF W. W. NORTON & COMPANY
INDEPENDENT PUBLISHERS SINCE 1923

This is a work of fiction. All incidents and dialogue, and all characters with the exception of some well-known historical and public figures, are products of the author's imagination and are not to be construed as real. Where real-life historical or public figures appear, the situations, incidents, and dialogues concerning those persons are entirely fictional and are not intended to depict actual events or to change the entirely fictional nature of the work. In all other respects, any resemblance to persons living or dead is entirely coincidental.

Printed in the United States of America
First Edition

Manufacturing by Lakeside Book Company
Book design by Hana Anouk Nakamura
Production manager: Delaney Adams

ISBN 978-1-324-12483-2

W. W. Norton & Company, Inc., 500 Fifth Avenue, New York, NY 10110
www.wwnorton.com

W. W. Norton & Company Ltd., 15 Carlisle Street, London W1D 3BS

Authorized EU representative: EAS, Mustamäe tee 50, 10621 Tallinn, Estonia

10 9 8 7 6 5 4 3 2 1

For my sisters, Kendyl and Calley.
I am me because of you.

HEARTBREAK AND OTHER ORGAN FAILURES

CHAPTER ONE

I WIND UP, READY TO LAUNCH MY PHONE ACROSS THE ROOM, BUT I remember where I am at the last second and my fingers stutter. Instead of accidentally ramming straight into the dialysis machine, the phone ends up plopping to the ground about a foot from my chair, bouncing only once so the screen lies facedown on the pristine white tile floor. Look at me, I'm like a professional sportsball player. Plus, I'm saved from having to explain thousands of dollars in damaged medical equipment.

Zoey sits up when she hears the bang, all traces of a nap long gone. The headband holding back her long blond hair is barely hanging onto her head. "What?" she asks.

"Careful, don't tug on your tubes."

"What?" she asks again. My big sister is nothing if not persistent.

I sigh, not wanting to explain the entire story only to reach the end and hear her change the question to *Why?* I need to break the loop before it starts. Before I can think of a new distraction, my phone buzzes.

"Kaley, phone," Zoey says, pointing to it on the ground.

"It's okay, I'll answer it later."

"Kaley, phone. *Phone,*" she insists. Then it buzzes again, sending her to the next level of urgency. "Phone!"

While I usually benefit from her homing pigeon–like obsession with my phone, especially because I lose it at least once per day, right now I don't want to look at my messages. But Zoey knows I am tethered to it, and therefore it is of the utmost importance to her as well. She does not understand my flippant attitude.

Glaring at my phone while it's lying there so innocently, I dare Blake to text me one more time. Then he can fully take the blame for my sister's impending meltdown *and* my freshly terrible mood. Zoey stares at it from her robochair, the beeping monitors unable to break her laser focus. Knowing I have only seconds before she tries to take matters into her own hands, I push down my frustration and get to my feet with a groan. Mom is in an important meeting with Dr. Hayes right now, and if Zoey sends the nurses into a panic by lunging from her treatment chair, guess who will get the blame?

The screen glows when I snatch it up, but I can't look at the messages anymore. What else can he try to apologize for that he hasn't already covered? Looking forward to his visit was the only thing getting me through the start of this miserable school year, and now he can't come home until Thanksgiving? I already bought us matching Halloween costumes!

Not to mention he also promised Zoey he would come with us during our sister trick-or-treat tradition. It was bad enough her old costume didn't fit, and I've only just started to broach the subject of a new rainbow skirt, but now I have to change the plan on her again. Already this isn't going as either of us envisioned. I sit back down in my chair with a huff.

Everyone rolls their eyes when I say we are making long

distance work. It's not like I don't expect it to be *work*, but Blake is never one to overpromise and underdeliver. He is the king of grand gestures. Last year, when he asked me to his senior prom, he snuck into my bedroom while I was at Zoey's appointment and put hundreds of glowing stars spelling out *Prom?* on the ceiling over my bed. He calls me every night without fail, and texts me "Good morning, beautiful" when my alarm goes off. I refuse to believe a few weeks of Blake in college can shake the year of foundation we have built, but that doesn't mean I want to talk to him right this second.

Especially during Zoey's dialysis.

Zoey knows I'm upset. I close my eyes and inhale to the count of four, exhale, then do it again. Once I've safely locked my emotions away in the little box I carry inside my chest, I finally look her in the eyes and smile.

"Mom?" she asks.

"Still talking to Doc," I explain. Zoey sticks her tongue out at that. "Hey now, you be nice to him when he comes in. You know you're his favorite patient."

She shakes her head. "Not today."

I get where she's coming from. I wouldn't be a fan of the guy who hooks me up to a machine for a couple of hours either. On days when Zoey only goes for a checkup, though, I swear she is a model patient. "What, you don't want to flirt with the handsome doctor?"

"Nope."

"Well, I guess that means I can." I give her a wicked smile, and her eyes widen before she realizes I'm kidding. Still, I hope it is enough to check her attitude before Doc and Mom come back into the room. No matter the outcome of their conversation, it's always more helpful when Zoey feels like cooperating. I'm the best at getting her to go along with things.

My lap buzzes.

"Phone!" she shouts. Okay, we've come full circle. Deep breath again.

I'm saved when the door slams open and Mom storms in. Mom avoids the chair next to me and paces the small space between me and my sister. I should have left my phone down there for her to stomp on. At least that would have taken care of one problem.

But now my problem is no longer a problem because we have a *family* problem. Those are always more important, and Blake needs to leave my headspace so I can help us all deal with the issue at hand. Mom's heavy breathing signals to me that she's too angry to even speak. Zoey is frozen in her chair, eyes wide trying to process the extreme emotions in front of her. I don't move an inch from my seat, waiting to see what will ignite a nuclear situation.

Mom is never like this in front of us. I know before she opens her mouth what the test results say. She is not a donation match for Zoey.

This was *supposed* to be a no-brainer. Mom would be a match, and we would all move on with our lives. I'd go to college with my Prince Charming—although this title is currently up for debate as of five minutes ago—Zoey wouldn't be tethered to a dialysis chair for hours multiple times per week and stuck with the world's most boring diet, and Mom wouldn't have to bust her butt working to afford all the treatments anymore. We could—gasp!—leave town if we wanted to. A novel concept, one that is quickly getting the book thrown at it.

Doc strolls in, hands extended, *Grey's Anatomy* jawline set in a concerned grimace. The picture of reserved professionalism. Exactly the reason we trust him with Zoey. "Julie, please. Come back to my office, there is some more we can go over. Let's not do this in front of your daughters."

Mom whirls on her heel to face him. "More to go over? What more can we do? You already said no living donors under eighteen, either."

My head whips around and my gaze shoots from Mom to Doc, then back to Mom. Wait, she discussed me as a possible donor? Without asking? I mean, I would probably do it if I was a match. But that's not the point.

The point is, Mom had a plan. Now, for the first time in my life, I wonder if she doesn't have one.

Getting to my feet, I scootch around Mom to Zoey's side of the small room. My arm weaves through the wires and tubes and rests on my sister's shoulder. She doesn't acknowledge me, her rigid posture a sure sign that if Mom doesn't calm down, Zoey will make sure everyone remembers she is present.

I can already see how it will go. Zoey will let out an ear-piercing scream, followed by some trademark handwringing, a few flaps for good measure, an attempt at yanking out her cannulas, then a lightning-fast punch to my head when I try to stop her, one that I may or may not be able to dodge. We'll be stuck here for another two hours at least while she calms down enough to get hooked up again and finish this week's treatment, adding onto the forty-five-minute drive home. I still have an AP bio report to write tonight.

"Mom," I whisper-yell. "*Mom.*"

She stops her ranting and looks at us, hand coming up to her forehead when she realizes what she's doing. By the time she pulls it away, her mask is in place. A huge smile lights up her face when she leans over and kisses Zoey on the crown of her head. Then she does the same to me. "How rude of me! I came flying in here and didn't ask how my favorite girls were doing!"

I feel some of the tension leave Zoey's body, but I still don't think we're out of the woods yet. "We're fine," I say, well rehearsed with our script. I am always fine. There is no other answer to this question.

"Listen, I just need to chat a little more with Doc in the hallway before we go," Mom says.

"Home," Zoey says.

"In a bit. Can you be patient?"

Dr. Hayes speaks up. "I really think we should go back to my office—"

"Home."

"How about a book?" I suggest.

Mom looks at me gratefully. "There's a few early readers in my purse. I'll just be a sec."

She and Doc duck out of the room but stay just outside in the hallway. Mom won't go far from Zoey right now, and at least I'm not on my own for meltdown control. Their murmuring voices are calm, though I know Mom is anything but. I disentangle from Zoey and head to Mom's purse, which is sitting under a chair.

Digging through wrappers from hundred-calorie snack packs, I find two books. I linger there longer than I should, and just as I hoped, the private conversation carries. It's all information that Mom should eventually share with me anyway, but sometimes I prefer to get it straight from the source. Lately her information hasn't been reliable, and I find I don't appreciate the censorship. It's like she'll start to have an honest conversation with me about Zo, then remember it's a weekday morning and I'm heading off to school and suddenly she's lecturing me on my homework instead. It's about *my* big sister. Obviously it affects me too. Eavesdropping is simply proactive. I peek my head out and spy Mom and Doc down the hall.

". . . on the list as soon as possible," Dr. Hayes says.

"Don't talk to me about the list like I'm an idiot," Mom says, deadly calm. I can't help but wince, and know Doc is about to get his butt handed to him.

"We still have time. It's all procedure—"

"You know as well as I do about the medical bias. People with disabilities are at a lower tier for transplant considerations. All this BS assumption about quality of life is just an excuse for doctors to actively discriminate against my daughter and face no consequence—"

"Jules," he interrupts. "Don't jump too far ahead. There is still a chance Zoey's father is a match. Didn't you say he should be getting his results back this week as well?"

She crosses her arms and stares him down. Dad was just supposed to be the backup plan. We all assumed Mom would be the match and we could get this all figured out before I left for college next year. But I have to hand it to Doc Hayes, he's one of the few people who isn't scared by that look. If anything, he leans into it.

"And not one more word to Kaley about getting tested," he continues. "She is a child. Morally, I cannot put her in the position right now to wonder about the ramifications of being a match or not before she turns eighteen. From here on out we are operating under the assumption that—"

"Kaley!" Zoey shouts, and I jerk away from the doorframe. Her patience is about to run out, so I bring the books over to her and hold them up.

"Which one?" I ask.

She points to the pony one, which I knew she would, but I still have to ask every time anyway. The spine is so worn that it falls open in my hands. I've read this thing more times than I can count, and I don't even need to see the words to tell the story.

As I read aloud, I replay the conversation I just witnessed in my head. My mouth talks about a rainbow unicorn, but my mind is reeling. I don't know why I always assumed that if Zoey *had* to go on the transplant list, she would jump to the top of the list. Kind of like how we cut the lines at Disneyland.

I remember feeling so smug as we walked past the hourlong wait at Splash Mountain. *My sister is a VIP, everyone get out of our way!* She was special, and she brought me along with her, which made *me* special. The ride operator told Zoey and me to hop in the front, which almost sent Mom into a panic, but she and Dad accepted a spot right behind us. It was our last vacation as a family of four, and quite possibly the literal last time Dad had our backs.

Zoey squealed when we crested the top of the long, dark

tunnel and found daylight again. I saw the drop coming, and I snatched her hand into mine and squeezed, hard. We were falling, but together it didn't seem so scary.

From what Mom said to Doc, it sounds like not only is Zoey forbidden to cut the ride line, but she isn't even allowed into the kidney theme park. Ugh, gross. Kidney theme park? Maybe this is not the best metaphor.

Zoey closes her eyes while *The Tale of Princess Unicorn* washes over her. I pause at the end of chapter one, and her attention snaps back to me.

"Remember when we went to Disneyland?" Years before this all started. Before a simple strep infection turned our lives upside down with post-infectious renal failure. A different life from the one we've been living for the past fifteen months.

"Yes."

"Remember Splash Mountain?"

"Yes."

"We should go again someday. You, me, and Mom, when all of this is over."

"Yes. Zoey. Kaley. Mom." There's a long pause as she mentally relives the previous vacation. "No Dad."

"No Dad." Can't even fake a good time at the Happiest Place on Earth.

Actually, maybe Mom is underreacting about the whole kidney-match situation.

CHAPTER TWO

ZOEY LIES WITH HER HEAD IN MOM'S LAP ON THE BATHROOM FLOOR. Her mouth is wide open while Mom works the floss between each tooth, diligently, lovingly, but sometimes the gums can't help but bleed. Mom's hands move slowly, as if weighed down by the news we got today. Still, they must complete the nightly ritual, the same as it has been for the last nineteen years. Clip fingernails, take to the toilet, turn on the nightlight, tuck into bed. I try not to think of it as a tick-tick-ticking countdown for when Mom will be too old to do it anymore.

I step over them and snag a hairbrush off the counter, and my sister's eyes track me. Her silent question asks, *Where?*

"I'm going out. Birthday celebration at Beth's." I pull my hair into a tight ponytail and give my reflection a once-over.

My mother interrupts my critical inspection. "What time will you be back?" Throwing the floss away, she reaches for Zoey's toothbrush next. Tapping her jaw, she says, "Open up."

"It's Friday. So, by curfew." And not a minute sooner. Reaching down, I thrust my hand out and wait for Zoey to fist-bump me.

She grins through a mouthful of toothpaste. I can tell what she wants to say—*Hell yeah!* Her knuckles crash into mine. Tomorrow I'll return with tales of misspent youth that need to stretch large enough to encompass both of us. I can't think about the hospital anymore. I don't want to call Blake; I'm not ready for him to know. Mostly, I'm not ready to admit the facts out loud.

So, a kegger in the woods it is.

An impatient horn outside sends me running from the room, down the stairs, and into the star-filled night. Leah's ancient minivan idles in the driveway. She's been my ride-or-die since we were kids; her house is the quiet haven I escape to when things get to be too much. She just gets it, without me having to explain.

A few weeks ago, she wiped my tears after I said goodbye to Blake when he left for Oregon, and the time before that was after the trip Mom, Zoey, and I took last year to the group home a few towns over, "Just to see, now that Zoey is eighteen." I don't know which time I sobbed harder on Leah's front porch. Feeling my heart ripped out when Blake left was unbearable, but touring that group home was a deeper sort of agony. Zoey didn't even realize why we were there. We didn't get to speak to any of the residents. The staff, if they deserved the title, ushered us through a dingy, lifeless house then instructed Mom to fill out some paperwork. "There's a long waitlist," one of them warned. "Couple years, at least, but sometimes spots open up early if someone passes away. We'll let you know when you can drop her off," she said, gesturing to Zoey. I almost threw up. The three of us ran out of there as fast as we could, and I vowed to never look back.

I try the handle on the van's sliding door and it sticks a bit. With a groan, it finally rumbles open and the familiar faces of my small-town Idaho upbringing stare back at me, crammed cheek-to-cheek in the cramped space. Whoever isn't double buckled is sitting on the floor. Looks like I'm fulfilling my promise to ride and maybe die with my best friend after all.

The squad whoops as I throw myself onto the backseat floor of Leah's car, and I grin in return. It's my first time out since Blake left, and I feel a twinge of guilt at neglecting my friends. I shimmy into a spot next to Hannah as Leah peels out of my driveway. The van lurches violently and I pray the wheels stay bolted on.

"I couldn't believe it when Leah told us we were picking you up!" Hannah yells right in my ear.

I try not to wince at her enthusiasm. "Yeah, sorry I've been a little MIA."

"I'm just happy you're here," she says, squeezing my arm. "It's going to be a blast."

We're off like a rickety rocket, flying down the two-lane highway to the edge of town. All the windows are down, and the night air whips through the crowded car. Three other conversations are circling around me. The second and third rows of the minivan are filled with Leah's soccer teammates, most of them juniors who just look happy to be included. One of them, Melanie, yells, "Are we almost there yet? I'm too sore to hold myself up much longer!"

From my spot on the floor, she appears wedged sideways in the last row and braced against the car frame, her arm propped over little Amy's head, holding her body off the smallest girl on the team. From what I've seen of Amy on the field during the scrimmage last week, that girl probably threatened Melanie within an inch of her life not to squish her. Both girls are cracking up harder than when they heard the chant Zoey and I came up with to entertain ourselves at the practice game. We still might not understand the rules, but our role of heckling the not-Leah side, the blue team, was clear. Zoey decided that *zoo* was the perfect rhyme for *blue* and followed up the whole thing with an elephant trumpeting sound.

"It's not my fault!" Melanie yelps after we hit a particularly large pothole. "I *had* a spot!"

"Hey, I wasn't going to make my bestie sit back there with all you animals. Please." Leah punctuates her point with a foot on the gas.

"Why couldn't she sit up front?" Amy wheezes. Melanie is sprawled across the back row now, probably with an elbow in Amy's diaphragm.

"And where would we put the keg?" Hannah says, flipping her hair over her shoulder. "Safety first."

Leah lovingly pats the keg that's securely buckled in and riding shotgun. These younger kids have a lot to learn. "You should respect your elders," she says.

I've forgotten this feeling of delicious escape. Why don't I hang out with them more often? Lately it's just been me at home, waiting by the phone like some pathetic . . . I slap the pocket of my zip-up jacket and realize I forgot my phone. Crap. Blake is going to panic when I don't respond later and give him the full update. I can't ask Leah to turn around and go all the way back, we will have a riot on our hands.

As if reading my mind, Leah asks, "And how is the boyfriend doing?"

"Oh, fine." I'm not ready to admit to her that I'll be half a

Halloween costume. My tone gives it away, of course, and she sees right through me.

"That bad right now, huh?" She loves us together, I know, but she's worried I'm stretched too thin, no matter how many times I reassure her that he isn't going to break my heart. He's been my rock through this whole kidney debacle, even as we navigate this new territory doing long distance. It's like he can guess my deepest feelings, even when I'm too afraid to say them out loud, and he never, ever judges me for them.

Leah is more of an action girl rather than a deep-discussion friend. "I already had to put you back together before school started, and I'd rather not do it again." Nothing like a best friend for blunt honesty. No wonder she and Zoey get along so well. Sometimes it even feels like two against one at our sleepovers.

"Long distance getting the best of you?" Hannah asks, sincere sympathy in her tone.

"No." I exhale. "It's just that I was really looking forward to seeing him in a couple weeks, and now he says he can't make it home until Thanksgiving. Too busy with school and studying."

Hannah bites her bottom lip. "You know, my sister tried to hang on to her relationship after high school. He found someone else, but instead of breaking up, she said it was like a slow fadeout."

Leah jumps to my defense. "Oh, come on, Hannah. You know Blake. He's obsessed with Kaley. He's not going to ghost her the first month they're apart."

As for me, I've been obsessed with him since always. Okay, maybe not always, but definitely since the time he gave me and Zoey his fruit snacks at the lake. It was scorching that day, made even more uncomfortable by the fact I had one foot in childhood and another in adolescence, straddling the divide with unspeakable awkwardness and a bathing suit that didn't quite fit right. Every other family in town had the same idea Mom did to get the kids out of the house—although I doubt any other parents were trying to distract from the fact that their husband had just up and left the week before. We crammed a *lot* of activities into those first few days of denial. Still, despite Mom's best efforts, Zoey and I knew on some level what was going on.

I pretended I didn't. I tried to get Zoey to pretend as well and go along with the delusion, but the concept of lying was and still is a bit of a stretch for her. Plus, even back then she understood more than people gave her credit for.

"Dad home? Dad home soon? Dad home now?" she kept asking as we waded into the murky yet cool water. I kept a tight grip on her hand. All around us, kids splashed and shrieked their summer joy. I had been given strict instructions; we were not allowed to go past our knees, and I was not allowed to let go of Zoey. Neither one of us knew how to swim. Mom always said she would get around to signing us up for lessons, but when most days were filled with therapies—physical or behavioral—to keep our family from drowning, there was little time left for learning other survival skills.

I waved with my free hand at Leah and Beth, who had made it out onto the floating dock. They were busy showing off for some of the boys in our class by doing jump tricks into the water. They waved back but didn't swim over to us.

While I was distracted, I hadn't realized Zoey had pulled

down her bathing suit and was trying to squat on the water. "Potty," she announced. Everyone on the shore was witness to my sister's bare behind.

Embarrassment flooded me and I frantically tried to yank her back up. "No, Zoey!" I yelled. Tears of humiliation and anger filled my eyes. "You know better than that! We do potty at the potty!"

The chatter behind us stopped, and I heard someone call for my mom. "Julie? Julie!"

Mom had been deep in conversation with Leah's mother. The look on her face when she realized what was happening was more resigned than angry. She hurried over and yanked up Zoey's suit before plucking her from my grasp and hauling her over to the cement bathroom building near the parking lot.

I was left standing in the lake, unable to look over my shoulder and back at my friends who no doubt had witnessed the whole thing. A few of the moms were chuckling. "We've all been there," they said when she and Zoey got back, but it was just to make my mom feel better because I know for a fact their kids didn't do it as teenagers. I trudged over to where Mom had laid out our towels and slowly sat down, wishing I could just disappear.

A shadow fell over me and I looked up, squinting. Blake was standing there, holding out his hand. Two foil packets of fruit snacks rested there. An offering. "For you guys," he said.

"I'm okay," I insisted, unsure of accepting anything from him.

"You can be okay and still eat fruit snacks," he said. "I do it all the time."

I took them from his hand with a small smile of thanks. He

gave a funny salute then took off toward the water. I watched him swim with a freestyle stroke, his arms and torso much longer than the kids in my grade. He made it to the dock in record time.

Zoey appeared and sat down next to me. I opened and then handed her a snack pack without a word. Side by side, we ate fruit snacks and watched the dive show. Zoey gave everyone a perfect ten.

I gave one only to Blake. And he's proven time and time again since then just how much he deserves it.

"I keep telling myself we only have to get through one year of this," I say to my friends now. "Then I'll be there with him next year in Oregon." It's my mantra, really. *One year. One year.* And after my freshman year when I'm out of the dorms, he promised we would get an apartment off-campus and live together. He's going to be top of his class in his business program, and I'm going to figure out what the heck I'm majoring in.

Blake says he doesn't care what I choose, as long as I'm happy.

"Is that the only place you're applying?" Hannah asks. "I feel like you could get in anywhere you wanted to."

Before I can answer, the van hits another pothole and I'm launched two feet into the air. Slamming back down onto the questionable carpet, I yelp in pain, and the collective groans around me prove I'm not the only one rattled. The tires find gravel and slow, their crunch letting me know we're off the main road and heading into the woods now.

"Yeah." I cough. "Going to see if I can get in early decision too."

"If you're really planning on making this relationship work, and banking your whole college experience on it, I think you need to remind him what he's missing," Hannah says, voice low. "Don't let it slow-fade."

"Huh?" My head throbs. I think I collided with an armrest.

"If Blake can't come to you, you should find a way to go to him. Before it's too late."

Too late? Would there ever be an instance where I am too late? Hannah doesn't know Blake like I know Blake. He is the calm in the chaos that is my life. My fingers itch to text him that, but I can't. I'll do it first thing when I get home.

His cancellation is simply part of an adjustment period. We have to go with the flow and be a little flexible. We're both dealing with a lot. He's the one that suggested the pre-planned visits. Hell, he's the one who has planned out the next four years for us. One canceled visit is small potatoes.

My traitorous heart whispers, *But it's the first visit.*

Wherein my brain responds, *Shut up, it's not going to set the tone for the year. Dramatic, much?*

The van lurches to a halt and I climb out of the clown car on shaky legs with nine other people. My white sneakers land in the dirt. A glowing bonfire roars straight ahead, and the rhythm of the music blasting through a nearby speaker dares me to dance. Hannah, Leah, and the other girls are already on the move, drawn like moths to the flame—if there were a type of moth that knew how to drop it low. I physically can't, not with the anxious spiral in my brain threatening to drag me under.

Hannah turns and looks over her shoulder, finding me lagging. "Come on, Kaley!" She shimmies her shoulders, then pretends to catch and reel me in like a fish. Despite the cringy choreography, she still does the moves like a pro. I guess you don't get to be a cheerleader if you can't keep a beat. Winding back her imaginary rod, she looks like she's in for the fight of her life when I don't budge.

I'm more of a sit-on-the-sidelines-and-watch type of person. Dancing is a foreign language where the grammar rules seem to change with every song. My body does not cooperate under the best of circumstances, and the thought of my limbs flailing around for everyone to witness makes me want to curl up in a ball and squeeze my knees to my chest until I'm calm again.

Hannah's ex, Charlie, hops in front of me out of nowhere. "Reel me in, baby!" he shouts to Hannah, pretending to be caught on the hook. I know for a fact that he kept *her* on the hook all last year, until she wised up and dumped him. It makes zero sense that he could fail to realize that the sweet, bubbly brunette is quite the catch.

Hannah rolls her eyes and turns her back on him to throw the pretend fishing pole into the fire.

"I'll win you back," Charlie promises. "I think we might be meant for each other, Hannah. I just didn't know it until too late. You can't forget what we shared—"

"Believe me, Charlie, your dick wasn't all that memorable," Hannah calls over her shoulder.

A blush rises to my cheeks. They had sex? And Hannah is acting like it's no big deal! She doesn't even care that she just announced it to basically the entire senior class. Blake and I still haven't—I mean, I like doing *things* with him—

A red cup is thrust under my nose. "Gah!" I say, and jump.

A familiar face smiles. "Looks like you need this."

"I don't take drinks from strangers," I bite out. Declan doesn't pretend to be wounded; he simply rolls his eyes at my dramatics.

"Your mama taught you well," he says. "How is she doing? And Zoey?" Declan grins. I'm here to forget the hospital, not relive it, so I ignore his questions.

"You haven't texted me back in a week!" I admonish. "I asked if you were going to make it back for the party." Plucking the cup from his hands, I stare at his face, searching his features under the stubbly jaw and scruffy hair for a hint of remorse.

"Hey, I told my cousin I was coming. You two are attached at the hip. I figured Leah would pass the word along."

"I thought you'd chicken out," I admit. "But I guess you and Beth ended on good terms?"

"Am I ever on bad terms with anyone?" Declan asks. "Besides, she knows I can't be tamed."

"Or taken seriously." Declan is a tornado. Leah bet me he would end up arrested before graduating high school—he was in the class ahead of Blake's—but he shocked all of us, not only by sweet-talking himself out of some time in court but also getting into college by the skin of his teeth. She still owes me twenty bucks. He pops in from Boise State every once in a while to do laundry at his parents' house and check up on the "youths," as he insists on calling Leah and her friends.

Beth's voice pierces through my thoughts. "Declan!" she calls. "We need a knife to cut the cake!"

"Excuse me," he says with a wink. "Duty calls. Can't deny the birthday queen." He pulls a switchblade from his pocket like a murderous Boy Scout. I have to hand it to him, though, he is always prepared, no matter what the situation calls for.

This might have been the cause for my once-upon-a-time very, *very* brief lapse in judgment when I developed a crush on Declan. It was the summer before seventh grade, a season of experimental makeup, poor wardrobe choices, and deciding that "bad boys" were hot. I admitted it to Leah, and she didn't speak to me for three days.

Much to her relief and my surprise, this hormone-fueled mess resolved itself when Zoey and I caught him spray-painting penises on the brick wall near the library. Zoey pointed at his masterpiece and asked, "What's that?" I looked from her, to Declan, to the phallic mural, and decided this was not how my happily-ever-after scenario was *ever* going to play out. I rolled my eyes at him holding that stupid can of spray paint, grabbed Zo, and walked into story time.

Leah appears in time to sidestep the knife. "Watch where you're pointing that!" she demands, but Declan's already striding away across the party. Turning to me, she asks, "Want to be my pong partner?"

I take a big swig of my beer. It's awful. "Did you forget I have terrible hand-eye coordination?"

"Oh no, you mean you're not perfect all the time?" Leah asks. The smirk on her face lets me know she's kidding. "Contrary to your terrible opinion of yourself, I just wanted to have fun with you tonight. It doesn't matter if we lose."

"Well, it matters to *me*," I grumble.

Leah laughs and slings an arm over my shoulder, steering me

around the bonfire where the beer-pong table is set up. Hannah and Charlie face us on the other side, with Charlie looking triumphant at his choice of teammate and Hannah trying to look irritated but failing.

We're losing, both badly and quickly. Leah hands me all her cups to drink because she's the designated driver. Although, between the beer and the game, I haven't laughed this hard in months. The last time I almost peed my pants, it was because some rude man behind us in line at the grocery store was complaining about how loudly and grossly Zoey was eating a banana. "It's a public place, for chrissakes. Doesn't anyone have manners anymore?" Before I could put him in his place, Zoey opened her mouth to give him an up-close-and-personal peek at the mashed-up abomination inside and started walking toward him and groaning like a zombie. He backed up so fast his cart smashed into the endcap and sent magazines flying. I'd never seen a grown man so flustered as he sprinted toward the self-checkout. Even the cashier was cracking up, and she gave Zoey two stickers that day.

My head is spinning a bit now. "For my next trick," I announce, flinging the ball toward the mostly-intact triangle of cups. "Oops." It lands in the bonfire.

"Does that mean we win?" Hannah asks.

"Looks like it was headed that way regardless," Leah agrees.

"Celebratory kiss!" Charlie says, trying to pull his partner closer.

Hannah whacks him away. "Get off me."

Charlie heaves a long-suffering sigh and gives me a wounded-puppy look across the table. "Thanks for trying, Kaley.

You're such a good friend to give us this moment. Good to know you have my back."

"But I didn't—"

"Where are the extra pong balls?" Hannah calls out, rolling her eyes at Charlie. "Who's got some?"

Mr. Always-Prepared approaches the game table, a teasing glint in his eye. Reaching into his back pocket, Declan pulls out a spare pong ball for Leah's and my supposed comeback.

I consider him for a moment. "Do you happen to have a spare kidney in there too?"

He tosses the ball, and it lands in the front cup without even hitting the rim. Show-off.

"That counts for us! Our point," Leah says.

"Kaley—" Declan starts, and I know I've accidentally opened the door to the Land of Stuff I Don't Want to Talk About. The word *kidney* just sucked the air out of my lungs, like a hatch passcode that leads to outer space. Now it's going to be a whole thing, and it's going to bring the party down.

"Sub in for me, yeah? I just need a break." I'm able to brush past him and head toward the trees. Our shoulders touch for a moment, but my eyes stay trained on the ground as I slip into the dark, quiet forest. Treading softly, I can finally draw a full breath again when I'm by myself.

Glass shatters in the distance back at the bonfire. I instinctively duck, even though Zoey's meltdown at dinner was hours ago. All the emotional buildup from the hospital had to go somewhere, and it happened to manifest as a plate launched at my head while we ate Mom's famous lasagna. Before I know it, I'm running.

All the beer sloshes in my stomach, and I realize I'm acting like an idiot. I'm far enough away from the party now that I can't hear anyone else, and for a little while I can pretend to be lost. Leaning back against a tree, I slide to the ground and crane my neck upward for a glimpse of the stars. The enormity of the day hits me in flashes, with fears I cannot outrun or hide from.

My fingers find their way into my mouth and I chew my nails bloody.

My sister is sick. And we don't know when she is going to get better.

CHAPTER THREE

WHY WON'T YOU FIT? **THE FOURTH TIME IS THE CHARM WHEN I** successfully shove the spare key from under the mat into the lock and turn. Leah's van rumbles away once I have the door open, a much quieter exit than her arrival at my house five hours earlier. To her credit, Leah didn't ask me a single question about where I'd disappeared to during the party. "Let me know when you wanna leave," she said when I reemerged from the forest like a feral animal. "We can head out anytime." But I stayed until curfew to try to keep my promise to Zoey.

My heart hadn't been in it at first, but Declan made it his mission over the course of the evening to improve my hand-eye coordination and fulfill my dream of being on the winning pong team for once. Even when I started to get frustrated, he refused to sub in. "You got this! I believe in you!"

Hannah said it was a shame she had never managed to recruit Declan for the cheer squad. Declan had told her he only believed in things that mattered, then Charlie jumped to Hannah's defense of the football team, which somehow derailed into Charlie promising to quit the team to be on Hannah's cheer squad if she took him back. Leah ended the debate by starting the chant Zoey and I had made up at the soccer match and got the entire party to sing along with her.

Suffice it to say, I still lost, but I did manage to enjoy myself—and sink two cups in a row, a previously unheard-of level of success. Too bad this didn't translate to key-in-door technique. Maybe I should ask Declan if he has any advice for that.

My bed is calling my name while I kick off my filthy sneakers. Mom left a light on in the living room for me, like she always does. Before I stumble upstairs, I follow the warm glow down the hall. I'll have to shut it off and sprint back in the dark before the monsters can snap at my ankles, but I appreciate the gesture. It isn't her fault I did more than enough running tonight.

My feet refuse to skip over where the floor creaks. Whispering a silent curse, I trip in my socks again as I round the corner. It almost becomes a real curse when I realize I'm not the only one awake in the house right now. Mom is sitting on the couch, leaning forward with her face in her hands, shoulders shaking with inaudible sobs. Her spine curves, each vertebra prominent through the thin pajama top. Fragile. I don't want to shatter her. Because then she'll have to try to glue herself back together for me.

She's always had the answer. She's always in control. Everything that's ever been thrown at her, she's handled with steady grace. Nursing school? Do what you gotta do. Divorce? No problem. Handling the role of both parents for two daughters? The transition was seamless. Streamlined, even. I've never had doubts or wondered if she was making the right decision for us. We rarely fight—what good would rebelling against my family do? At the end of the day, it's the Larssen girls versus the world. With my version of rebellion, a few backwoods bonfires aren't going to change anything. I feel like it's probably more than Mom ever got.

If anyone needs to blow off some steam, it's her. This afternoon had really and truly *sucked.* But she'd tried her best to hold it all in. Keeping quiet and keeping her walls up. I wish I was as skilled at keeping my feelings in check, because sometimes it really does feel like both Zoey and I lack any sort of filter. Filters, in Zoey's case. Ha. Kidney humor.

But Mom's not laughing now. She's actually letting herself crack just a little bit, and I'd rather not interrupt anyone's mental breakdown if I can help it. I have full faith that she'll have a plan, and a plan B, and a plan C, plus all the contingencies come morning.

I back up down the hall until I'm at the front door again, opening it just to slam it shut before stomping up the stairs to my room. Smoke from the bonfire seeps from my clothes and I can't get them off soon enough, not bothering with the zipper on my hoodie and yanking off both it and my shirt all in one clumsy motion. My arms get stuck overhead, but I can't let go of my last piece of dignity and yell for help. After a good two minutes of struggle, I finally free myself. Off go my jeans, and I yank on an oversized shirt, but I still stink. It's in my hair and on my skin, branding me with a reminder of my attempt at escape. I'll deal with it in the morning.

The belly-flop onto my welcoming bed ends with a phone jammed into my boob. "Ow!" That's where I left it. The screen lights up with unread notifications. With bleary eyes, I try to make sense of the words, but my brain no longer functions. Probably a blessing at this point. I throw my phone toward the other end of the room to become tomorrow's problem, and much to my surprise, I succeed. There might actually be a dent in the drywall. Possible cracked screen aside, the pride at my aim turns to dread when I realize the sharp thud might have woken Zoey up and freaked her out. Rolling from my stomach back upright and to my feet makes my head spin, but I won't sleep until I know she's okay.

Just as I suspected, Zoey's eyes are open when I creep into her room. They glitter in the glow of her rainbow night light. The blankets are pulled up to her chin, and before she can scream, I whisper-yell, "Shh, shh! It's just me!"

There is no irritation on her face at being woken up in the middle of the night, only relief that I'm here with her. She gives me a huge smile and giggles. The sound is magnetic, pulling me to her side. "Can I sleep here with you tonight?"

She nods and scootches over. I climb in beside her and lie on my back, staring at the ceiling. There are no glowing words made from stars in here, just bright colors. "Story?" Zoey asks.

I promised her tales of misspent youth, but I'd done nothing to brag about tonight. "Not really," I say, rolling over on my side. A gentle hand touches my shoulder, and she starts humming, not a song I recognize, but a soothing rhythm just the same. A lullaby all her own, just for me.

I'm hungover the next day, but I don't even need to hide it from Mom because she's too preoccupied to notice. She didn't even raise an eyebrow when she found me in Zoey's bed this morning. All she said was, "Breakfast in five. Hurry up and get downstairs." The trek to the kitchen was miles long, but I made it, barely, staggering in like I finished last place in a marathon.

"Did your dad change his number?" Mom demands.

Sitting at the table and nursing my cup of coffee, I wince at the volume. Can't she see that I'm trying to piece my body back together?

"Not that I know of, but he hasn't called in, like, two weeks." Besides, Dad is not the phone call I'm avoiding this morning. I still haven't called Blake back.

"I've called him six times and left two voicemails!"

"You know he doesn't always get service at certain points in the park."

She fixes me with a glare. "That doesn't mean he gets to go off and be Smokey Bear without a plan for emergencies." Sniffing me, she continues. "Speaking of smoky—"

Instinctively, I lean back while hoping the bonfire stench covers up the leftover booze leaking through my pores. *Quick! Deflect!* "Did you tell him you aren't a match for Zoey?"

"I'm trying to," she says through clenched teeth. A muscle in her jaw twitches, and I'm worried she's going to crack a molar. Witnessing this side of her makes me wonder if I imagined the scene on the couch last night. This is Mom in action mode. The only problem is that she currently has nowhere to direct the energy, so it's building.

"I'm sure he'll get back to you soon," I say, still trying to keep the peace. Old habits are hard to break. It's not like I was able to keep things from blowing up between them anyway. I don't know why I defend him, when all he's done is run off to Crater Lake and get a job where he doesn't have to interact with *anybody*, including his own family. Must be nice to check out of real life and get lost in the woods instead. I mean, I did the same last night, but at least I came back.

My platitudes ricochet back when Mom turns her frustration on me. "We don't have time to wait, Kaley. I need to know what his test results are so we can make a plan."

The counter vibrates, and Mom snatches up her phone before either one of us registers that it doesn't say Will on the caller ID, it says Blake. Her face falls and she wordlessly hands the phone over to me and heads upstairs, no doubt going to get Zoey dressed for the day. It's Saturday, no doctors' appointments to attend, but we still need to follow my sister's routine.

I hit the Answer button. "Blake? Why are you calling my mom?"

"I've been trying to get a hold of you since yesterday, Kaley!" he says. "What happened? Are you okay? Is Zoey okay? Did you get bad news?"

What had I ever done to deserve this boy? Of course the only reason he can think of that I would ignore him all night is that something devastating happened. The worry in his voice hits me like a punch to the gut. He was probably up all night, despite telling me earlier he is overwhelmed and behind at school.

"Maturity and communication." That's what I tell people when they ask how we're making long distance work. I should have called him yesterday when we got home from the hospital, but I knew that Blake would jump straight to action mode and try to fix it for me, asking questions that I don't have answers to yet. I didn't have it in me to go around and around again, especially after listening to Mom panic all afternoon. I should have just told him I needed time to process and let loose, but a tiny, immature part of me was still mad that he bailed on the visit, and I kept putting off my text to him.

Obviously that was the wrong call.

But instead of fessing up about exactly where I was last night, I do an awful thing. I play the Zoey card.

"Yeah," I tell Blake. "We found out Mom isn't a match. Trying to figure out the next steps now, but it is overwhelming." It is the truth, technically. But a lie by omission, just the same. The half-truth evokes images of me spending the night consoling my family, phone lost under the wreckage that is my life. Blake will not assume that me being overwhelmed involved getting drunk at a birthday party in the middle of nowhere.

The Zoey card is basically a Get Out of Jail Free card. The move no one questions, because if they do they sort of look like a terrible person. It's one that can get me an extension on an assignment, leeway with adults in life, and an excuse for any questionable behavior. To be honest, I put up with a lot in my day-to-day. I shouldn't feel guilty about using one of my teeny-tiny perks of being a sib. But I've never used this card on Blake before. I've never had to.

"I wish you would have told me," Blake says, much calmer now. "I'm trying to be there for you." He doesn't seem to realize the bigger picture of this yet, and I can't bring myself to tell him that my plan for U of O early decision was contingent on Zoey getting Mom's kidney ASAP.

"I didn't want to freak you out." The truth.

"It's okay, you are spinning a lot of plates." It was pong balls, but close enough. "I just want to be sure that you're being cared for too." I could swoon. It's just the way he sees *me*, even when I'm trying to be perfect for everyone else, giving them the version of me that best fits whatever the situation calls for. I may carve a path of least resistance through life, smoothing it out so my sister won't stumble behind me, but I don't have to pretend when I'm around him. He picks me up when I'm the one who trips. He never falls. Steady. Reliable.

"I'm on Mom's phone right now. Can I call you later?" I say.

"I'll be in the deep, dark library pit with my study group." He needs to catch up on all the work he missed worrying about me yesterday. Cue my guilt at being a bad girlfriend. "But Riley usually gets service down there, in case of emergency. I'll text you her number."

Her? My throat tightens. This is the first time I'm hearing about what a good friend Riley must be, such a chill, cool girl to be fine with handing out her number so a hot-mess senior can call her boyfriend and pretty much continue to lie to him. "Okay. I love you," I say. That, at least, is not a lie.

"Love you too. Make sure you do your self-care. Go out for a walk. Take your vitamins. Remember your meditation!"

Even from far away, he's trying to look out for me. Psh. Hannah doesn't know what she's talking about. Slow fadeout, my butt. Would a boyfriend on his way out be acting like this? "I'll try," I promise, even as I get up to rifle through the pantry for some junk food, forgetting that we can't have any in the house right now.

"I just want what's best for my girl. I'll talk to you later and text you when I can."

After a few rounds of "No, *you* hang up!" I hang up, and before

I can catch my breath the phone rings again. "Mom, phone!" Yelling upstairs makes my head throb, but her boss is calling.

"Is it your dad?" Her voice is full of hope, and I have to squash it.

"No. It's Victoria."

She curses, then she's sprinting down the stairs to take the call, curling iron in hand even though her hair is stick-straight. She's mid-curl for Zoey, then. "Victoria!" Mom says. "Yes, yes, I'm here . . . Oh, I hope she feels better soon . . . until eight tonight? Well, all right . . . Yep, see you soon." Mom puts the phone down and turns to me, purple bags under her eyes telling me she is in no shape to work a ten-hour nursing shift at the hospital.

God, even when she does sleep, she probably dreams about that place. When she's not there for work, she's there for Zoey's treatment. Or therapies. Most of her life spent under fluorescent lights and freezing air conditioning. The insurance is worth it, Mom likes to remind me. We couldn't afford anything without it.

Accepting her fate, Mom pours herself another cup of coffee and straightens her spine. Then she hands me the still-hot curling iron. "At least a shift will distract me from your father," she says. "Kaley, I need you to—"

"Watch Zoey today," I finish for her. As if she forgot I've done this for the last five years. Except for the emergency times when Leah's grandma watches her if something pops up while I'm at school. I love Gran, she's the best. She calls me and Zoey her extra-special bonus grandchildren. I say it's because I'm extra and Zoey is special.

"That's my girl," Mom says, brushing my greasy hair out of my face. "There's leftovers in the fridge for dinner. Don't forget her three p.m. medications." Back to business as usual. If I hadn't seen her on the couch last night, I never would have suspected a thing. I kinda thought she might have come up with a plan by now, though. We're coming up on twenty-four hours since the news and I have yet to hear any viable options.

"Mom?" My voice wavers more than I'd like. "What are we gonna do?" Either Dad is not a match, and we're screwed, or Dad *is* a match but doesn't want to donate, and we're still screwed. Best-case scenario is that he is a match and is going to donate, and not telling us is some sort of sick joke.

"Get through today. We'll figure something out, I promise."

We. Like I have any clue what to do to fix this for Zoey. It's my job to be Mom's sounding board, and I'm getting suspicious that she's out of ideas. I want to strangle Dad for not calling her back and leaving us all in limbo.

A vision flashes through my mind of Mom hightailing it out of the hospital, a spare kidney shoved in her lunchbox. I wouldn't put it past her. Groaning, I say, "We're gonna end up on the five o'clock news tomorrow, aren't we?"

"Be good." Then she's gone.

Once the front door shuts, I need to go check on Zoey. I find her upstairs, sitting innocently in her room. "Hey, sweets. Oh, Mom did finish your hair! Looks cute." Good call not to leave Zoey unattended with the hot iron, though. "Listen, Mom had to go to work, and I need to take a shower. You'll be good for twenty minutes?"

Zoey nods.

"Want me to put on a show for you?" It's not that I don't trust her, but the likelihood of her getting into anything decreases by a lot when she hangs out with her favorite Saturday-morning cartoons. They're a great influence, especially on the magic of friendship. She shrugs, and I take that as a yes. Back downstairs I go, with Zoey in tow, get her settled on the couch, work the remote, then back upstairs to finally wash off last night. These stairs are quite a workout. Is this actual sweat? And does it smell like beer?

My dirty-blond hair takes forever to lather, rinse, and repeat, but it leaves time for my brain to wander. Hannah's words haunt me, playing on all my insecurities even though I know she's wrong. But maybe she's not completely incorrect. There's a reason everyone says high school relationships don't last, and maybe I've been an idiot by refusing to acknowledge the realistic difficulties of long distance. Maybe because I've been thinking about it as temporary, I've been downplaying the effects. We're only a few weeks in and he's canceling visits, and I'm already keeping stuff from him. Blake's the person I need to trust the most with the hard things, right? Is it me? Am I the problem? Oh God, am *I* doing a slow fadeout by being too preoccupied with my own problems, albeit accidentally?

I comb through my hair with my special conditioner that Mom thinks costs too much. When I watch the remnants of the woods spiral down the drain, with maybe even a leaf or two from my feral sprint through the trees, I feel a better version of myself emerge fresh and clean. If only my inner doubts could be scrubbed away so easily.

The water is starting to run cool by the time I'm done shaving my legs. Lost in my meditations about my own failings as a girlfriend, I must have been in there longer than I realized, or our hot water tank is about to fail. It's been on its way out for three years but still hanging on, so I'm assuming it's me. The handle turns off with a small squeak of protest and I'm reaching for the towel when I realize it feels quiet.

Too quiet.

Somewhere in this house, someone is absolutely up to no good. Except instead of a two-foot-tall child who can still be foiled by babyproofing, there is a five-foot-five person possessing adult strength with the same sense of toddler mischievousness and the single-minded focus to see a potentially dangerous plan through.

Working the towel over my body, I lose the internal debate on whether I have enough time to get dressed. Erring on the side of caution seems to be the best idea, and I wrap and secure the towel under my armpit. Did I lock the front and back doors earlier? I definitely did. This wasn't going to be a repeat of the Great Escape of 2018. My feet carry me out of the bathroom and hustle downstairs. Was Zoey trying to cook mac and cheese again? No, I could trust the fire alarm to go off.

My hand grabs the banister at the bottom of the staircase and I use the momentum to whip myself around the corner and halfway down the hallway. Even though I'm expecting it, the empty couch in front of the TV in the living room sends me into a panic. Pinkie the Unicorn is up on the screen, mocking me with her maniacal laughter.

"Zoey!" I call.

No answer. But I do hear a splash.

Yep. A splash. I'm not hallucinating, and it's coming from the laundry room. I hightail it across the kitchen, my steps turning into a cartoon-like slide before I get there. Barely managing to stay upright and waving my arms like an inflatable, my body crashes into the closed mudroom door. A giant puddle is leaking from underneath, and it is on its way to flooding the house.

I wrench it open. A shocked Zoey stares back, standing in an inch of water that is overflowing from a packed washing machine. It appears she found every piece of clothing in the house and crammed it in before pushing every button at once. Detergent crunches under my toes like sand. The completely empty cardboard Tide box is trying to dissolve on the floor next to the dryer.

"Don't. Move."

I try to take a step forward toward the washer. If I can get to the hoses behind the machine, I can twist them off before this gets any worse. My first two steps are successful, but my third takes me down. I fall. Hard. My towel loses its grip just as I do, and before I can blink I'm completely naked with a bruised butt sitting in Lavender Fresh floor water.

"Uh-oh!" Zoey says.

Bringing my knees up to my chest and burying my face in my hands, I let out an unearthly shriek. I even frighten myself. The urge to keep screaming overwhelms me, but I push it down. *Deep breaths. Lock it deep inside.*

Swallowing the bile in my throat, I crawl to my hands and knees, testing the surface before standing up. Next, I haul my slippery body up and over the machine and *bingo.* With a quick twist, the water stops flowing. My heartbeat thunders, worry and rage all at once.

"What the hell were you doing?!"

Zoey looks stricken, betrayed by my tone. I don't care. Mess aside, she could have gotten seriously hurt. Slipped and broken her leg. Or—just the thought makes me want to vomit—fallen, hit her head, and drowned in an inch of water.

"Twenty minutes!" I bellow. "That's all I asked for. Sit down, watch a show, and *don't wreck the house.*"

Tears well up in both our eyes. I can hardly see straight, but I have to get her out of the water first. I push forward, my feet sliding as if I'm on skates. This isn't safe. I don't trust myself to get us both through the puddle in one piece. When I finally reach Zoey, I plant my feet as best I can and use more strength than I knew I had to lift her up and place her butt on top of the dryer. The utility closet is within arm's reach now, and I open the door to grab the mop.

I shiver, naked and soaked, contemplating my life. Then I get started.

CHAPTER FOUR

"SORRY, KALEY." ZOEY LEANS HER HEAD ON MY SHOULDER, AND WE stare out at the backyard. I'm dressed in an old pair of sweats and a T-shirt that Zoey didn't get her hands on from the back of my dresser, so at least I'm not putting on a show for the neighbors. Everything else, though, looks like it has been through a monsoon. A rainbow of clothes is strewn across the lawn chairs, porch furniture, rickety playset, and back fence. It all flutters a bit in the breeze. Sun warms my face but there is a bite in the air that says fall is truly here in the Pacific Northwest.

I know I should tell Zoey I forgive her, but I can't just yet. "I told you to watch a show. What part of that sounds like do laundry?" My sister has never attempted to do laundry in her life. Why today, of all days? Did she think inhaling soap fumes would cure my headache?

"Help," she says, shrugging her shoulders.

I digest the response for a beat, turning over her answer as if holding it in my hands and examining it from all angles. Sometimes it's an issue with my question. Other times, it takes me a while to see the perspective she's coming from. But my patience is used up, and I fling the answer back to her without usual consideration.

"How is trying to flood the house helping?"

She sits up straight, and my shoulder is both lighter and colder. Looking me straight in the face, I catch a flash of hurt cross her features. A face with rosy cheeks and smooth skin I would kill for—this girl has never had a pimple in her life. Then she leans forward and gives a dramatic sniff. "You stink," she informs me.

"Well, it's not *my* fault I smell like lavender on steroids—"

She cuts me off. "No."

I'll never admit it to her, but a small part of me loves it when we bicker like Leah and her family. Maddening as it is, I feel proud of her when she can hold her own. For the briefest second, I let myself imagine that after we are done fighting, my big sister will drive me to the mall and we can spend the rest of the day shopping for new clothes while she tells me the latest makeup trends. Then we will go out for coffee, and I'll tell her all about what's going on with me and Blake while she gives sage advice about boyfriends.

Instead, Zoey yanks a piece of my wet hair and forces my attention to where she's pointing. My outfit from last night lies drying on the grass. "You *stink*," she emphasizes.

Oh. Oh! "I stank from last night," I realize. "You knew I didn't feel well and were trying to help me out today." Now I feel like an idiot.

"Stink."

I don't know if she's reiterating her point or calling me a stinker for not getting it sooner. "You're right on all counts," I concede. "But next time, you need to ask me first for help. No surprises."

She looks away, avoiding my eyes. She's either embarrassed

or processing. When she fully turns her back to me and crosses her arms, I know it's the former.

Sighing, I say, "It's fine. I forgive you." Zoey doesn't budge. "Wait, now you're mad at *me*? How does this track?" Still, nothing. Then, I offer my olive branch that I know she won't be able to resist taking: "How about I show you how to do the laundry?"

Slowly, she turns and gives me a big grin. Then I take my nineteen-year-old sister inside and give her step-by-step instructions on how to run a wash cycle. She gives me a hug and says she loves me. I make her promise again not to try it without me.

An alarm goes off on my phone. I can hear it, but I can't find it. Walking from the laundry room through the freshly mopped kitchen, I glance at the oven clock to find it's already three p.m. Where did the day go? Crap, Zoey's blood-pressure medication.

She has followed me into the kitchen and is glued to my right hip. "Kaley, phone."

"Yeah, I know." I grab the pill bottle on the counter and empty her dosage into my hand. "Here, take this first, then you can go find it for me."

Usually there's some form of protest to go along with swallowing the yucky pills, but she's already focusing on the hunt and downs the medication before she's off to find the origin of the now earsplitting alarm. Out of sight, I hear her feet stop on the stairs halfway up and then she comes back down. A vague memory surfaces of kicking something hard as I sprinted out of the bathroom earlier. I must have punted my phone down the stairs. Poor thing. At least the alarm still works.

Zoey returns my precious to me with a smug smile, content with a job well done. "Thanks, sweets." I cancel the alarm and at least ten notifications pop up on the screen. Instagram. Snapchat. Missed calls. Voicemails.

Blake, from last night and this morning. *Good morning, beautiful,* and *Goodnight, gorgeous. Checking in. Love you. How was the appointment?* Having talked it out with him already, I leave those alone for now and check my social media. @bananahan tagged me in two photos. The caption reads, *Getting our balls wet.* I'm half-turned from the camera, laughing at something Leah is saying while we stand at the beer-pong table, and despite the poor lighting, it is still clearly me. Underneath in the comments, @Let_them_eat_Blake wrote, *Looks like fun! When was this?*

@bananahan: *Last night! Sorry you had to miss. Bet your college friends aren't as cool as us!*

My breath leaves my lungs in a whoosh. The world tilts underneath me as I check the timing on the missed calls. Three last night, two earlier this morning, and one just an hour ago. I have to explain. Before I can call him back, a text pops up.

We need to talk.

What does this mean? Zoey's eyes are on me right now, and I've already blown up once today. Focusing on her face instead of Blake's text helps the tunnel vision clear and quiets the roaring in my ears. She needs an *organ.* I'm having relationship drama of my own making. Perspective.

Mom and I tell her what she needs to know about her disease, but I'm not sure how much she understands other than the routine and the mechanics of her treatment. The scope of her medical issues is hard for her to wrap her brain around. But I bet if I told her about Blake's text, she would be more enraged about my shaky relationship status than about her lack of donor. She's never met her kidneys, but she does know Blake. It's just that simple to her. Zoey is always on my side. I try to be the sister she believes me to be and hold it together.

Finger shaking, I press the Call button. Blake answers on the first ring. "Hey, Kaley." Is his tone off? Why does he sound so serious?

Hi, Blake seems too formal; *Hey, babe* makes it seem like I don't respect the gravity of my lies. "Hey," I squeak. It's all I can get out anyway.

He sighs. "I'm sorry," he says.

"What?" What on earth is he sorry for?

"I know that me canceling our Halloween weekend must have been terrible news at the same time you found out about your mom not being a match. I didn't mean to pile everything on you at once, and make you feel like you couldn't tell me things. You deserve to be able to take your mind off the stress any way you want. I'm *glad* you had support from your friends, and I hope the party helped. I just want you to know that I'm here for you. *Always*. I just wish you would let me in a bit more. I don't want to fade into the background during the hard times."

Friggin' Hannah and this slow-fade nonsense! I feel about one inch tall. "Blake, *no*. I shouldn't have been so sketchy about last night. I promise, nothing happened, I just got beer drunk with the usual crew. You were waiting around to talk to me, and I blew you off for a party and I shouldn't have. I feel like the worst girlfriend—"

"Kaley," he interrupts. "We're fine. I just needed to talk to you to let you know it's okay. Your sister and this situation put a lot of stress on you; it's never your fault. We're figuring out this temporary stage in our relationship as we go, right?"

I swallow back the lump in my throat. "Right," I croak. His ready forgiveness only makes me feel worse about my behavior. Somehow this morning, I've gone from being mad that he can't come visit to questioning if I'm accepting the reality of long distance, to finally this desperate need to prove just how much I love him. "You are not slow fade. You are surround-sound Technicolor on fast-forward."

"I take it that's a good thing?"

"The best," I assure him, wishing more than anything it wasn't just words.

"Talk soon, babe?"

"Of course. I'll be here." Stuck. Watching everything fall apart. "I love you. Bye."

It's more than the guilt that I've treated him like crap for the past twenty-four hours. These traitorous doubts and anxieties that have been whispering in my head since last night *can't* win. I need to shut them up for good before I self-sabotage this whole thing. If I don't act fast, they're going to get louder.

I need to find some way to get to him, reassure him that despite everything going on around me, he is still a priority. As of yesterday, Zoey's situation is only becoming more complex. Friday-night bonfires and new study-buddy friends are kid stuff compared to what we'll face this year. I owe it to him to talk it out together, in person, and plan as a *team*. Like adults. Blake will see just how strongly I'm factoring him into *our* future together.

Unfortunately, my newfound mature mindset does not come with adult funds, or a car. Mom would never agree to a spontaneous visit out there. He's nine hours away, and we are in the middle of a crisis. But dammit, *I'm* having a crisis too. Could I convince her that I needed to do a college tour there? No, she'd see through that in a second and she'd never let me borrow the car.

But maybe I can solve everyone's problems at once.

My half-formed, detergent-addled thoughts try desperately to coalesce. As of this morning, the plan for Zoey if Dad doesn't cooperate will either involve Mom in a high-speed chase with a lunchbox kidney, or me with a stroke of brilliance wherein I upend the entire medical community bias and enable Zoey to cut the general transplant line. Let's get real. Despite inhaling a lot of fumes, I don't believe either of those will work.

Then, an idea hits me upside the head like Zoey on a bad day. Why don't I just volunteer to drive out to Oregon, drag Dad from his hiding place, and then demand his kidney in person? He can't ignore my face like he can a phone call. And since I'm already out there, I'll swing by U of O campus to *prove* to Blake how much I love him with more than just words, if you know what I mean, and then victory lap on back as Zoey's hero.

I'm not supposed to call Mom at work unless it's a real emergency. Therefore, the speed at which she picks up the phone at the nurses' station is quite expected. After assuring her that Zoey is okay, her first question is, "Did you hear from your dad?"

"Not yet," I tell her. "But listen. I have an idea. Tomorrow morning, I'll drive out there and just talk to him in person. Get a real answer and plan for Zoey. I'll fix it for you and be back in a few days." After pulling off a grand gesture of '90s rom-com proportions at my boyfriend's dorm room, of course. And having my first sleepover with a boy.

"A few days?" Mom asks. "Why would you need a few days?"

Her initial answer is not a no. I exhale with relief. This could actually work.

"I didn't think you'd want to spend so much time with your dad," she continues.

"It's fine, Mom. Let me do this for Zoey. Plus, I'll be making the drive back and forth from Oregon all next year, too, remember? It will be good practice."

"He hasn't even tried to call?"

"No." Unlike Blake. There's a warm certainty in my chest that I picked a man nothing like my father.

She sighs. The jumbled voice of the hospital intercom sounds in the background while she considers my offer. Another emergency, hopefully reminding her that we need to stay ahead of our own ticking timeline. Zoey is not a code blue yet, and I'll do everything in my power to have her stay that way. "I'll think about it," Mom says.

That's still not an answer, so there's room for me to bargain. "If there's still no contact from him by tonight . . ." I start.

"I hate the thought of sending you off on your own to handle him." She says it like there's another option if Dad remains incommunicado, but we both know that Mom won't leave Zoey for longer than a shift at the hospital, much less overnight, and Zoey can't travel because of her dialysis. I'm our best shot. "But maybe you're right," Mom continues. Whoa. She's trusting me with this? "We'll work out the details when I get home—*if* I still haven't heard from him."

My fist pumps in the air. Unable to hear Mom's end of the conversation, Zoey gives me a questioning look but leans over to offer me a high-five anyway. I take her up on it as I hang up the phone with my other hand.

For the rest of the afternoon, I start working out my timeline. Eight-ish hours to Dad's cabin. Bing-bang-boom, get a straight answer out of him to make a medical plan, then make it to Blake a few hours later. It's doable. Strong-arming a person into giving up an organ probably works better in person than over the phone, so I'm guessing it won't take long, leaving me plenty of time to prioritize Blake. Crater Lake National Park is less than three hours from U of O, which is basically two and a half, which is basically two hours if I want it to be. I just have to hightail it down Highway 58 after Dad's. When Blake sees my face in his dorm room, every wonderful memory of us will come flooding back. Once I feel his lips on mine, the world will right itself and maybe I won't feel like an insecure piece of crap anymore.

I keep an eye on my phone just in case Dad tries to call, praying he doesn't. The odds are low as I scroll through evidence of our previous contact over the past few years. A phone call every weekend, though sometimes it's Friday afternoon, Saturday at eleven p.m., or Sunday at the crack of dawn. It's sporadic, and not in the fun, keep-me-on-my-toes way. If I don't answer, he just texts a question mark. I text back the full excuse, filled with emojis that go unappreciated, and he responds with *ok*. Question mark. Ok. Does he know how to type anything else? A few weeks ago, I started sending memes instead. That made him even more confused. I think he avoids looking at anything I send him now, which I am aware is bad timing.

The front door bangs open just as Zoey and I are settling in on the couch to watch a show. I'm usually exhausted after watching her all day and getting her ready for bed, but tonight I'm a live wire. Mom's sudden arrival launches me to my feet. No call from Dad, which means my road trip to Oregon is a go.

"Kaley, come give me a hand," she calls from the entryway.

There's more banging as I hurry down the hallway. Whatever she brought with her sounds bigger than a kidney. Oh God, she brought an entire body home, didn't she?

It's not a person. My shoulders sag in relief. However, it weighs as much as a medium-sized child.

"Lift the handle with me," Mom instructs. "Let's get it inside and on the floor."

"You stole a portable dialysis machine?" The expensive piece of medical equipment reminds me of the pictures of the first Mac computers in my history textbook. "Why?" Other than letting Zoey do dialysis at home instead of at the hospital, it wouldn't fix our problem like a kidney will.

"Not stole. Borrowed," Mom says, slinging off the tote bag on her other arm and setting it down gently. It opens to reveal bags of dialysate, the fluid needed to run the dialysis and push Zoey's blood around to clean it. Lots and lots of dialysate and saline.

"Does Doc Hayes know you 'borrowed' it?" What is the difference between larceny and grand larceny? How many years in the clink is my mother looking at? I'll bring my sister to the trial, and we can stare down the jurors and play the highest-stakes Zoey card ever and try to get Mom a reduced sentence.

Why yes, Your Honor, she's an upstanding citizen when it comes to most laws, it's just that some of those pesky rules should not apply when it comes to failing kidneys.

"Of course he knows I borrowed it! Jesus, Kaley. A wealthy former patient donated it to the hospital. Dr. Hayes gave it to us to use this weekend."

When she says *former patient*, does she mean former as in, received a kidney transplant and no longer needs it, or *former patient* as in, died and left it in their will? My heart pounds in my chest. I don't like where this conversation is heading, possible cursed dialysis machine aside.

"We're all going to go to Oregon together!"

I officially take back my magnanimous offer to help lower her prison sentence. "But . . . you don't go on trips anymore." Much less across state lines.

"No, but I'm done sitting around," she says, as though ten hours on her feet today at the hospital counts as sitting around. "I thought about what you said, and you're right. You inspired me to take action too."

This is not good. "Mom, as much as I want Zoey to get a kidney, I don't know if a visit with Dad is the best idea for her. It will take her ages to stop talking about him if she sees him in person. A trip like this is going to tear her heart open again."

"I'm not making you do this on your own, Kaley," she says.

Please, God, just let me do this on my own. "The trip has too many logistics with all three of us," I tell her, holding up one finger and scrambling to come up with reasons she might listen to. I'm also going to pretend I'm not a little offended that she doesn't believe I'm capable of doing this by myself. I hold up a second finger. "I have a bio report due next week, and you know I can't miss as many days as last year; my guidance counselor will have an aneurysm. I'll be faster by myself. And three"—I hold up a final finger—"I'm not getting punched in the head by cranky Zoey in the backseat when she gets too tired and out of sorts from changing her routine."

She holds up a hand, cutting me off. "We won't make the drive in one day. We'll stop at a hotel overnight when we're almost there so she's not too exhausted when we see your dad."

Great. And how does that improve the logistics? Can't she just let me do this one thing for us?

"We'll get to the hotel with plenty of time for you to do your homework and for Zoey to dialyze," Mom promises. "Then we will get to your dad's early Monday morning, have a quick conversation, and hopefully everyone will go home happy. Everything back to normal by Tuesday."

I rub my temples, trying to stave off my returning headache. Regardless of my side quest to see Blake, there is a pit of worry in my stomach that forces me to speak up. "Are you sure about this home dialysis? What if something goes wrong?"

"Kaley, I'm a nurse. I know what I'm doing. I'm perfectly qualified to do this, especially because she will only need dialysis once while we're gone, and then we'll be back home and back to regular routine. Zoey will see Doc Hayes on Tuesday as usual, and hopefully he will get Zoey on the transplant surgery schedule once Dad confirms. Aren't you excited?" She gives me a big smile, while I'm still speechless, watching my original plan dissolve into thin air.

Mom sidesteps the dialysis machine on the ground and heads down the hallway to the kitchen. “I’m starving. I need to eat and then we’ll go pack.” Her voice fades as she leaves me standing by the door, but I can still hear her. “Oh, and Kaley! Thanks for mopping today.”

CHAPTER FIVE

MY FINGERS DANCE IN THE WIND AS MY ARM TRAILS OUT THE OPEN window. Old-school Taylor Swift pours out from the car stereo and all three of us are sort of singing along. The sun is higher in the cloudless sky than I wanted it to be when we left, but at least we're on the road now.

Long hair whips into my mouth and I half choke, half gag. Right during my favorite part of the chorus, too. Why *do* you gotta be so mean? I flip down the visor and try to lasso my hair into a decent ponytail.

Through the mirror, I see Zoey behind me, lost in thought as she looks at the wilderness rolling past. There really is a whole lot of lack of civilization in Idaho. The portable dialysis machine is buckled in its own seat on the driver's side, looking like a budget R2-D2. An overflowing bin of snacks occupies the middle seat while our giant, shared suitcase is stuffed in the trunk.

A semi-truck moves over to pass us on the two-lane highway. Why does Mom insist on driving five miles an hour under the speed limit? When it is my turn to drive, I'll have to make up for lost time. If everything had gone to plan and I were by myself, I'd be halfway there by now. A frustrated sigh escapes me.

The oversize cab is now parallel with us, and when I look across Mom through her window, I catch the driver's eye. He glances at our car with utter confusion and concern as he takes in the Larssen family in all our slow glory, eyes lingering on the dialysis machine. I give him a little wave.

Signs for Boise State pop up as we near the closest major city. "Go Broncos," I mutter, dripping sarcasm. Most of the kids who graduate from Redson High end up here—close enough to come home every two weeks to do their laundry. Ahem, Declan. I wonder if he's back at school yet or still being pampered by his mama.

Mom's lips flatten, and I know the argument is coming. The one area of my life that I'm willing to hold the line for, and hopefully she realizes now that I'm serious about it and won't be changing my mind. There's nothing she can say that we haven't gone around and around with this summer anyway, and I'm bracing for the guilt trip. "Family is important," she says. "It's already going to be an adjustment for Zoey that you'll be away at school most of the time. How are you going to tell her that you'll only see her on major holidays? What if there is an emergency?"

Like it's *my* fault my boyfriend chose a school so far away. I'll take the blame, though, for having the audacity to want to be with him. As Zoey's kidney issues have taken a downturn, I still hang on to my original plan out of sheer stubbornness, my fingernails splitting as I claw at the cliff. Four years. I only want four years.

But what if Zoey isn't better by next fall?

I squeeze my eyes shut just as surely as I squeeze the traitorous thought from my head. She'll have the kidney transplant soon. She'll be fully recovered and happy for me by the time I even apply for early decision to Oregon. With none of the frequent appointments and pain-in-the-butt medical stuff to worry about, Mom can return to the original plan of switching to three twelve-hour shifts a week. Leah's grandma can chill and watch TV with Zo and make sure she doesn't burn down the house on those days. The rest of the time Mom will be home with her. It's not like she's going to be with some stranger, or, God forbid, that disgusting group home we toured. I shudder reflexively, the memory still as horrifying as last year. I will never allow my sister and her bright light anywhere near a place like that, where people are shoved away and forgotten by their own families who don't want to deal with them. A sad, depressing place where they're kept alive with the most basic needs met but prevented from really living.

But back to the plan. If Zoey doesn't get Dad's kidney and has to do dialysis long-term . . . well, I don't want to go down that road, not until we talk to Dad. All I know is that Gran is definitely not qualified for anything intense next year—she's plucky, but I doubt the reflexes are there to handle Zoey's frustration/discomfort/general hatred of all things dialysis-related.

Funny, because I have a frustration/discomfort/general hatred of where this conversation is heading with Mom.

"Boise State has some great programs. I'm just saying, you should look at options closer to home too."

"U of O has better options. And Blake," I argue back.

"It's only October. We don't know what next year looks like yet, and you know how I feel about following a boy—"

"And I know how *I* feel about following *this* boy. Why don't you trust me to make decisions for myself?"

Mom runs her hands through her hair, her signature move

when she's short on patience. "You don't even know what you want to study!"

"Blake!" Zoey pipes in.

Hm. Yes. She does have a point. I *would* like to study Blake, in all academic pursuits. Anatomy, especially.

Honestly, I'm not sure what my true calling is just yet, but I'm excited to have time to try all the classes and figure it out. "See? Zoey is team Oregon too. You're outnumbered, Mom."

"I just want you to be realistic, Kaley."

Realistic about my own prospects? Or what's coming for our family? I decide this is too big of a subject to debate while the stereo ushers us from Taylor's country era into one of her pop-perfection masterpieces. I lean forward and turn it up, cutting Mom off from her worst-case-scenario spiral. She's been having a lot of those lately, and it's been harder and harder to pull her out of it. She grimaces, annoyed at my transparent actions, but when Zoey and I belt out the words, she finally picks up with us on the chorus.

She does a little shimmy in her seat, a move that Zoey copies by bouncing around behind me. My gaze darts between the two of them, questioning how it's fair that they got the dancing genes in the family and left none for me. Both of them just feel the music and let themselves get swept away. It's been a long time since I've seen them dancing together.

When the song fades out, Zoey asks, "All done?"

"Nope, we aren't there yet," I answer. "Lots and lots of songs to go."

"Soon?"

I look over my shoulder at her. "Nope. Just focus on your

driving." She picks up her imaginary steering wheel and grips it tightly. The car leans left and Zoey crisscrosses her hands around in a circle, just like Mom. "Don't forget to hit the gas." She kicks the bottom of my seat. "Too fast, too fast! Now the cops are on us."

Zoey squeals with laughter while I check the GPS map. One hour down, eight to go.

Mom's phone rings through the car Bluetooth. It's not Dad; it's some person named Cole on the caller ID. She immediately hits the Ignore button, but it's too late, I've already seen it.

"Mom, who is Cole?"

"A friend. Nobody you know."

Duh. But who is Cole to Mom? He's not, like, a date or anything. She doesn't have time to date. She's either with Zoey or at the hospital. Still, I need to know for sure. "Mom, do you have a boyfriend?"

"Lord, Kaley. No."

"Then why did you just reject a call?"

"Because I don't have time for chitchat right now." Her gaze flicks to the rearview mirror, where Zoey is eavesdropping on the conversation. Whatever it is between her and Cole, she doesn't want my sister to know.

I sort of believe her, because how can she have a boyfriend if I can't remember her ever getting dressed up and going out after Dad left? How do adults even navigate this sort of thing? It's quite possible that my dating cluelessness is hereditary. That would explain a lot. Thank God for Leah to steer me in the right direction. Without her, I would have done the dating equivalent of walking into traffic.

Blake had nervously invited me to his house to "hang out" and "study" one Saturday last September, offering to help me with math homework.

"But I don't need help with math," I'd said, standing in the middle of the cafeteria holding my tray. "And Leah and I already have plans."

Leah stood at my side, eyes wide, watching the exchange between me and Blake instead of heading over to our usual table. "No, we don't!" she said. Was she kidding? We had been looking forward to our *Buffy* marathon all week. Then, she stomped on my foot, and I tried to keep up.

In my defense, never in a million years would I have expected Blake to be interested in me, even though I'd been pining for him for years. He was a senior, on the periphery of our friend group, yet elevated above us mere mortals. The golden boy everyone loved, not just because he was hot and talented but because he was so genuinely kind. He even started an annual fundraiser for the local animal shelter. So yeah, excuse me if I assumed Blake was just trying to help the poor junior in his math class before the first exam. The same proverbial fruit-snacks offering as before.

"Oh, so . . ." Blake trailed off, waiting for me to jump in.

"She'll be there," Leah confirmed. "Three o'clock work?" She didn't need to confirm the address. Everybody knew where the richest family in town lived.

"Sounds good." He flashed me a grin with that freaking trademark dimple and I couldn't respond. I just stood there, frozen. I might not have needed math help, but I sure needed help remembering how to breathe.

There was a knock on the door that fateful Saturday morning, and when I opened it, Leah was standing on my front porch with a suitcase full of clothes, makeup, and hair tools. She whipped out a flippy little pink skirt and waved it around her head like a lasso. "OKFD!"

"Oklahoma Fire Department?"

"Operation Kaley's First Date!"

Shoving past me, she barreled her way up the stairs and into my bedroom. All the noise drew Zoey's attention, and she popped her head out from her own room. "Leah!"

"Hey, ZoZo. Wanna help me get your sister ready for the first day of the rest of her life?"

Zoey nodded, not quite sure what was happening but happy to be included. I hadn't breathed a word of my date to her or Mom, afraid Blake was going to cancel at the last second.

Like I'd summoned her, Mom appeared at the top of the stairs. "What's this about a date?"

My cheeks flushed. "Leah is exaggerating. It's a 'hang out and study.' At Blake Parson's house."

"Blake Parson? *The* Blake Parson?" Mom teased.

"Yes!" Zoey yelled, pumping her fist in the air. "Blake!"

Gazing out the car window and biting my lip, I wonder if Mom had felt left out that day. Why hadn't I told her until the last minute? I'd like to think that if Mom had a date at some point, she would have let me and Zoey dress her up and get her ready. Hopefully she doesn't feel like she has to hide any of it from us. Lord knows it's been long enough since the divorce.

But why else would she be so secretive about this Cole

character? "Wait a minute," I say. "You didn't let Leah's mom and aunt give you a makeover montage and exclude your own daughters from it, did you?"

Mom sighs. "What on earth are you talking about, Kaley?"

It has been ages since I remember her hanging out with her friends. She basically goes from work to home to Zoey's appointments. Unless. . . . "I did notice you got some fancy new scrubs, Mom. Trying to impress anyone at the hospital?" I ask, waggling my eyebrows suggestively. I'd offer to let her borrow the tried-and-true flippy pink skirt, but she'd claim it would get her fired.

"My old ones are too baggy now."

Oh. That is a less fun reason.

Zoey shoots her hand up to the car ceiling like she's an overeager student. "Oh! Laundry," she suggests. "I do it."

"Not a bad idea, Zo," I agree.

I must have fallen asleep at some point because the next thing I realize, Mom is pulling off the highway exit and accidentally running over the rumble strips. My fingers clutch the armrest at the deep, resonant sound that seems to go on forever beneath my feet.

"Whoopsie!" she says. "Sorry, everyone."

"No wub wubs!" Zoey yells. I agree with her. Those things are the worst type of sensory overload. It's like waking up to imminent death. My heart rattles in my chest at the shot of adrenaline, stronger than any cup of coffee. I'll switch spots with Mom after we gas up and skip the energy drink.

Zoey and I are both feeling on edge as Mom pulls into the gas station. When I see it, my panic eases a bit. "Hey, at least I don't think we'll get murdered here," I say.

"Kaley!"

"I was just complimenting your gas-station choice and the lack of broken windows. And look! All the pumps work." Unexpected for the middle of nowhere. I'm pretty sure we crossed the border into Oregon a while back. It is still the boonies, but sugar and the lack of sales tax call to me from the little adjacent store. "Zoey and I will go pee and grab some treats while you fill up."

"There is plenty of food in the car. Hardboiled eggs and unsalted pretzels. Dried fruit and protein bars too." Zoey diet–friendly. Ugh. Except I know Mom packed her own treats in her purse. Hypocrite.

"Noted. But not the same as Swedish Fish, right, Zo?" That candy follows the rules. Low salt, low potassium.

Zoey has left me in the dust and is already heading toward the convenience store. Not even the sound of thumping bass as another car pulls in behind ours can distract her. I admire her dedication to our cause—Viva la corn syrup!

Three passengers and a driver exit the Jeep as I'm hustling after Zoey. They don't look like they belong here either. The two girls wear high-heeled booties and I spot a designer purse. The guys have matching baseball caps, perched on their heads at opposite angles so their girlfriends can tell them apart, I guess. One of them is complaining about the lack of gas-pump attendant while I yank open the door to the store.

The bell chimes and an older woman behind the counter gives me a warm smile. How does she keep herself entertained all day, surrounded by cigarettes and the occasional two-minute visitor? It must get pretty boring. I bet we are the most exciting thing to happen to her all day.

Scanning the tiny shop, I don't see Zoey's blond head right away. She's here somewhere, though.

"To the right, dear," the lady says, knowing exactly what I'm looking for.

I find Zoey squatting down, staring at the candy but not grabbing it. She's on a strict diet at home to help with her kidneys, but Mom is also fanatic about making sure she's healthy overall. Sugar is a rare treat, and she doesn't know where to start. "What are we thinking?" I ask. She puts a finger to her chin, pondering. Picking one is impossible. "Two for each of us?"

"No."

"Three? Then we can go halfsies on each one. That's six different treats." She nods. Mom will only let her nibble on each one, but it's still worth it. "Okay, you pick them. You know what I like. And remember, you're not allowed caramel, chocolate, or peanut butter. I'm going to pee. You need to go?" She waves me off. Treats are the focus right now. I'll ask again after we check out, but right now my bladder is screaming at me. Zoey rarely has this problem anymore, a small perk of failing kidneys.

The toilet is crammed in a closet at the back of the store, but at least it's clean. I pee quickly and wash my hands but stop to fix my hair in the mirror. It still looks like a tornado hit it from my earlier attempts to tame it in the car. I finger-brush it as best

I can before pulling it up into a bun. Feeling more like myself, I return to the shop.

Across a few aisles, I see Zoey chatting with the kids from the Jeep. Back home, pretty much everyone knows Zoey. Living in a small town means that she's like a local celebrity. The downside is there are hardly any resources for her, but at least I don't worry as much for her safety when she's out and about. From where I'm standing, the interaction looks innocent, but the hairs on the back of my neck rise.

Closing in on them, I catch a snippet of their conversation. "—eat it all in one bite," the guy with the left leaning hat is saying. He's holding out a huge chocolate bar that he unwraps when he sees Zoey's hesitation. "Take a video," he tells Righty.

The friend shifts uncomfortably. "I dunno, man."

"Well?" Then I see a phone come out of the girlfriend's designer purse. Lefty flashes her a grin. "Thanks, babe."

"What the hell are you doing?" I ask calmly, and the squad jumps.

"She looked hungry. Just trying to help her out," Lefty says, eyes wide and innocent.

"No, you weren't." My rage simmers in my chest, but I keep a lid on it. My locked box of emotion helps me keep a level head. *Get Zoey out of here and safe.*

This living embodiment of Axe body spray is not used to being called on his crap, especially not in front of his underlings. He straightens up with a glint in his eye. "Are you accusing me of something?"

I stick to the facts. "Yeah, of being a dick."

The girlfriend steps forward. "Don't talk to him like that."

"Come on, Zo. Grab the candy you want and let's get to the car." Zoey's hands are full as we push past the wannabe tormentors to get down the aisle toward the checkout.

"You should keep your retard on a tighter leash," Lefty calls out.

My self-control snaps. "One second," I say to Zoey as she lays the candy on the counter. With even steps, I stride back toward the group, raise my hand, and slap the offender across his face so hard that his hat and sunglasses go flying from his head.

"*Ow!*" he wails, clutching his cheek, all former bravado gone in an instant.

Frozen, I look down at my tingling hand in shock. I've never hit someone before. Dodged hits plenty and had enough land on me that I know what hurts, but I always thought I was better than displays of violent emotion. But based on how good that felt, maybe I'm not. I kind of want to do it again.

The girls are backing away from me now. "Oh my God, you *assaulted* him!"

Righty recovers first. "My dad's a lawyer, just wait until I tell him—" Ah, the real reason he's allowed to tag along with this group.

"You cracked my three-hundred-dollar sunglasses!" Lefty says, voice several octaves higher than it was when he was taunting Zoey with the candy bar.

"We need the security tape!" Righty calls up to the cashier. "Did you see that?"

The woman smiles. "I didn't see anything. And I don't believe our security cameras are up and running today." She turns her attention to Zoey. "Candy's on me today, kid."

They're still wailing when I drag Zoey out of the building and over to the car.

"Everything all right?" Mom asks. "Wait a minute, what did I say about all the candy?"

"It was on the house, Mom. Just get in the car." Zoey has already dropped two packages during our sprint and is clutching the other four with both hands. Skittles scatter around our feet, cheerful pops of color on the greasy asphalt. A rainbow trail of destruction. It should be our criminal calling card. They'll call us the Rainbow Rebels.

"I still need to use the restroom—" Mom starts.

The crew bursts out of the shop like murderous paparazzi, their cell phones out to record us while they yell about how they're the victims.

"What on earth?" Mom asks, completely stunned.

"Come on! We gotta *Thelma and Louise* it out of here. Unless you have a spare three hundred bucks hidden in the glovebox?"

Mom plants her feet and puts her hands on her hips. For a sickening moment, I think she's going to refuse to get in and force me to explain myself. Then, Righty yells, "You can't just leave! I'm going to sue you for everything you have!"

I can't help myself. "They weren't even *your* sunglasses, you suck-up!"

Mom's lips purse into a line so thin they disappear. "Right. I'm driving."

It's technically my turn behind the wheel, but I don't argue and slide into the passenger seat instead. Zoey has barely closed her door when Mom puts the car in high-speed reverse, does a one-eighty spin, and narrowly misses clipping the bumper of the

Jeep. It's so precise and calculated that I wonder if she wanted to do worse but chose the high road. The feral pack scatters out of the way as Mom guns it forward.

The car doesn't slow down as Mom steers to the onramp, executing a drift I've only seen when Blake plays video games. Where did she learn that? I want to speak, but my tongue is stuck to the roof of my mouth and my heart is in my throat.

"Whee!" Zoey says, sliding to the middle seat and knocking all the snacks onto the floor.

"Zoey, are you buckled?" Mom asks.

"No."

"On it!" I say, half diving over the center console and reaching for Zoey's lap. I shove her to the side and get her seat belt secured.

"Stay down," Mom says, and I feel her ease off the gas. I flatten myself as best I can and turn my head to look out the window. The trees are no longer a blur, and I spot the nose of a cop car sticking out from behind a sign. I debate spinning around and scrambling for my own seat belt but opt for casual stillness instead. Nothing to see here. Just a mom taking a Sunday drive.

From the corner of my eye, I see the cruiser pull forward just a bit, hesitation evident as the cop decides whether to trust his instincts. The choice is made for him, though, when the red Jeep comes flying up behind us and laying on the horn.

Mom doesn't speed up, just keeps a nice and steady pace down the highway. The cruiser's siren turns on and I imagine he's pulling in behind the Jeep. I pop my head up enough to see the drama through the back window while our biggest fans slow their car and pull to the side of the road. A relieved, slightly hysterical laugh escapes my lips.

"We're not clear yet," Mom says through clenched teeth.

We're clear enough for me to return to my seat, though, because my neck has started to cramp. It isn't until three miles later that Mom's shoulders fully relax, and she stops clutching the wheel at ten and two. Zoey, worn out from all the excitement, leans against the doorjamb and snores softly. She clutches her unopened candy prize in her hands. Silence cocoons us, but I have to break it. I have to know. "Holy crap, Mom. Where did you learn how to be a stone-cold criminal?"

"I'm not a criminal," Mom snaps, keeping her voice low so as not to disturb Zoey. Then she sighs. "But I used to drag race with your dad, once upon a time . . ."

The revelation startles me. Staring at her now, I try to picture what she must have looked like twenty years ago behind the wheel. Maybe with black eyeliner and chipped nail polish, hair whipping around her face as she careened down backroads at ninety miles an hour. The hardest part is conjuring up Dad sitting next to her, turning up the radio to blast his emo rock while entranced by the wild creature who would one day spend her days trapped with piles of medication and stacks of paperwork.

She hardly ever talks to him, not unless it's strictly business involving child support or medical decisions. She never talks *about* him either. Our high-speed chase must have cracked her fortress just enough to slip me that little detail, but even as I savor it, I can see her building her walls back up.

"What should we say to him?" I blurt out, desperate not to let this newly discovered version of who she is fade into obscurity. I like her. Not only would we have been friends if we shared a timeline, but she would have been a bad influence on me in the best way.

"I'm not sure yet," she says. Her blunt honesty surprises me. Usually, she pretends to have it all together. "Any suggestions?"

I think for a moment before responding, "There is no way to segue, is there? It's going to be awkward no matter what." The absurdity of our mission was almost forgotten in the drama of the gas station. At least now asking for an organ will not be the most ridiculous part of this road trip.

"True." She reaches forward to turn up the radio, deciding that the conversation is over.

I'm not done. "I can do most of the talking," I offer. "He'll have a harder time fighting with me, if he decides to make it a struggle. I'm getting a straight answer out of him one way or another."

Instead of turning up the music, Mom's fingers hesitate on the dial before stretching to open the glovebox at my knees. A thick stack of papers, folded into thirds, rests inside. "I did bring this, just in case," she says, like a confession.

I'm gonna need an up-close look at these mystery documents. Maybe they are photocopied love letters from before they were married, to remind Dad that he loved her—and us—once upon a time. Or it could be different versions of a speech Mom tried to prepare. Oh, I bet it is a complete write-up from Doc Hayes detailing Zoey's prognosis. Either way, she's offering me information I can learn without eavesdropping, *and* asking my opinion about it. I rarely gather my intel legally, so it's possible she's considering our narrow escape as a new chapter in our mother-daughter relationship.

Legalese in stark, black print stares at me as I open the paperwork. My eyes skim the words, and then I have to go back and read it again from the top.

"This . . . this is a termination of guardianship."

CHAPTER SIX

MOM NODS ONCE, SUDDENLY VERY INTERESTED IN THE EMPTY ROAD IN front of us.

"You're letting Dad off the hook for Zoey? Permanently?"

"If he needs a little extra motivation to agree to the donation, it might be best for everyone."

I slump in my chair. Child support for Zoey didn't end when she turned eighteen. Instead, my parents transitioned to becoming co-guardians. Zoey is the link that ties my parents together for life. Dad could insist on a divorce, move to a different state, and give up his visitation in preference for financial support, but part of me was glad he could never fully leave. If something bad ever happened to Mom, there was still a backup for Zoey. Even though he isn't involved with Zoey's day-to-day life, they decided to cooperate on this for Mom's peace of mind. She runs the show; he's on paper to make sure Zoey doesn't end up a ward of the state. To my knowledge, he's never overstepped this arrangement. But what if he really does want out of our lives completely? Life suddenly feels very fragile.

"And you thought this was a good conversation to have while we are careening along in a metal death trap, capable of crashing at any second?" I click my seat belt in and tug to check it. "You're really going to let him sign that?"

"I'm not going to lead with it as an option, but yes. If push comes to shove, I'll have him sign it."

"Jesus, Mom!" How can she talk like that?

Mom reaches over and clutches my arm, her fingers digging into my wrist so hard I drop the papers into my lap. Desperation seeps from her, and I can see how hard she's trying just to take it one step at a time. She never wavers when it comes to all of Zoey's needs. She fought tooth and nail for accommodations with the school district, against scummy insurance for occupational and behavioral therapies, and against every ignorant word that came out of stupid people's mouths for my entire childhood.

We still don't know what we're walking into. Is Dad a match? Is he even willing to donate? Why won't he give us a straight answer? I can't blame her for planning to throw everything against the wall and see what sticks. My plan to simply appeal to his human nature suddenly seems very naïve.

"I . . . I'm glad you told me."

Her grip on my arm loosens. "I wanted to be honest with you." Her face still seems guarded, but her tone is more relaxed. "I'm happy I raised such a smart, mature young woman. You're so wise beyond your years."

Should I record those words to play back to her tomorrow once I've committed grand theft auto to go hook up with my boyfriend? The getaway plan is looking more and more like simply ditching Mom and Zoey at the cabin for a few hours once I know my sister is getting the kidney. I imagine we'll all be celebrating—yay kidney yay, maybe even with a group hug—then I'll drop down and duck out, snagging the car keys in a sprint that I'm hoping doesn't land me on my face in the driveway. There's really no way I can make it subtle. The confusion on their end will be something almost worth sticking around to see. I'll bet Zo thinks it's hilarious.

Zoey yawns, stretching after her cat nap and interrupting my scheming.

"Potty?" she asks.

"Didn't you just go?" Mom says.

"Oh, ah, we got sidetracked. It was my fault."

"There's no stops for a while," Mom says through the rearview mirror to my sister. "Are you sure you actually need to go?" With the dialysis, Zoey barely has any urine output, and her bladder has a hard time telling her the truth. She will declare she has to go immediately, then change her mind by the time she gets to the bathroom.

"Hurry!" she urges.

Mom curses and pulls the car over to the highway shoulder. "Okay, come on. Let's go pee on a bush. I have to go too." She helps Zoey out of the backseat and they walk a ways from the road, but when I get out of the car I can still see them. Mom is helping Zoey pull down her pants. For a horrified moment, I think this will only end with everyone covered in pee and tears, but they get the angle right. Zoey looks like she's sitting on an invisible horse while Mom struggles to keep her upright.

Horses. Damn, everything makes me miss Blake.

Leaving the papers on the passenger seat, I walk around the front of the car to get into the driver's seat. Thankfully it's my turn to drive, and I need this distraction because my phone won't cut it. It's too tempting to pull up Blake's social media and doomscroll until we get to the hotel, which is *not* what I'm doing right now waiting for Mom and Zoey to get back to the car. I'm scrolling through my *own* picture archives, and there is no obsessed-girlfriend rule about that. I'm only through June when my thumb cramps. I bet my thumb would feel better shoved in his cheek dimple.

I shoot him the throwback picture I landed on. It's the two of us at the fair, along with a heart emoji. He sees it and leaves me on read for almost a full minute. When he responds, it's with the first selfie we ever took together. I had just fallen off a horse, so I have a very fuzzy memory of taking it with him.

Our first date had started off just about as smoothly. Blake had answered the front door to lead me into his house's cavernous entryway and said, "Hey! Where's all your stuff?"

I froze. This was a study date, and my books were at home, on the kitchen table, where Leah had insisted I leave them. The seconds ticked by, and I couldn't respond. Didn't this giant house have a secret trapdoor that could just swallow me up? A secret torture chamber in the basement? Nothing could be as agonizing as this silence.

"Do you want to see the horses instead?" Blake asked finally. He would later confess that he was afraid I thought his house was creepy, and that the realization we were alone there had me replaying every true-crime episode I'd ever watched.

Meanwhile, I was trying to play the cool girl. Blake's family was rich, but I hadn't known how rich. They were show-horse people. His mom was anyway. He explained it all on the walk "through the grounds" over to the stables.

He opened the sliding barn doors and ushered me into the warm space. Sunlight streamed in from skylights, illuminating the dust particles suspended in the air. The occasional muffled snort broke through the silence, but it wasn't the tomblike quiet of the house. The smell of sweet hay and something a bit mustier invaded my nostrils when I took a meditative breath to calm my heart. Blake stood right next to me, watching me take it all in, and I knew I couldn't tell him that large animals really freaked me out.

Rather than let my face give away my hesitation, I walked into Blake's sanctuary. *Slap-slap-slap.* Flip flops really were a terrible choice, but I was in too deep to back out.

"Atlas is my favorite," Blake said, pointing to the other end of the barn. "Want to meet him?"

The animals shifted in their stalls as they realized they had company. If Zoey had been there, she would have been losing her mind, convinced there was a unicorn stashed somewhere. I hustled after Blake. *You can do this. Just feed Atlas a carrot, give him a pat on the nose, and move on.* A horse stuck his nose through the bars on his stall as we passed it, and I let out a little scream.

Blake put a hand on my shoulder and gave it a gentle squeeze. "Try not to make any sudden movements," he said, speaking in a low tone. I felt a little calmer. "Don't startle them."

Well then, they shouldn't startle me.

"Half our horses are rescues," Blake explained. "We also get a few fosters now and again, get them healthy and trained after they've been beaten and neglected. I just can't believe anyone could hurt them, but it's amazing once they start to trust again." At the end of the barn, Blake clicked his tongue, and

Atlas shoved his head through the bars. "Hey, buddy." My crush stroked the nose of the animal with zero fear.

Holding my hand out from five feet away, I approached on tiptoe. "Hi . . . dude." Fingertips brushed a velvety nose. *I'm doing it!* Then Atlas snorted, and I jumped back out of range. "I've had a lot of practice dodging bites," I reassured Blake. "But do you have any smaller horses?" Maybe it was a size thing. Smaller might be less intimidating, and I preferred a situation where I could hold my own in a fight.

Blake's face lit up. "Yeah! I think you would get along with Strawberry Shortcake."

Dubious, because what kind of a name is that? At least Atlas I could respect. But *Strawberry Shortcake*?

"She's old and patient. She might even let you ride her. Stay here, I'll grab you a pair of Mom's boots."

Well. That escalated quickly.

Thus, with a series of people-pleasing events that could only be described as exponential—a term Blake and I would go over in our graphing assignment a few days later, in fact—I ended up atop a dessert horse that was anything but sweet.

"You're a natural," Blake said after boosting me into the saddle. My thighs chafed and the borrowed boots pinched my toes.

"You're not going to let go of the leash, right?" My voice trembled, but I managed to smile at him. I was rewarded with another peek at that dimple.

"Nope, I got you." Blake Parsons had me, and I was a goner.

In more ways than one.

But Strawberry Shortcake had had enough of pretending her

rider was in charge and shuffled her feet underneath my inexperienced butt. Called out with nowhere to hide, I panicked, tried to overcorrect, pulled my feet from the stirrups, and slid off a stationary horse.

I landed in a heap. I don't know who was more shocked, Strawberry Shortcake or Blake, because they both stared down at me. Then, ever the hero, Blake leaped into action. He walked the horse away from my crumpled body and ran back over to my side. My knight even pulled my skirt down from where it flipped up and over my sexiest underwear—my *black* boy shorts—to protect my modesty.

"Are you okay? Did you hit your head? Don't move. Keep your neck still."

My ears rang, but if I tried hard enough, I could make the two Blakes kneeling over me merge into one.

"I am such an idiot. Of course I should have had you put on a helmet first." He shook his head, beating himself up for my absolute lack of grace. "It was my responsibility to keep you safe. I'm so sorry."

I lay there, enjoying the feeling of his large hands on either side of my head, and smiled up at him with the stupidest of grins. He wanted to play Dr. Prince Charming, and I was one hundred percent into letting him.

"Can you talk?" he asked, and I realized I'd been staring up at him for a *very* long time by that point, thinking, *Someone get the smelling salts and a Victorian fan because I am a damsel in distress.*

"I think I'm fine," I whispered, sounding weak enough to be

afflicted with consumption or dysentery or whatever ladies who fell off horses back in the day were complaining about. Would a hand across my forehead have been too much?

His worried face cracked a smile. "I've been trying to ask you out for weeks."

"Huh?" Such refined elegance.

"You make me nervous. I never know what you're going to say."

"Well, I have a pretty good idea of what I'll say right now if you ask me out." I struggled to sit up, and Blake carefully pulled me up by my wrists so our faces were inches apart.

"Kaley, will you go out with me?"

I screamed, "Yes!" and launched myself into his arms, giving him the kiss of his life. Near-death experiences have a way of doing that, I suppose.

Now I'm on a wild road trip a year later to tackle him yet again. This time, hopefully, without a concussion.

Looking at the photo of us, I almost text him and ruin the surprise. My fingers even get so far as to type out, *I can't wait to see you soon,* before I realize what I'm doing and erase it. The temptation is too much. I open the glovebox and go to toss my phone and the guardianship paperwork back inside, but my attention snags on some colorful pamphlets stashed in there too.

At first, I think they're dialysis info handouts, but I don't recognize the name on the front. *Fides.* Whatever *Fides* is, these people on the front cover sure are excited about it. They're hugging, and the tagline underneath reads "Building Community." Sounds vaguely churchlike, probably one of those pamphlets that people stick on parked cars. A tree died for this garbage. I want to toss it out, but being a litterbug after bemoaning the death of a tree is completely hypocritical. I look out the window to see Mom and Zoey hiking back to the car and throw the pamphlet back into the glovebox. Their shadows stretch in front of them.

We're behind schedule.

CHAPTER SEVEN

"WHAT DO YOU MEAN, YOU CAN'T FIND OUR RESERVATION?" MOM demands at the hotel front desk.

The receptionist eyes our battered suitcase, lingering on the dialysis machine perched next to it. Mom and I made quite the scene lugging it through the rotating door a minute ago. It is a real pain to carry with atrophied legs thanks to being in a car for over six hours. There is real regret in his voice when he continues. "I think there's been a mistake because I have you down for Sunday night *next* week. Normally we could squeeze you in, but there is a conference here and all our rooms are booked until Thursday."

I can't help but ask, "What company booked a retreat for the middle of nowhere?" Because really, what is there to experience an hour from Crater Lake, besides the national park? I bet they're just cheap.

"You can try the motel fifty minutes back," he suggests.

The thought of backtracking makes me want to scream, but I see Mom considering it. It already took forever to get here, and I can't stand the thought of adding another two hours total to the trip. "We can just rest for a bit and then push through," I suggest. "Get to Dad's tonight." And closer to sneaking out to see Blake tomorrow. "Zoey is already late for dialysis," I point out. "It's also dinnertime, and we're starving."

"He just said there's no room, Kaley," she says, moving away from the desk and grabbing the suitcase handle.

My stomach growls. "No. We don't need a room, just a pit stop. I can finish and email my bio report here while you plug the machine in for a little while for Zo. Then we'll be on our way." I talk loud enough for the receptionist to overhear and let out a long-suffering sigh. "But I guess we can load it all back up in the car and drive back an hour instead. I just hope it isn't too late. For her," I add dramatically.

I wonder if I'm laying it on a little thick with playing the Zoey card, but the receptionist looks like he's wavering. Zoey trips into a lobby couch and seals the deal for us.

"One of the smaller meeting rooms should open up in five minutes," he says. "You should have adequate privacy. The code is eight-zero-zero-eight-five." Boobs? The code is boobs?

I beam at him. "That will be perfect. We'll only be around, oh, three hours." Like I said, a pit stop. "Oh, does it have an attached bathroom too? We'll need a drain."

He blanches but nods, knowing he can't take back his offer. Besides, we will be secured out of the way, nobody will notice us. It could even be positive PR for the hotel. *Look how magnanimous we are! Saving a single mother and her two daughters from the consequences of their own actions.* If I saw that in a commercial, I would definitely book my vacation here.

"The smallest conference room is down the hall and on the right. If you hit the pool, you've gone too far."

This place has a pool? I'm about to take off toward the direction he's pointing, but Zoey has me beat. Girl can motor when she wants to, which makes it more annoying when she drags her feet when I have somewhere important to be.

"Girls!" Mom snaps. "Suitcase and snack bin. And Kaley, help me with the dialysis machine with your free hand." Loaded down like pack mules, we look like we're planning to zone a tent city within the hotel. We reach the locked door and Mom asks, "What was the code again?" I stare at her for a beat before punching it in. "Thank goodness you're so good with numbers," she says.

I turn the handle and pull it open. Twenty faces stare back at me. We are at the head of a PowerPoint presentation, in which someone is explaining the definition of a "downline" based on the current slide. "Whoops, sorry. My bad." Five minutes. The receptionist had said the room would be free in five minutes, a detail both Mom and I chose to ignore.

The presenter gives us a bright smile. "No problem! Are you here for the intro class? I'm afraid you've missed it, but tomorrow we'll do a review before the team bonding exercise. We can catch you up then, can't we, ladies?" She addresses the last part to the group of women in the audience, who all nod at the same time. Creepy.

"Nope, just here to borrow the room. But we'll wait in the hall while you finish up." Mom backs us out of the room and shuts the door.

"Who are those people?" I ask. "Some kind of cult? They all look the same."

Mom grimaces. "Worse, I think. Multilevel marketers. We need to hurry the hell up and get out of here as soon as possible."

A few moments later, the door opens, and the women file out. They're all dressed in yoga pants and pink T-shirts. I bet if I yell Melissa or Jessica, at least four of them will turn around. Instead, I keep my mouth shut and focus on reading the back of the shirts. *Transforming Lives, One Bite at a Time.*

I slap my hand over my mouth to keep from cracking up. Mom's gaze follows my own and I see her fight a smile. "We need to steal one for Zoey," I whisper.

"Don't you dare," she warns me, laughing softly.

Zoey leans in to get in on the joke. "What?" she says at full volume.

"The shirts. They say 'One Bite at a Time.'"

She thinks for a moment, then quick as lightning latches her teeth onto my bicep. See? She's quick when she wants to be. I instinctively flinch, but she doesn't bear down. I hear her chuckle and I know she gets the humor. "Baby Zoey," she remembers, straightening up again.

My sister has mostly outgrown her biting phase, but there were times growing up when she downright terrified me. She was bigger and stronger for a long time and would go from fine to overstimulated in the blink of an eye. As I got older, I understood that her meltdowns were not her fault, but it didn't suck any less to have to explain to my teachers where my bruises came from. Eventually, everyone knew and would just stop asking. There wasn't a lot they could do about it. Bite marks took longer to heal than punches. Zoey's rage at not being able to communicate what she wanted manifested in half-moon marks that sometimes bled. On her own arm, mine, Mom's.

On second thought, I think we all deserve a T-shirt.

The presenter is the last one out of the room. Her name tag reads EMILY. Dang, that wasn't in my top two guesses. "It's all yours!" she says. "You ladies look beat, though. Long day? Are you sure we can't talk you into joining us for dinner? Nutrition is important." My eyes widen, and I know what's coming next. "I left a few free samples in there if you're hungry. Come find me later and let me know your favorite flavor!"

Zoey seems to think the woman has a mute button, because she reaches out and pokes Emily right in the chest. "I like . . . your shirt," she says. Then she gnashes her teeth together.

Emily jumps. "I'll just get out of your hair!" Then she scurries down the hall after her minions.

"Come on, Zoey," Mom says, nudging her into the room. "Time to get you hooked up."

Zoey immediately starts dragging her feet, leaning into me and putting her weight on the arm that's not lugging the portable dialysis machine. This means she's pulling on the tote that has all the dialysate and saline bags, and if those pop, we're in big trouble. "Get off," I grunt.

"Too tired," she whines. Drama queen.

"You've been sitting in the car all day," I point out. "And you napped for, like, half of it."

Caught out, she straightens up and stomps over to the far corner of the room. Folding her arms, she sits down in one of the chairs in a huff.

"Thanks for your cooperation," Mom says wryly. "Oh good,

there's an outlet." She gets to work getting Zoey hooked up. Zoey, for her part, acts like a surly preteen but doesn't fight it. She's never done her dialysis away from the hospital, and I feel a surge of pride in her flexibility.

It takes a while for Mom to set up. I know she knows what she's doing, but I watch her with eagle eyes anyway. After sanitizing herself and Zoey, she plugs in the machine and gets it going. The whole system is a mess of tubes and hookups and needles, similar to what Mom spends her entire day doing at the hospital for other people. It feels different when it's for Zoey, though. I wince at the sound of the lines snapping as she gets out all the air. Finally, it's the worst part and the needle goes into Zoey's arm. She doesn't yell this time, and Mom successfully ducks a swing.

Mom straightens back up and sneaks a kiss in on Zoey's cheek. "That's my girl! All done."

Zoey grumbles but doesn't wipe the affection off her face.

Taking in the complicated process I just witnessed, I ponder an alternate reality. "Can you imagine how hard this would be if you weren't already a nurse?" I don't know how anyone does casual dialysis from home on a daily basis.

"Hm?" Mom looks up from the medical binder where she's writing everything down. "Oh, yes. It's always easier treating other people, though. The stakes feel so much higher when it's your own family." She gives me a wry smile. "I also have a lot of practice dissociating at work. It helps me buckle down and do my job with a clear head."

I can't even keep my next question in. "But when do you let it out?"

"Don't you have a bio report to get to?" Mom asks, dodging the question. "Zoey, how about you help Kaley finish her homework."

I let it slide and turn toward my sister. "Can I read you my bio report out loud?"

Zoey closes her eyes instead of answering, but I take that as permission to be the entertainment while we're stuck here for the next few hours. Clearing my throat, I start. "Cellular Processes: An Investigation into Diffusion and Osmosis." It's party time.

The report is mostly finished, except for clarifying the methodology and editing the entire conclusion. That is the tricky part. I hate endings—wrapping it all up and having to justify the entire point. Is it acceptable to just write, "It is what it is"?

Zoey interrupts every other sentence, but it forces me to go slowly and fix things. By the time I write the last line, I've got this report memorized. I should start reading my math homework out loud to her as well; maybe it will sink in. I didn't do as well in last year's precalc class due to certain—ahem—distractions. I'm willing to admit I'm lacking a few foundational concepts. It's still early in the year, though. I'll catch up. I hope. Maybe all my teachers will excuse me due to my life-and-death situation—Zoey's quality of life and my own slow death if I don't see my boyfriend soon.

There's a pull toward him, stronger now that we're only a few hours apart. Can he feel that I'm closer? Are his thoughts drifting to me whenever he has a quiet moment today? When we crossed the state line, did he feel a little prickle on the back of his neck? I've been reading too many romance novels lately.

Thrillers, too, now that I think about it. I guess any romance can be a thriller if the other party doesn't know what's going on.

Shaking my head, I focus on hitting Send on my email. I need to remind Mom to call the attendance office tomorrow. How do I convince her to preemptively excuse me for Tuesday as well? I have a feeling we'll be stopping at that motel on the way back on Monday night. My surprise Blake agenda will massively set back Mom's timeline, so if I can be officially excused before she finds out, that will save me a failed-quiz grade. I feel like at this point, I should be able to call the school myself and just play a Zoey card, but I've already played so many that they might lose their effect.

At least I didn't play a Zoey card to get out of this bio report. Can I get extra credit for that? I shut my laptop with a delicate click. "Done!"

"Great job, honey," Mom says, looking up from Zoey's medical binder. "I'm going to grab us some food and we can eat when Zoey's finished."

"Burger," Zoey votes.

"No way. You already had treats today," Mom says. "More than I gave you permission to eat. I had to pry the remnants from your hands."

"And now the dialysis has to clean out all the junk," I finish for her. But where was Mom going to find some unsalted chicken and vegetables for dinner—the gas station down the road? I told Mom she hadn't thought this road trip through.

"We could have had burgers if your sister hadn't given you candy. I'm not adding all that salt into your system on top of the food dye."

Whatever. Zoey clearly thought it was worth it at the time. I'm pretty sure if I ask her what she preferred, blue tongue or dead cow, she will pick the former.

"I'll stay here with Zo."

Mom levels me with a stare. "No shenanigans from either of you while I'm gone."

I cross my heart, and Zoey does the same. I really and truly intend to keep that promise, but it's not my fault if other people are idiots. Not five minutes after Mom's departure, someone knocks on the conference room door. "Occupied!" I yell.

The knocking persists, and I set aside the unicorn book I'm reading aloud to Zoey. I'd recently tried to get her into thrillers as well, so we would both be entertained, but after three nights of nightmares, Mom made us stop.

I yank the door open and there's a petite redhead bursting with excitement. "Oh good, I hoped someone else would still be in here! I'll have to get the code from you for the rest of the week."

She tries to duck under my arm to get in the room, but I block her. "There's been a misunderstanding. We have this room for the next hour and a half."

"I just want to go over my notes before the next presentation. I have a couple of questions—"

"Kaley! Who?" Zoey asks.

I read her name tag. "Mary."

"It's Mary-Langston."

"Langston isn't your last name?"

"No, my name is Mary-Langston McKinley."

Jesus. That name definitely isn't on my MLM bingo card. "Isn't that confusing?"

"Confusing for who?"

"I guess it's convenient. Mary-Langston McKinley. Multilevel marketing. It's all the same acronym."

"I haven't heard that one before!" Mary-Langston giggles. "You gals are pretty funny. Want to hang out while we wait? The post-dinner roundup is supposed to be a blast."

Why not? I don't have anything better to do right now other than answer a few texts from Leah. I open the door wider and motion for her to come inside. "It's boobs, by the way."

"What?"

"The passcode."

Mary-Langston looks confused, then shocked when her gaze lands on Zoey, mid-dialysis. "What happened to her?" she blurts out.

"She ate too many One Life bars."

Mary-Langston slaps a hand over her mouth.

I nod seriously. "Yep. And she's been hooked up to that machine ever since. She still can't give them up, though. That's why we're here. Dedication. We still have faith that we'll change our lives one bite at a time."

"Wow. I had no idea that could happen." Her perky tone has sobered with doubt as she tries to figure out if I'm lying to her about her beloved "nutrition" bars. "But what about, you know, the rest of what's wrong with her?" Mary-Langston asks.

My eyebrows narrow. The high road stretches out in front of me, with explanations of why Zoey is the way she is, and how it is actually completely unrelated to the kidney issues, but I've been driving too long today.

Instead, I lean forward conspiratorially. "Essential. Oils."

Mary-Langston rears back as if I'd punched her. "No, that can't be the case!"

"Now Big Oil is trying to silence our family. I'm only telling you because I trust you, Mary-Langston McKinley."

She nods seriously, eyes wide.

"One Life Nutrition promised us protection. There's a whole other side to this you've never seen. The conspiracy goes all the way to the top."

"Of the government?"

"Of the pyramid."

Dun. Dun. Dunnnnn.

I can't keep a straight face anymore and finally crack. "Naw, I'm just messing with you."

Mary-Langston needs to exhale, because if she keeps holding her breath, I'm afraid she's going to pass out. After another few seconds, she lets it out in a whoosh, but her face is reserved. I get ready for a look of dawning comprehension and for her to start laughing with me.

"Are you serious?" she asks.

This isn't good. "I just told you I was joking." Should I apologize to her? I kind of feel a little bad. But really, she started it.

"Do you, like, need help?"

"I just told you it wasn't a real secret, Mary-Langston." Her name is kind of addicting to say now. I can see why she insists on the full name. Maybe I'll force everyone to call me Kaley-Marie next year in college, just to reinvent myself, but I'm not sure it has the right ring to it.

"I can help, you know," she says. "Look into things. Ask around, see if it's happened to anyone else."

Oh Jesus. "I'm not recruiting you to our cause."

Mary-Langston puts a comforting hand on my shoulder. "I'm sorry your family has suffered."

She's sweet, in a going-to-end-up-in-a-commune type of way. I should try to deprogram her before it's too late, but before I can go back and fully explain, Mom shows up with the food.

"Zo, Kaley, you girls okay?" she asks, eyeing our visitor.

Mary-Langston turns to Mom and sashays over to wrap her in a gentle hug. "Y'all have been through so much and are such a wonderful family. I'll be praying for you. Stay strong."

Mom's arms hang at her sides, weighed down by bags of food while wrapped in Mary-Langston's arms. She shoots me a bewildered look and mouths, *Help.*

Zoey saves us. "Dinner!"

Mary-Langston pulls away. "Oh, I'll leave you to your meal. It was such a pleasure meeting you. I'll see you at the next seminar. We still have so much more to talk about." With a little wave of her fingers and "Toodles!" Mary-Langston leaves.

"Are you going to tell me what that was about?" Mom demands, dumping the takeout bags onto the closest table with a thump. A familiar smell wafts toward me.

"Where did you get a roasted chicken?"

"I went to the hotel kitchen and special ordered one. They were more than happy to accommodate a guest, especially one with special needs and dietary restrictions. Even told me I could charge it to the room."

"The conference room?"

"I'll be writing up an exceptional review on Yelp."

A sigh escapes me and Zoey at the same time. "At least I'm

not the only rational person in this family, Zoey." I turn to fist bump her but find her eyeing the spread Mom is setting up. Not a sigh of solidarity then, but of hunger.

"How much longer for her hookup, Mom?" Zoey hates that she can't eat while doing dialysis, but usually it's in the middle of the afternoon, not close to dinnertime. It must be agony right now.

Mom glances at her watch. "She has about another forty-five, at least."

"Everything will be cold by then! How about fifteen?"

She hesitates. "Thirty and we'll call it a day. It's been a long one." I like it when Mom's in charge instead of Doc Hayes.

When we're all finally eating, Mom picks at her food in between cutting up and serving Zoey's portion. I know she's thinking about the next few hours of the journey and the grand culmination of showing up at Dad's front door. They haven't seen each other in person in at least five years. I haven't seen Blake in five *weeks* and I have no idea what I'm going to say when I knock; I can't imagine what she's feeling.

Zoey picks up on the tension in the room, as she often does. Reaching one hand across the table, she grabs Mom's hand before reaching to the side to grab mine. She holds us there for a beat, linking our family together. My heartbeat slows and I feel better.

"Ready to get going, crew?" Mom asks.

I nod. "Let's do this."

"Do it," Zoey says.

CHAPTER EIGHT

"WE'RE GOING TO GET EATEN BY A BEAR."

"Don't be ridiculous, Kaley. You really think a bear is going to attack a moving vehicle?"

Mom slows down to pay attention to the speed bump. We crossed the entrance to Crater Lake National Park twenty minutes ago, and there are absolutely zero signs of human life, furthering my theory that they'd all fallen victim to the wild. Headlights are our only illumination on this deserted road, which is lacking even moonlight to make the surrounding woods less spooky. It's the perfect place for a predator to lie in wait and jump unsuspecting, slightly-lost visitors. The brush up ahead and to my right wiggles. "It's coming for us!"

I picture the news headlines the next day and think about the two wildly different ways I could be remembered. *Kaley Larssen was unfortunately bitten by rabid bear while on vacation with her family. She died running away.* The alternative: *Kaley-Marie bravely protected her family from a wild predator by trusting her gut and never backing down. Read the full article here.*

The blur of brown fur that suddenly appears on the road proves my point. Thankfully Mom, swayed by my theory although she'd never admit it, puts the pedal to the metal to blow past our attempted attacker. The car jumps forward as we refuse to become a statistic.

Except, like a deer in the headlights, I find myself staring at a deer in the headlights. "*Ahhh!*"

Mom realized her mistake a second before I did, because she's already slammed on the brake while yanking the wheel to the left. Somehow the car sideswipes the deer instead of hitting it head-on, and the wheels spin out into the dirt. Zoey lets out a scream that matches mine. When we stop, I'm staring straight at a gigantic tree that would have won this fight hands-down. *Four-hundred-year-old conifer crushes family car in a symbolic instance of technology vs. nature. More at eleven.*

Thanks to Mom's stunt driving, we are all still in one piece. Even the deer.

Except the poor thing is lying on the road, not moving. There are no blood spatters to aid forensics, but things are not looking good for our innocent victim. "*Law & Order SUV*," I mutter.

"Mom, tummy!" Zoey screams, still in full fight-or-flight mode. She's all amped-up, kicking the back of my chair with ferocity. Whereas the burst of adrenaline will leave me shaky, Zoey rides a high between excitement and violence. Considering this is our second exhibition of Mom's driving skills today, I have a feeling she's tending toward violence this time.

"Really, now?" Mom says. Her voice doesn't even shake. Her hands still grip the wheel and she's steady. A stone-cold boss.

"Are you sure you're gonna throw up?" I ask. If we take Zoey out of the backseat now, there's a good chance one of us is going to get decked. I'm betting it will take her around half an hour to come back down and not be a mess of flailing limbs.

A muffled retch precedes her answer. "All done."

The smell hits my nose. "Yep. Got it all out. Great."

Mom sighs. We're so close to Dad's cabin, if the maps are to be believed. I, for one, believe it's a very big *if.* I have reason to believe that the navigation system has been driving us in circles since we entered the park. Between the deer and the accident, I wonder if the universe is trying to tell us something.

"Let's get you changed, Zo," Mom says, getting out of the car. When she opens the door to the backseat, Zoey aims a kick her way, but Mom intercepts it, grip strength trained with years of preventing Zoey from hurting herself.

I exit the car and position myself to be on standby next to her. Another foot flies up toward Mom's face, but she deflects it. "Get some spare clothes for her from the suitcase in the back," she says to me through gritted teeth.

Walking around the car, I pull the handle to pop the trunk. I'm a little surprised it hasn't opened on its own accord during our *Fast and the Furious* escapades, especially considering how stuffed it is after repacking it post-hotel. Mom really threw everything in here in her frantic state while leaving the house this morning. Is that a space blanket in the corner? And hiking poles? I take more inventory while I struggle to haul out the big suitcase. A bag of dried beans. An electric-toothbrush charger. Three tubes of sunscreen.

The suitcase lands on the ground and I let out a grunt. "Jesus, Mom. What did you pack?"

"I wanted to be prepared for anything," Mom snaps, a little breathless with her current efforts. "Just grab some clean pants and a shirt for her. It's all down her front."

There's tension in the zipper as I bring it around the bag, and the top pops off to reveal slightly more organized chaos, a contrast to the camping supplies for the world's weirdest apocalypse stashed in the trunk. "Hurry!" Mom says. "She's a mess, and so is the seat."

I snatch the first thing of Zoey's I can see—her Elmo pajamas. At least there's a good chance she'll cooperate and put these on. "Heads up!" I toss them Mom's way.

Movement out on the road distracts me. At least, I think it was movement. The dead deer looks suspicious, and I need to take a closer look, just to be sure. Yep, there! Is that a leg twitch? Or maybe I'm too optimistic.

Her eyes are open and glassy, reflecting the headlights that bathe her in a depressing spotlight. "I'm so sorry," I whisper. Bears are one thing, but this little deer was not a threat to anyone. In all practicality, though, am I supposed to drag it to the side of the road? I'm not sure about protocol regarding roadkill and driving hazards. Or should I let nature do its thing? Predators had to be on their way, drawn to Zoey's upchuck scent and dead deer. We have to get the hell out of here.

Against my better judgment, I lean over, grab a front leg and a back leg, and give an experimental tug. For an animal that is so slender, deer are surprisingly heavy. I'm successful for about three inches, then fall back on my butt. "Oof."

I don't even see it coming. One second, I'm trying to be a good Samaritan, and the next, there's a hoof trying to land in my eye socket.

My head snaps back on instinct thanks to years of dodging Zoey, so the flailing kick only grazes my face instead of knocking me out cold. It still hurts like hell. My hands fly up to cover my eye. Piercing agony sears through my brain and I fall flat on my back.

Through the haze of pain, I'm aware when the deer scrambles to her feet and bounds off into the bushes. Stunned, then. Not dead. The world goes quiet as the shuffle behind me at the car ceases. Zoey and Mom are probably just as shocked as I am. It weirdly feels like a miracle. I've never seen anything resurrected.

My eye throbs. The last thing I want to do is stand up, but there's a set of headlights bearing down on me now, and the rumble of a big truck approaching. I roll to all fours and stagger to my feet, like, *Hello, there's a person here! Barely.*

The truck stops a safe distance away. I don't know if I'd risk stopping if I saw the same horror scene in front of me, so props to the driver. With one hand over my injured eye, my good eye squints to catch a clear glimpse of them. I'm seeing spots, and a masculine voice calls out, "Can I help you folks?" He kills the engine and dims the lights.

"No, thank you, we've got it under control!" Mom shouts back from over near our car. The spots in my eyes clear and reveal that Zoey is standing there in a shirt and a pair of clean underwear, the suitcase has been upended in the struggle, and clothes are scattered around them. I glance down at my own ruined outfit. Yep, we totally have it under control.

As if sensing our lie, the guy hops out of his truck. "Are you injured, miss?"

The more I listen to his voice, the more I want to trust him. "It's not too bad, I'm fine."

He suddenly halts his forward stride. He shoots a glance

over to Zoey and Mom again, then back to me. Yanking off his baseball cap, he reveals curly brown hair underneath, and he runs his fingers through it in disbelief.

It's impossible to mistake him now. "Hi, Dad."

First impressions are never the Larssens' strong suit. I firmly believe we are "third time's the charm" people. The first time is never good because there are too many factors to account for, including changes to Zoey's routine and the pressures of meeting new people. The second time, we tend to try too hard to make up for the disastrous first time. By the third time we've relaxed enough to let our real selves shine, and everyone loves Zo.

The trick is getting another invite *after* that first impression.

My vision for this first impression after all these years was to breezily knock on Dad's cabin door, present a bold plan of action, and have him fall in line. Notice how none of that includes vomit, a vengeful deer, and a spun-out vehicle. Now he gets to play white knight, and I'm not going to stand for it. I take a deep breath, ready to unleash, but Mom steals my thunder.

"William."

"Jules."

"Long time," she states.

"I know." Dad doesn't ask permission; he starts gathering up the clothes around the car. I watch him out of my one good eye, brain struggling to process the image of both my parents in the same frame.

Zoey, who is now fully dressed in clean clothes, doesn't say a word. She just clutches Mom's arm with owl eyes. The full explanation for this poorly executed visit is on the tip of my tongue, but no one is talking anymore. There's no way he doesn't know why we're here.

He hands me a clean T-shirt before zipping up the suitcase and walking over to throw it into the back of his truck. The vehicle doesn't have any official decals on it—it's his personal truck, not a work one. Why was he out driving on the back roads at ten o'clock at night?

"Follow me when you're ready," he says. He hops into the cab of the truck and waits for the rest of us to get organized and play a round of musical chairs.

Without the suitcase in the trunk, there's enough space to place the dialysis machine gently in the back, wedged between the dialysate tote and all the other crap that Mom deemed necessary to pack. Zoey's former seat has a towel on it to soak up the accident, and she's now in the dialysis machine's old spot. Mom and I can't get into the car yet.

There's dirt and mud all over my shirt. Trying not to get it in my hair, I attempt to gently take my T-shirt off. Before I get halfway, Mom says, "Here, let me help." I haven't needed her help like this since I was four, but I accept her expertise.

Shivering in my bra, I yank the clean shirt on as quickly as I can. It's backward, but I don't care. Mom balls up the dirty shirt and throws it in the plastic bag with Zoey's puke clothes. At least she thought of one useful item during her frantic packing.

The searing stinging just under my eye has dulled to a steady throbbing as I find my seat again. If anything, it's an afterthought compared to the painful run-in with Dad.

"Everyone buckled?" Mom asks, turning on the car.

I turn around to check Zoey, realize I can see with both eyes again, and answer for us. "Yep."

Mom pulls the car out onto the road at a crawling pace and lines up behind Dad's truck. We don't look at the map anymore, trusting the red taillights to lead us to our destination. It's only about fifteen minutes down a winding path when we roll to a stop.

Up ahead and to the left is a cabin from a storybook, but not with a Hansel and Gretel murdery vibe. Smoke rises from the chimney and the forest huddles around the walls. Warm light glows through the windows, welcoming us to this place removed from time and space. No wonder he barely gets cell service out here. Dad is already out of his truck, hauling the big suitcase up the steps like it weighs nothing.

Mom sighs and unbuckles her seat belt. "Ready to do this?" A muscle in her jaw flexes, and I can see how hard she's fighting to control her emotions. I follow her gaze to where she's locked onto the little sanctuary. It's his sanctuary, all right—a home away from *us*. It no longer looks adorable or welcoming. Dad is trying to throw us off with this no-questions attitude and a warm bed. It feels like a blow to our collective pride to accept anything from him other than the organ we came for.

Zoey yawns, which sets me off with one of my own. "Can you pretend to get along?" I ask Mom. "Just for a night. For me and Zo." To Mom's credit, they never fought in front of us growing up. Whispered conversations are all I can remember, but I could *feel* it. The tension always hung thick in the air between them, with me in the middle as the comedic and practical relief who thought if I could just anticipate what they wanted and become the version of myself that everyone needed, I could hold the family together.

Distract Mom and make her laugh, hang with Zoey and turn down other playdates, help Dad in the yard as his silent shadow. I flipped through these personalities like a deck of cards, because otherwise I might stick on one too long and the rest of my family would think I favored one person over the others.

Despite my efforts, it wasn't enough. We weren't enough. Dad moved here, Mom absolved us of any wrongdoing by declaring it was for the best, and I watched the light go out of her eyes.

Her gaze is lit up now, though, with a fire that looks ready to burn the cabin down. "Arson is a federal crime if it's in a national park," I need to remind her. "Although, I hear fed prisons are nicer than state ones, so if you're gonna do it, now is the time."

"Arson?" Zoey asks.

"It's when you set something on fire on purpose, sweets. When you want to watch it burn," I explain.

"Bad."

"Usually. But maybe it's worth it."

Mom whacks my arm. "Don't teach her that, Kaley."

"It's not like she'll play with matches!" Then I think about the laundry incident and change my mind. "No running with scissors either. Or guns. Don't set things on fire, even if Mom sets a bad example."

"Kaley!"

"What? Set a good example and promise us you won't light

a metaphorical *or* physical fire tonight, and we can all sleep a little deeper."

"Fine. I promise." Mom exits the car, storming up to the front door and leaving me to hustle behind her with Zoey. We leave everything else in the car. Our suitcase is already inside anyway.

Dad steps out of the cabin before Mom gets inside, and for a second, they're almost chest-to-chest. He leaps back like he's been burned and clears his throat. "There's a full bed in the loft with clean sheets. Just made up the couch too. I'll leave you to it." He's been busy while we sat and argued in the car, but his no-nonsense plan makes no sense.

"Where are you going to sleep?" I blurt out.

He holds up a wad of nylon material in his hand. "Hammock. Out front." Zoey's brevity is obviously inherited.

"Will, we aren't trying to kick you out—"

Dad cuts Mom off. "Wouldn't be the first time. Sleeping out under the stars, I mean." With heavy steps, he clomps in his hiking boots down the front stairs. "I'll knock in the morning," he says over his shoulder.

That's that. I know better than to argue with him, it's basically pointless. Still gripping Zoey's hand, I tug her inside the rustic space. "Pretend we're on vacation. Oh dang, it actually is adorable in here."

A little wood-burning stove sits in the corner, the wrought-iron potbelly sticking out proudly into the sitting room. It isn't a room, per se, but the entertaining space? Then again, I doubt Dad has many visitors to entertain. Whatever. There's a couch with some blankets and pillows, no TV to speak of, a table with four chairs, a bare-essentials kitchen, and a closed door in the opposite corner that probably leads to a bathroom. A compact, winding staircase leads up to a loft that overlooks the downstairs. The roof is so sloped I doubt Dad can stand up fully once he gets to the top.

"I'll take the couch," I offer.

"Don't be silly. You and Zoey take the bed. I'll be just fine on the couch." Mom takes my face gently between her hands. "First, let me have a look at your eye."

"I'm fine!" I insist. "It just grazed me. No concussion. I've had worse." We both know that's true.

Mom stares me down. "It looks like it hurts."

"It does," I admit. "But I bet it will feel better by morning. I just want today to be done."

Mom gestures toward the suitcase that sits beside the front door. "Grab your jammies, brush your teeth, and go to sleep. It's been a long day."

"Only if you promise to do the same."

She gives me a stiff smile. "I will." I hear the lie in her voice. She'll be up half the night, going over all the imaginary conversations in her head until just before dawn, then she will crash for two hours but be up making breakfast before we wake up.

Unable to help myself, I wrap her in a spontaneous hug. Her shoulders are too narrow, and I feel her bones hard against me, resisting the offer of comfort. The stress of these past few months weighs heavy on a frame that refuses to bend.

Zoey joins in to make it a group hug, and for two precious

breaths, we all meditate in the moment together. Then Mom leans over to give both of us a kiss on the forehead. "Go. Scoot."

Fifteen minutes later and with six head bumps on the roof between us, Zoey and I are tucked into bed. Zoey rolls over to face me, staring while she sorts out her thoughts. I wait.

"Dad? Mom. Go home soon?"

"I don't know. It's complicated. Hopefully, we'll all talk tomorrow, and then head home once we make a plan." Not too soon, though, because I still need to sneak away and make sure Zoey and Mom do *not* hijack that trip as well. There's some lingering guilt at forcing Mom and Zoey to stay here with Dad for a few extra hours, but not enough for me to consider aborting the mission. It's one of those ask-forgiveness-instead-of-permission scenarios. The thought sends butterflies swirling in my stomach, and I want someone else to share in my plan.

"Can you keep a secret?" Zoey nods seriously. "I'm going to surprise Blake."

"Blake." Her face splits into a huge grin. She misses him too. Then, she puckers up and pretends to kiss the air, smacking her lips until I laugh.

"Quit teasing."

Blake swore that Zoey hated him for the first month of our relationship.

"Zoey doesn't hate anybody," I assured him. "I'm pretty sure she isn't wired that way." But after three weeks of my usually bubbly sister giving Blake the cold shoulder, I started to wonder if he was right.

Blake pulled out all the stops to impress her. He took us all on ice-cream dates, told Zoey and me to pick out as many books as we could carry from the bookstore, watched a double feature of Zoey's two favorite My Little Pony movies, and she still mostly ignored him.

"Is she jealous?" I asked Mom. "Of me spending so much time with someone else."

Mom paused, her hands covered in bubbles from doing the dishes. Blake had stayed for dinner and won my mom over by dessert—which he'd baked from scratch—along with flowers for the three of us. Suffice it to say, two of the women in our house were smitten. "It might be hard for her to watch her little sister pass a milestone she will never achieve." I remember her voice broke a little on the last part. She used her wrists to wipe her eyes but still managed to get soap on her cheek.

My shiny, happy new-relationship bubble popped, and I fell back to Earth, weighed down by guilt. Zoey had crushes, hormones, and desires swirling around inside her too. Even a period each month, synced up to mine now, which was a whole bundle of fun. How maddening it must feel for her, with full comprehension and consent just out of reach. And what had I been doing? Freaking rubbing it all in her face for three weeks!

I was the worst sister in the world.

She was tucked in on the couch when I found her. "I'm so sorry, Zoey."

"What?"

"I've been insensitive, forcing Blake on you. You don't have to like him. You can feel however you want about him. I don't have to keep bringing him around, I just wanted the two most important people in my life to get along, but that's what *I* want, which is selfish—"

Zoey reached out to grab my hands, which were flapping around my face as I got worked up during my apology. "No hurt Kaley."

I wanted to cry. "Of course you didn't mean to hurt me."

"No." Zoey tried again. "Blake no hurt Kaley."

"Blake has never hurt me—oh!" The truth hit me like a train. Zoey was being the protective older sister and looking out for me. She didn't trust Blake not to break my heart, to walk out like Dad did. The sheer normality of the moment took my breath away, and a warmth radiated through my chest. It took a full minute before I could trust myself to speak again. "You're a good big sister, looking out for me."

Zoey lunged and before I could blink, she'd wrapped me up in her arms for a hug.

"Look, sweets. Whatever happens between me and Blake will happen. Maybe we'll be together forever, maybe we won't. But how about we try to enjoy his company while he's here?" Zoey still looked skeptical and rolled her eyes. "At the very least, I think he's a good person, don't you?" My sister huffed and shrugged her shoulders. Progress.

Next time he came over, Bake, Zoey, and sat I around the coffee table on the floor, brightly-colored gel pens scattered between us. Zoey's brows knit together in concentration, tongue poking out the side of her mouth. She finished with the green pen and tapped Blake's arm before handing it over, sharing her favorite color.

"Why didn't you tell me that coloring books were the key the whole time?" Blake asked me. "Zoey, were you putting up a fuss to try and make me look bad or something?"

When Zoey completed her picture that afternoon, she signed it and gave it to Blake to take home. I wonder if he still has it hanging up in his bedroom.

Maybe he brought it to his dorm room. I'll find out tomorrow when I see him.

"Don't tell Mom I'm going to visit," I warn Zoey. "It's a secret." Secrets with Zoey are a hit or miss, depending on how excited she is about it. I'm trusting her not to blurt it out over breakfast tomorrow, hoping Dad's presence is enough to distract her. I probably shouldn't have said anything at all, but secrets between sisters are sacred.

"We have some stuff we need to work out. I'll only be gone for a bit."

She nods, but looks up at the ceiling, distracted. Here I am, focusing on just my drama again.

"It's weird seeing Dad again, huh?"

"No birthday. No Christmas. No, no, no."

"Yeah, Zo. It's been a while. And I gotta say, that reunion did *not* go as planned." I shift my head on the pillow and try to get comfortable. Rolling over to see her puts pressure on my injured eye, but I do it anyway. "Do you wish we saw him more?"

In the dim light, I watch her bite her lip, considering my question. "Yes. No. Kaley and Mom sad mad."

"Sad mad is the perfect way to put it. That expression is going into my personal vernacular from now on. But I'm not talking about me and Mom, I'm asking *you*. We didn't give you much time to mentally prepare for this. I'd expect you might be feeling a bit of emotional whiplash."

She doesn't answer for a long time, and I wonder if she's frustrated with me for prying. Her brain is in processing mode, whirring away with a thousand-yard stare. Information is loading . . . loading . . . loading . . . Then she just says, "Tomorrow."

"Good idea. We should all sleep on it."

CHAPTER NINE

I WAKE UP ALONE IN BED, AND QUICKLY REALIZE I'M THE LAST ONE awake. The murmuring voices of Mom and Zoey float up to the loft, but I don't hear Dad yet. Yawning, I rub my eyes and let out a yelp. Jesus. With one finger, I touch my left eye with feather-light contact just under my lower lashes. It borders on unbearable. The swell feels like a mountain, and I'm afraid to look in the mirror. Procrastinating, I change out of my jammies and throw on some jeans and a shirt. Better, but only a little. Might as well face the music.

My fears are further confirmed when I make it down the spiral stairs with limited depth perception, and Mom gasps. "Look at your eye!"

"I'd rather not, thanks." Or maybe *eyed* rather not. I giggle, then wonder if maybe that hoof scrambled my brain.

"Go wash your face and come have breakfast."

I do as she says, but I should have gone with my first instinct—not to look—because I cannot unsee the creature reflected back at me over the tiny sink. I let out a screech. "I look like a gargoyle!" My swollen black eye twists my expression into a grotesque caricature, my face is puffy from sleep and junk food, and my hair stands on end like I'm a lightning-strike victim. At this point, I'd welcome a bolt of electricity to end my suffering.

Through the haze of horror, I remember that I'm going to see Blake today. He'll take one glance at me through the peephole, mistake me for an OSU student, and I'll be dragged off by campus security. My plan had been to dress up and breeze into his dorm room, strutting my stuff and showing him what he's been missing. He'll see today what he's missing, all right—that trip to Notre Dame Cathedral. He did always say he was bummed he skipped it on his European tour last summer. Now's his chance to experience it in real time.

Taming my hair is the easiest place to start. While I'm normally content to throw it into a topknot, for the sake of professionalism today I pull it back into a high ballerina bun. Now that my hair is off my face, does it draw more attention to my eye, or less? I'll figure it out later. My teeth are next and then finally, I cup my hands under a trickle of cool water and splash a bit on my face. It doesn't burn as bad as I thought it would. By the time I dab with a purple towel—who knew Dad liked purple?—I can see clearly out of both eyes.

Feeling more confident, I open the bathroom door straight into a body waiting on the other side. "Jesus, kid." My fingers fly to my eye and I'm self-conscious all over again. "I brought you these." Dad hands me a bag of peas that look like they've been in his freezer since he moved here, maybe even from the previous owner. They're wrapped in a baby-blue towel. Does he have other frozen vegetables in his fridge? Does he intend to eat these peas, or is their sole purpose to be an ice pack? How often does he use them? Has he ever accidentally gone to cook dinner and been like, *Oops, can't cook these. These are the first-aid peas.* He always hated cooking when he lived at home.

He clears his throat, and I realize I've been staring at the bag. "It's for your eye," he explains, like I can't figure that out.

"Thanks," I snap.

He turns to go back into the kitchen but stops. "It happened to me too. Except I got kicked in the ear. It rang for a week."

Despite my attitude, I have to ask, "When?" Dad was always so selective with his stories growing up, and every morsel of information he chose to share felt precious. I hate that I still crave these scraps. I want to suck the question back into my lungs, but it hangs in the air between us.

"A buck got himself caught in a fence."

I wait for him to continue, but apparently that's it. Awesome. I pause for a dignified moment, refusing to chase after him like a little kid. I hold the peas to my eye and let out a hiss. It hurts, but a minute later I feel nothing other than comfortably numb. I'm ready to face my family.

The silence is painful when I approach the kitchen. The doe should have kicked me in the ear as well as the eye, because tinnitus would be an upgrade to this. We're all waiting for Dad to speak first, demand answers, something. We descended upon him late last night with no explanation and took over his house. Yet he stands there at the counter, sipping his coffee and staring out the window at the trees. Zoey seems equally baffled by him, staring at him with such a lack of self-awareness that she's hardly blinking. Mom pretends to busy herself and loads up a plate of breakfast for me.

"How do you feel, dear?" Mom asks, setting a plate of bacon and eggs in front of me.

"You should see the other deer," I joke. No one laughs. I bite my lip and look at my plate, stomach churning at the sight of the greasy food. I'm so full of nerves with all this awkwardness, my body is rebelling. "Uh, can I get a glass of water?"

"Sure, let me find a cup." Mom starts rummaging through the cabinets, then slams one shut. She's not holding a glass. It's a bottle of wine.

"You're drinking again, Will." There's no accusation in her voice, just resigned sadness.

Dad snaps out of his trance and turns to look at her. His face betrays no emotion, but he answers, "No, I'm not."

"You're going to stand there and lie right to my face? In front of our children?"

"I'm not drinking again. Haven't touched the stuff in years."

"The bottle is *open*."

"It's not mine."

"Then whose is it?" Mom demands. Dad doesn't answer right away, and I see the dawning comprehension on her face. "Oh," she says, a little breathless.

The blue and purple towels. The extra set of clean sheets. The open wine. A decently stocked fridge. I bet if I look a little harder in the bathroom, there will be some bobby pins scattered around. Small hints of a feminine presence in his home, enough clues that show she's marked her territory.

For the first time since we got here, Dad's mask of reserved calm finally slips. He swallows audibly while Mom waits for an explanation. "It's not serious."

Mom scoffs. "Of course it's not. You can't take anything in your life seriously."

Does this mystery woman know that we exist? How long

have they been seeing each other? Is she also a park ranger? I need answers quick in case I get kicked outside when they start yelling. Maybe now is the time to bring up Cole, and I can level their playing field while getting all the information I need. Sliding my plate toward Zoey, I scooch closer to her as quietly as I can. The stool still scrapes across the floor, reminding our parents that they have an audience.

Zoey chooses this moment to strike. "Hi, Dad. Hi. Hi. Hi."

He startles, and I realize these are her first words to him since we got here. She never calls him Dad over the phone. She'll usually say hello, then wander off, leaving me to entertain him on my own. "Hi, Zoey."

"Zoey Baloney," she corrects, then returns to her breakfast.

An acknowledgment of the nickname he used to call her, before he left. Was it a dig at him? Should I try to give her a high-five? I admire her strategy; it seems to have thrown him way off kilter.

"Hi, Zoey . . . Baloney."

He may have forgotten, but she never will.

She doesn't look at him again. I'm not about to remind him about Kaley-bo-bailey, and I would appreciate getting back to the regularly-scheduled parent fighting.

"I know you didn't come all this way to berate my choice of company, Jules. Why are you here?"

Mom puts the wine back on the shelf and runs her fingers through her hair. When she turns to face Dad again, she's got her nurse face on—deadly focused. "I'm here because you *won't answer your damn phone.*"

Tell him, Mom!

Dad rubs a hand down his face. "I was going to call you back. Today, in fact."

"Why won't you just tell us what the tests said?" I blurt out. I've kept quiet long enough. "You're either a match or you're not. But you can't just leave us in limbo. This is bull—"

"It's hard to explain," Dad interrupts, not meeting my eye, which is good because I'm starting to see red.

"Oh, I get it," I retort. "You didn't know how to tell us that you're a match, you just don't wanna give it up!"

"Kaley, enough. I'm handling this," Mom says.

"It's not that," Dad says. Of course, he's going to try to defend himself, as if anything he says can excuse the fact that he's denying his daughter a life-saving surgery. He hasn't been there for all the dialysis appointments. He hasn't been there for all the diet changes. He hasn't been there to explain why absolutely everything is harder for her and *it's just not fair*. It's his fault she'll go on the transplant list, and I'll never forgive him. Never ever ever ever.

"William, why didn't you call me back?" Mom asks. "How do you think it makes me feel that I can't get a hold of you in an emergency? We're still co-guardians."

Dad hangs his head. "I didn't know how to explain myself. I just needed more time. If there was a real emergency, I figured you would call the Ranger Headquarters and they would radio me."

That *would* have been the logical route. Much more so than an impromptu nine-hour road trip just to yell at him in person. But I gotta say, I'm on Mom's side with this one. She's turning red, struggling to find the words to convey what she is feeling against his flippant attitude.

"Must be nice," I say. "To choose to check out when it's convenient. To let Mom decide if something is an emergency or not. To be the one who reacts instead of acts."

What a life, to trust that other people are doing the right thing, so you don't have to worry or even think too hard about it. Zero accountability. All he has to do is throw the minimum amount of financial support at the problem, and poof! It no longer takes up space in his brain. Mom should threaten to switch places with him. Live out her *Boxcar Children* dreams in the quiet woods and expect someone to radio her "if it's a real emergency."

Except she would never do that to Zoey, so she might as well bang her head against a wall and expect Dad to get a headache. He doesn't respond, but sits there, staring, as if he's never really seen me before. There's a good chance that's actually the case.

"I think we need to finish this conversation away from curious ears," Mom says.

We are in agreement on that. "Hey Zo," I say, "how about you head up to the loft and you can wear my headphones and watch a movie on my phone?" There are a couple of her favorites already downloaded that I save for situations just like this. Well, not this exact situation, because we've never done *this* before, but I'm thankful that I usually anticipate the worst.

"Actually, Kaley, I need you to take Zoey outside for a while. Your dad and I need to talk."

"You're icing me out? Seriously?" I've been to almost every

doctor's appointment. Learned about all the dietary changes. Given Zoey her meds. Kept her entertained. And this is how Mom wants to play it? "You can't expect me not to have a say in all of this. I've earned it."

"Yes, you have," Mom agrees. "Which is why I'm trusting you to deal with Zo while I deal with your father. We're a team, remember?"

I push my full plate away and hop off the stool. "Fine. But I'm telling you now, I'm getting really sick of only being treated like an equal when it's convenient. One of these days you're going to have to make up your mind on if I'm a teammate or if I'm your kid, because I'm not going to keep doing this back-and-forth thing."

Mom stares me down, hands on her hips. "I'm as transparent as I can be with you. What I need right now is for you to let me handle this."

Zoey is still stuck on the movie promise. "Mickey?" she asks, not getting off her perch until there's a better offer of entertainment on the table. I think we should all be able to stay, Zoey especially because it is about her, but I'll admit that this drama might be more PG-13 instead of PG. Maybe even an R if it deteriorates enough. Zoey might learn a few new words to yell at the park, and then suddenly it will be *my* fault if she says them around little kids. Personally, I'm a fan of a well-placed swearword, but Zoey has trouble with appropriate context. Except that one time she totally dropped an F-bomb when some lady knocked over a shoe display at the mall. I was so proud of her that day.

I turn away from my parents and sigh, resigning myself to my usual method of gathering intel. "Yeah, get your shoes on and we can watch Mickey outside." And maybe check my text messages too. There's got to be a spot to get a signal somewhere, but I haven't found it yet. There's zero chance I'm asking Dad for anything right now, even if it's the password that allows me to connect to civilization.

Zoey has her shoes on the wrong feet, but we're not going far. I push open the door and say, "After you." Before I follow her, a flash of hot anger surges through me, and the only team I'm on is mine and Zoey's. Turning back over my shoulder, I lock eyes with Dad. "Zoey needs your kidney ASAP. Figure it out."

My sister is not about to let me have the last word, because she shouts, "Thanks!" from the front porch to our shocked parents. I laugh at her quick wit, rage diminished as quickly as it came on. She either understands way more about this than we give her credit for, or it's actually a heartfelt thanks, which is equally funny right now.

From our spot on the front-porch bench, I listen to see how this is going to play out, but it's annoyingly quiet. "Come on, Zoey. Ninja mode." She grabs my arm, and we creep down the steps. Hunched over, we make our way around the corner of the cabin to stand underneath the kitchen window. All of a sudden, my phone starts pinging, six times in a row before I can pull it out of my pocket and silence it.

"Kaley, phone!"

"Shh, Zo, I know," I whisper. But she's staring at me expectantly, so I sigh and check the notifications. My heart leaps when I see three texts—one from Leah, one from Declan, and one from Blake.

Of course I click on my boyfriend's text first. *Kal Imiss*

youe soooo much. My heart soars. The urge to jump in the car and speed all the way to campus overwhelms me. He sent the text at 1:48 a.m., which means he's probably wondering why I haven't responded all morning. Poor Blake, up studying hard in the middle of the night, yet still thinking of me. There's a forty percent chance it was a drunk text, but I'm giving him the benefit of the doubt.

Babe, I can't tell you how much it means for me to hear that, I text back. *I miss you more than anything. I can't wait to see your face.* I stop myself from writing *soon* at the end. I'm dying to give him a hint that I'm coming, but the surprise on his face will be worth it. I hit Send, but the message gets kicked back as "not delivered." Waving the phone over my head, I try to get a signal again.

No luck. I read Leah's message next, which says, *Where you at, girl? Get that kidney yet? On your way to U of O? If you don't answer Imma know you're nice and busy with the boy. *winky face**. Sent at 8:02 a.m. It's almost nine now, so she's just about to leave our AP bio class. She's going to hold those notes hostage until I give her the juicy details about the trip.

I respond to her anyway, even if the text isn't going to send. *Might have hit a temporary road block, will know more soon. Can't leave to see Blake until I know what's up. Dad being shady. Also is dating again? Not the reason for being shady, but weird nonetheless.*

Of all the information in the text, I know the snippet Leah will respond to, first. I can just see her answer—*Well, does the girlfriend have a spare kidney you can borrow?*

Declan is last. At least I know it will be over a week before he'll check my response, so there's no hurry. *Yooooooo why did you duck out of the party before we could do the dance-off I was gonna win? You're avoiding me?*

Well, he used the right *you're*, at least, and even though I like to reward good grammar, I can't bring myself to think of a response. There's too much to unpack about seeing Dad, and historically Declan has been too flaky for me to trust him with the important things. Except he really did come through for me at Beth's birthday party. It feels like I saw a completely new side of him. No, that's not right. Not a new side of him, because Declan is always up-front with the world about who he is. Maybe I just witnessed a side that I'd purposefully ignored until now.

For therapy's sake, I type out a response that is not going to get sent: *Just on a crazed road trip to get my sister a kidney, visit my estranged father, avoid getting kicked by another deer, and maybe have sex with my boyfriend for the first time. NBD.*

How's that for an explanation, Declan?

I exit out of my text messages while Zoey tugs at my arm.

"Kidney," she says, drawing my attention back to the matter at hand. Voices overhead are getting louder, and I think she's right, we'll hear something good soon.

". . . yes, Will, now."

"I'm a match," he answers. My heart soars. "But I can't donate right now." What on earth does that mean?

Mom's voice is quieter, so I can only make out a little bit. Something, something ". . . timeline."

Dad grumbles, then Mom's pitch gets more frantic. "Tell me you've already started."

"I'm trying, Jules. Haven't touched one in forty-eight hours. Wanted to know for certain I could do it before I gave anyone false hope."

Excuse me? What the actual f—?

Their voices are clearer now. I think they're standing right next to the sink, which is helpfully near the slightly open window above our hiding place. "I can't believe you've been smoking again, Will. What did you do, give up one vice for another? Or did you really believe you wouldn't be the one who had to donate? You could have stopped *months* ago, when this all started. Just in case I wasn't the match. Tried to be a real parent."

"Now, just a second," Dad's voice has an edge now. "I never said I wouldn't donate."

"Yes," Mom snaps. "Let's celebrate the donation we'll all wait with bated breath for you to follow through on, because you have *such* a great track record. You can't donate while you're smoking. You need to stop for at least six weeks, for your sake and hers to mitigate the risks. Zoey's going to end up on that list when you can't. Are you going to tell her, or should I? I can't walk this road alone with her, Will."

"I thought we agreed you'd get help for Zoey next year anyway. You said you were looking into it, what with the group homes." Dad is further behind than I realized, because that was decided a year ago by now. Done and dusted, a collective decision by the Larssen women that outside assistance for Zoey is a no-go.

"I still am."

What?

"Don't change the subject, Will," Mom snaps. "I'm not talking about that right now. We're talking about *you*. I'm not leaving here until we have a plan."

Wait. Yes, change the subject. Go back to the group-home thing. What is Mom talking about?

"I need to check in at work," Dad states firmly. "We'll talk about this when I get back."

Mom and I have the same thought because she yells, "Don't walk away from me right now!"

Then the sound of the front door slams from around the corner, and I whip my head around the wall to watch him, all caution aside in my absolute outrage and confusion. What did Mom mean she's still looking into group homes? My head is spinning as I watch Zoey's match for a kidney transplant snag the open carton of cigarettes from the porch railing and shove them into his pocket. No no no no, this is not happening. Zoey and I stay frozen in our hiding spot while the rumble of Dad's truck engine starts up. He wrenches the vehicle around the gravel driveway, treating it like a sports car, then flooring it out of here.

"Uh-oh," Zoey says, staring up at the house.

As I slowly lift my chin, my gaze finds Mom's face, frowning down at us from the window. She shakes her head and thrusts her pointer finger at the glass before saying, "You are in so much trouble." I could send her a message with *another* finger that would also be loud and clear, but my thoughts are still reeling from their conversation.

"Zoey and Kaley. Come inside right now," Mom shouts, like we're seven and nine years old and we're hiding outside because we don't want to come in for dinner. But I'm not hiding anymore. I'm furious.

After stomping around the side of the house to face Mom, who is now standing on the front porch, I plant my feet in the gravel and cross my arms. Zoey mimics me in a solidarity way, not a mocking way. How much did she understand of our parents' fight? She isn't in control of anything that's happening to her. Does she feel helpless? Is she mad? All the conversations about her surround her and nobody ever *asks*.

Mom sighs. "Just get inside."

"No. You need to explain to me and Zoey what we just heard."

Mom's face goes carefully blank. "I don't know what you think you just heard, but Dad is going to think about how to get the donation on track while he's at work. Hopefully we will pick up the conversation this afternoon, but we might not head home until tomorrow. Depends on how long it takes for him to get his head out of—"

"Don't gaslight me. You didn't think to tell me that you suddenly decided a care home was on the table?"

"Is this more talk from Blake's Psych 101 class? I thought he still wanted to be an accounting major."

I resist the urge to move. She thinks she's talking me down, distracting me, but in my head, I'm imagining shaking her shoulders so hard her teeth rattle. Boy, this trip is really showing a whole new side of me. Slapping a stranger at a gas station was just the beginning. I'm about to turn feral.

"Is this because I'm leaving next year? You're making me choose between my future or Zoey's," I snarl. "You knew I'd never be on board with this plan."

"Oh, don't be so dramatic." Mom waves me off. "That's not what I'm doing. I need to have a plan in case Zoey still has to continue dialysis for who knows how long. And thank God I have one now that this weekend has gone off the rails. Now it all depends on your father following through on quitting smoking in order to undergo the donation, which we know is a fifty-fifty shot. Remind me to give him the guardianship paperwork when he gets back, as an incentive."

Normally, I would agree. Keep the peace. See the logic in Mom's choices and take the emotion out of it. The care home is still just a backup plan, apparently. Who cares, right? Other than the fact that she kept yet another secret from me. What she's doing is practical. Except I saw Dad take those cigarettes. We're nowhere near the donation yet. What is going to happen next year? I stretch and stretch and stretch around her reasoning, contorting myself like I always do.

Then, suddenly, I snap.

Zoey and Mom sense it. Zoey takes a step toward me while Mom takes a step back. Zoey's hand on my shoulder is the only thing keeping me grounded to the planet. My body vibrates on a completely new frequency, and my brain floats outside of my head. After two rapid, shallow breaths, I'm on the move.

"Kaley, just talk to me," Mom says as I brush past her. She could reach out and physically stop me, but she doesn't. In a dreamlike trance, I'm propelled inside by my legs, all the way to the kitchen counter, where I pick up the car keys and nothing else.

Mom sees the keys in my hand. "Where do you think you're going?"

Away. But I can't open my mouth to answer her. My ability to communicate has been stripped from me. I can't trust her.

I don't trust Dad. I need Blake. He'll help me make sense of all this.

Mom lunges right to block my path down the steps, but I dart left and hop the porch rail. In typical graceful fashion, my back foot catches on the wood and my vault is more of a tumble. While I'm splayed on the dirt and trying to orient myself, a hand appears. I take it without question, and Zoey helps pull me to my feet. I force myself to look at her, and even though I still can't speak, her eyes show me that she gets what I'm feeling. "Go."

I auto-unlock the car and sprint toward it. I'm behind the wheel before Mom can catch up. She's not giving up that easily, though, because she's banging on the driver's side window a second later as I'm starting the engine.

"Kaley Marie, you do *not* have permission to take this car."

My middle finger gives the salute it's been waiting for, and I floor it. Gravel spews from under the tires and I make it a good way down the drive before I slam on the brakes. Reaching over to the glovebox, I pull out the thick stack of legal papers and that Fides brochure. I know exactly what it is, now. When I roll down the window, I can hear Mom shouting at me still from near the cabin. When my foot finds the gas again, I trail my hand out the window and let the papers flutter behind me like leaves.

CHAPTER TEN

I DRIVE FOR A GOOD TEN MINUTES BEFORE I CAN BREATHE REGULARLY again, realizing at the same time that I'm dangerously close to becoming hopelessly lost. Pulling over to the side of the narrow road, I hit the GPS screen. This thing barely works anymore, and I jam my finger hard trying to get it to function. I can't remember Blake's dorm address, but entering the University of Oregon campus should get me close enough. Some nice frat boy will give me directions once I'm there.

When the robot voice tells me I've already gone nine minutes in the wrong direction, I try not to take it as a sign for the next two and a half hours to come. Except I think I can make it in two. Thank God this trip was already half-planned because I don't know how I could have stayed at the cabin half-cocked. Mom's betrayal cut me in ways I don't want to think about right now. My only focus is getting to my boyfriend, falling into his arms, smelling his neck, and hearing him say that he will love me forever. Then I'll rip the band-aid off.

A National Parks ranger truck pulls up behind me and stops in a cloud of dust. This better not be Dad, coming to drag me back. Not even my luck can be that terrible; and based on the morning I've had, karma and the universe owe me a solid. What is the jurisdiction radius for a park ranger, anyway? Does Dad have the power to arrest anyone? Do I just have to get through the gates to be considered a free woman if I'm on the lam?

I slump in my seat, willing whoever it is to go away. I could pretend I'm an exhausted tourist, except for the fact that it looks like I'm living in my car, thanks to the sheer amount of snack wrappers and miscellaneous crap stuffed in here with me. If I don't get arrested for grand theft auto, a ticket for vagrancy will be on the docket.

A sharp rap on the window startles me. Instead of irritation, the woman standing next to the car stares at me with open, honest concern on her face. Oh, my black eye. Right.

Rolling down the window, I ask, "Can I help you, Officer?"

She doesn't smile back, but she does say, "I'm not an officer, honey. Just a ranger. Do you need help? Is there something wrong with your car?"

"Ah, no. Just got a little turned around. I figured it out. Front gate is that way, right?" I point my thumb over my shoulder, back at the way she just came from.

"Yes." She hesitates before continuing. "Are you *sure* there's nothing I can help you with?"

My mouth tries to smile, but it ends up as more of a grimace. "Nope, I'm good," I force out, as perky as I can muster.

"I'm not sure I'd feel good about just letting you go like this," she says. Her gold name tag reads RACHEL. Rachel is a good person, I can tell. But Rachel needs to mind her own business. "I've been where you are," she says, so quiet I almost miss it.

Well, crap. My people pleasing kicks in, and I spin a story to make her feel better. "I'm on a road trip to visit my . . . friend. It's been a long few days, but I'm really close now. Less than an hour, I promise. I just need to get to them." I could ham it up by adding *or else*, but that would be a bridge too far. Especially because I already feel like a terrible person for lying to her.

Rachel is wavering, so I let out a yawn. That part isn't a lie. I've lived a thousand hours since this trip started yesterday morning. "Hold on," Rachel says. She walks back to her truck and returns with a full, insulated thermos of coffee. "Take this."

"What?" I balk. "This is a nice thermos. I can't take this from you."

"Please. I'm just passing along the good deed someone did for me years ago. I promised myself I would do the same if given the chance. You can do the same one day and pay it forward. That cup of coffee saved my life."

Tears well in my eyes as I take the bright-purple thermos. I owe her a little bit of the truth. "I'm not a good person," I confess, thinking about leaving my mother and my sister in the dust. Mom might have deserved it, but Zoey sure didn't, even if she's the one who told me to go.

Rachel's gentle smile is undeterred. "It doesn't seem to me like you're giving anyone a hard time; you're just having a hard time. There's a difference."

If only Rachel knew the extent of it. My whole family is worse off now than yesterday. We should have just stayed home. Then I wouldn't have had my heart broken by Dad's smoking confession, or Mom's betrayal. This whole journey has been utterly pointless so far, moving us backward even though we've traveled hundreds of miles from home.

"It's just that nothing is getting any better," I tell her, my voice thick. It's too complicated to explain more than that. The back story alone would mean I'm out here all morning. Plus, I'd rather not be the water-cooler drama for all the rangers over the next week. Do park rangers gossip at a water cooler? Maybe for them it's around a campfire.

"But are you running from something, or to something?"

"Both? I don't know. But also, thank God I'm not, like, *actually* running." I shudder against my cushioned seat, imagining physical exertion this early in the morning. Yes, I guess it could always be worse.

Rachel laughs. "I've often found the difference is that running from something is stressful but running to something is exciting."

Funny how swapping out just one word changes the entire meaning. Right now, am I running to Blake, or from my family? Blake deserves to be the one I'm running to, despite the fact that the events this morning were my starting gun. He can't be my escape; I won't put that on him. He is enough on his own, existing as his wonderful self, and my own motivations need to be pure before I navigate the twenty minutes back through the park and get on the highway. I can't risk any more bad karma coming at me like a hoof.

"To him," I decide, swallowing the painful lump in my throat. "I'm running to him." I sit up straighter with my declaration. My tears have already dried, and I can draw a full breath now. My heart has stopped racing and I'm feeling steadier with clear purpose. "You know, you're pretty good at this, the whole words-of-wisdom thing."

"I try," Rachel says, smiling wryly. "For what it's worth, I think you'd have figured this all out pretty quick on your own."

I shrug. "Maybe. But it's still nice to get some free coffee."

"Drive safely. And I hope whoever you're running toward is waiting to catch you with open arms."

"Oh, he is," I say with a cheeky grin. Once he gets over his shock when I bowl him over at the door.

Rachel gets back in her truck but waits until I'm back on the road and driving the correct way before she eases out to continue in the opposite direction. I wave at her through the rearview mirror before her truck disappears from sight. Now that I'm oriented, I might as well bust out my coffee. I hit the Cruise button and steer with my knees to crack open the lid. I take a swig, and it scalds my mouth, punishing me.

"Blah!" I spit. A fresh stain spreads across my light pants. If I wasn't so pissed at myself, I'd be impressed at the quality of my new thermos. This thing holds lava. I'm set for the entire drive. I put the lid back on and put it in the cup holder, channeling my emotions into my lead foot and pushing my speed higher.

After a few minutes I'm out of the park gates and the flow of the nearly empty road lulls me into a state of calm acceptance. I handle the curves and let my thoughts wander. Mom will be furious right now. My phone has service again but still hasn't rung. The uneasy silence is worse than incessant ringing would be. If she were calling nonstop, I would know where I stand. A communication blackout is new territory for us. I turn off my phone before she finds a pocket of cell service at the cabin, so I can focus on what I'm going to say to Blake when I get to his dorm.

I love you, I'll say. Predictable. Cliché. *Take me*. What am I, a busty heroine from a romance novel? *I missed you*. Duh.

I'm sorry. An apology for sure, because after what I saw this morning, I'm going to have to tell him our countdown for our year apart is probably going to be suspended. Not indefinitely. Just until the transplant is over and I can know for sure again that I'll be joining him in around, oh, three hundred days. Not that I've been keeping track.

This is so not how I wanted this trip to go. I wanted to share the good news with him in person—"Dad's a match! Zoey is getting the kidney and will be back to normal in mere months! Everything is proceeding exactly according to plan and I'm coming to University of Oregon next year because my sister will *definitely* not be in some group home!"

I'm trying to stay positive while I settle in for the long drive, trying to imagine what the coming years will look like if I hold on to hope and Dad comes through in time. I'll have to go back and forth from Idaho as often as I can. Schedule out the long weekends. If Zoey doesn't have dialysis anymore it will be much easier for her and Mom to come visit me too. My soul already feels stretched taut between my family duties and my guy. Will it get easier over time, or harder? Mom's initial protests about me going to U of O seemed exaggerated, but now I'm not so sure. After two days on the road, the distance is no longer ambiguous, and frankly, it freaking sucks.

As I'm focusing on logistics, the image of Dad snagging those cigarettes and leaving us in the dust keeps popping up. A tear traces down my cheek, and I brush it away angrily. I refuse to lose hope, not yet, but I need to be honest with Blake today about the "maybe" for next year. Dad is a match, but there's complications. I'm not going to lie to Blake by omission again, especially not after he was so understanding two days ago. That's a dangerous precedent to set and he deserves the truth. No more self-sabotage. No more letting my anxieties have a say. We can handle it together—I have to believe our relationship is strong enough to tackle anything, even if it means our timeline is delayed.

I'm going to make this visit count. Salvage the original plan of this trip with an afternoon spent proving our eternal love—in the physical sense—*then* deliver the uncertain news. A deep sigh helps push the negative emotions down. I'm still in control of this situation, even when my parents are determined to set fire to my carefully laid plans. I'm fine. This is fine. I'll just pat out the occasional errant flame and nobody will know. Just a little while longer and I'll see him, trying not to smell like burnt hair.

This is a huge step for us, one that I hereby declare myself ready for. Life is short and unpredictable, and we should celebrate it while we can.

A squeal of excitement escapes me when I spot my first University of Oregon campus sign. The exit eases the car off the highway. I should stop for gas, but my forward momentum can't be interrupted. In just a few minutes, I'll be kissing Blake's face off.

The increasing number of pedestrians lets me know I'm on the right track and to keep heading toward the middle of campus. This place is huge—my entire town could fit onto the college grounds. The inhabitants all look so bright and shiny and carefree in the October sunshine. I pop on my sunglasses in an attempt to dim their light. Are all college kids so attractive? Is it a requirement? Because truth be told, yellow really isn't my color.

Four years here. Maybe three, if I have to spend a year at Boise State first because I can't trust my parents. And then after that, I don't know. I am fairly confident I'm not supposed to know yet, because having my entire life planned out at seventeen would be nuts. But being here will be my first opportunity to establish an identity as just Kaley, not "Zoey's sister." She wants that for me, right? Do I want that?

I shake my head to clear it of insecurities.

There—Carson Hall! That's it. And is that a parking spot outside his dorm? Finally. I pull in, and it reads ZONE C PARKING ONLY. Dang, I think I need an official pass. I back out and keep going. Farther down and a few turns onto some narrow side streets, and I think I'm on Greek Row. Cars are lined up on the streets even more densely than in the middle of campus, an endless colorful snake wrapping around battered houses that have seen better days. There's a couch on the front lawn of one. A freshly broken porch rail hangs by splinters on another home's patio. Is that a mattress on the roof over there? Must've been some weekend.

Just when I'm about to give up, I find my spot. For someone who rarely gets to practice, I pride myself on my parallel-parking technique. Mom taught me, and I never questioned until yesterday why she was so confident behind the wheel. Now I know she's been holding out on me, especially because she never passed along her drifting skills. Another perfectly rational reason to add to the list of why I'm no longer speaking to her today.

My complete focus is on lining up the car and sliding it into the barely big enough space, so I don't notice I have an audience. When I get out, there are three guys in sleeveless T-shirts clapping for me from their porch. I recognize some of the Greek letters hung over the doorway. Beta Zeta something?

"Gorgeous," one of them compliments.

"Teach us your ways."

"We've been playing a game all morning," a boy with a shaved head says. "Eight other cars have tried to take that spot and failed. And you did it in one try!"

I push my sunglasses further onto my face, so my disastrous eye doesn't make an appearance and ruin their cool impression of me. A faint blush creeps up my cheeks at the attention, but instead of thanking them, I blurt out, "You have nothing better to do than watch people park?"

He shrugs. "Well, we turned it into a drinking game."

My mouth parts in shock. "It's not even noon. On a Monday."

"What, are you new around here?"

"Um. Yes. I'm a prospective student. I'm coming here next year." Hopefully.

Shaved Head Guy's face splits into a grin. "Excellent! That means you're invited to the party tonight so we can properly induck you."

"I think you mean *induct*."

"Quack. Welcome to U of O."

I certainly don't intend on partying with a bunch of frat boys instead of being with Blake, but they can tell I'm thinking of an excuse to turn them down.

He jumps on my hesitation. "You'll have changed your mind

by the time you come back to get your car. See you tonight, High School."

Not likely. But if that means I don't have to keep driving around and looking for parking, I'll take it. "Can you point me in the direction of Carson Hall? I'm completely turned around."

"About a mile through campus. That way."

I'm on my way when I hear one of the other guys whine, "Well, now what game are we going to play? I don't have class until two. I was just getting a buzz on."

A chuckle escapes me. They seemed rather nice, not at all like how Blake described Greek life here. He had agreed to attend his father's alma mater but told me that joining his dad's fraternity would have been a step too far. It had been an awkward family dinner this summer when he sat his parents down and told them. I thought James was going to flip the table for a minute, but he settled on storming off with his glass of wine and not coming back until dessert was served.

Blake's mom, Elena, just rolled her eyes and ignored her husband. "He'll come around," she assured Blake. "He just wants what's best for you. His choices served him well, and he thinks this is the way to ensure this same life for you one day. Oregon is just the first step, then graduate school . . ."

Blake's mom was always the more reasonable of his parents. Normally she was on our side, ever since we first met. After I had shaken her hand, Elena had cocked her head and said, "You're in Blake's class? I don't recognize your name."

"I'm a junior," I had clarified.

Recognition had sparked in her face. "Oh, *this* is who you were talking about with your dad!"

Blake had blushed so hard his ears turned red, side-eying me. "Um, yeah, maybe. He was asking about the test, and Kaley you came up because you know we sit near each other—"

Elena put a hand over her heart and laughed. "She's the reason Dad is so worried about your grade. I can see why. Kaley, you're an adorable distraction. And quite funny, too, if I overheard right. You're the one with the—you have a sister, don't you?" Elena asks.

Small-town life. "Yes. Zoey."

"I'll have to officially meet her one day."

As I sat at the twelve-foot-long table trying to focus anywhere but Blake's family feud, I realized we never had gotten around to getting both our families together. I tuned out Blake's mumbling and looked around the Parsons' formal dining room, focusing on the giant chandelier hanging above our heads. There are a lot of earthquakes in the Pacific Northwest. Was that thing properly secured? The glittering opulence turned sinister, hanging above our heads like a guillotine waiting for the foundation to shake.

"Maybe I don't need antique furniture and thousand-dollar bottles of wine and five cars to be happy," Blake said.

Elena leaned over the table and patted his hand. "Of course you don't, dear. But keep your mind open and say yes to opportunities that come up this fall. This is a special time in your life to try a wide variety of things you would never expect to like."

Blake threw an arm around my shoulder. "I already know what I like."

My heart races now as I speed-walk across campus. My nervousness is replaced by impending joy at seeing him in person. My steps slow down, though, when I reach a crossroads. Which way is the right one? I need to ask for directions again. I refused to take my phone with me when I left the car, but now I feel a bit silly for being so paranoid. But what if Mom's able to track my location when I turn it on? I'm not going to risk it.

There are two girls walking toward me, so similar with their long, dark hair in waves around their shoulders and their matching green-and-yellow sweatshirts that they could be sisters. They aren't, though, because one of them says, "Oh my God, my mom will not stop spamming me with these stupid Facebook articles."

"Which conspiracy theory is she obsessed with this time?"

"I don't even know. Something about how those essential oils she loves so much have been taken over and corrupted by the pharmacy industry. 'What You Don't Know About Big Oil.' Jesus."

The other girl groans. "Can't you just, like, block her posts?"

I'm about to step out in front of them to ask them which way to Carson Hall but wait a few extra seconds for an opening in their conversation.

"I'll see you in a few."

The girl who is busy texting her mom back looks up from her phone in surprise. "Oh, I thought you were headed to the library to study with Riley."

"Yeah, I'm picking up my study partner's notes at his dorm first. He's over in Carson."

Perfect.

"That's really nice of him."

"Yeah, he's a total sweetheart. See ya, girl. Let's do coffee later."

"Don't get too distracted, Addie," the other girl says with a smirk. "You said he's cute."

I wait for Addie to walk past before letting a respectable distance stretch between us. Then I fall in line behind her, wondering if I should have just asked her for directions instead of assuming stalker status. If I had, maybe we would have fallen into an easy banter along the path to the dormitory. Then I'd really be able to prove that I fit in here. I've already been invited to a party tonight—not that I'm going, but still—and now I have the opportunity to make a new friend.

Instead, I'm chasing after Addie like a lost puppy. It's weird that I know her name, and that her mom misses her, worries about her, and sends her unhinged Facebook articles to show her love. She finally turns to look at me when she scans her card and holds open the door to Carson Hall. "Oh! Go ahead," she says. Does she know I've been trailing her the whole time, or is she just unfailingly polite? Maybe her mom is big on manners too. I head to the stairwell, which is a little dark with my sunglasses still on and make it up to the second floor. Now Addie is the one following me.

Blake's room should be . . . 209. I walk the length of the hall and stop in front of the door, picturing my boyfriend studying his little heart out on the other side, completely unaware he's about to get the surprise of his life. Addie stops to stand shoulder to shoulder beside me. "Oh, are you here for Blake's notes, too?" she asks. "I don't recognize you from class."

Before either of us can knock, the door is yanked open, and Blake fills the doorway. "I thought I heard your voice, Addie . . . Kaley? What—"

When planning this romantic grand gesture, I never accounted for an audience. I feel Addie's stare to my right, and a head full of curly hair pops up behind Blake's shoulder. "Dude, Kaley's here? *The* Kaley? The one you won't shut up about?" This must be Zack, Blake's roommate.

There are three sets of eyes on me, and I want to melt into the floor. I wanted a private moment with Blake, and he's looking at me like he's seeing a ghost, Addie is shifting uncomfortably beside me, and Zack is shouting about me living up to expectations. I thought I would throw myself into Blake's arms and we would passionately kiss, and all my stress and frustration would melt away. I hug myself instead.

Thankfully, Blake takes charge of the situation. He turns to Zack first. "Bro, clear out for the afternoon. I need the room."

Zack shoots me a wink. "Gooooot it," he says, voice full of innuendo.

"I'll come back later," Addie says. "Apparently this is a bad time."

"No, it's fine," Blake assures her. "Here." He shoves a stack of annotated papers into her hands, complete with the color-coordinated highlighter system I recognize so well.

"I take it you won't be at the library this afternoon?" Addie asks. Is it my imagination, or does she look a little disappointed? And another thing, if she was meeting Blake at study group, why did she need to stop by his dorm to get the notes ahead of time?

"No," Blake says. "I need some time with my girl." *His* girl. Ha.

Thirty seconds later, Blake and I are finally alone in his quiet dorm room. We stare at each other, and everything I planned to say flies right out of my head. Blake slowly lifts his hands, and instead of wrapping his palms around my jaw to kiss the life out of me, he gently pulls off my sunglasses. His sharp inhale at my black eye has me scrambling to explain.

"It's not what you think—"

"Did she do this to you?"

"No! Of course not."

"Not 'of course not,' Kaley. I've pulled shattered glass out of your hair. I drove you to the ER when we thought you had a broken nose. What happened?"

He doesn't ask why I showed up at his door. He is just worried for me, like always. I owe him an explanation first, otherwise he won't be able to focus. "I got kicked by a deer."

"That's not funny."

"It's the truth! On the drive over here, we thought we killed a deer. Turns out, she was just stunned. Pro tip—don't try to drag roadkill that isn't really dead off the road."

He stares at me. "You're serious?"

"*Yes.*"

Blake keeps his stern mask on for a beat longer, then he cracks. His chuckle sets my giggles off, and soon we are both laughing so hard tears roll down our faces. The locked box in my chest where I shove my feelings opens, and soon I'm sobbing with relief, hilarity, and exhaustion. The ever-present ache that has been around my heart since Blake left is lifted, and I realize I forgot how good it feels to feel good around him.

He senses my shift in mood and pulls me into his arms. His palms work magic on my back, rubbing soothing circles as I let everything out. "Shh, Kaley. It's okay. My wild girl."

Hiccupping like a maniac, I finally calm down to pull away and look up at him. "Hi," I say.

"Hi. I missed you."

"I missed you too."

"Apparently," he says, quirking a smile. "Long drive?"

"Yes! Did you know how far this trip was?" He stares me down as I state the obvious. "I couldn't wait until Thanksgiving to see you. I know you're studying for midterms this week—"

"Screw midterms. These past few days have been killing me, knowing that you're going through so much with Zoey right now and I'm not there for it. It hurts, not seeing you every day anymore." Blake shakes his head. "I can't believe you're really here."

"I wanted to prove to you that I'm still all-in on us, no matter what this year brings. You're it, Blake."

He groans, and finally, finally, finally kisses me.

CHAPTER ELEVEN

LYING ON BLAKE'S CREAKY DORM-ROOM TWIN BED, I DON'T KNOW which way is up. I'm wrapped around him like a koala and we're trying to tear each other's clothes off, which ends up with a lot of elbows and knees slamming into other body parts. But in this moment, I'm the star of my own CW teen drama. This is my epic montage, and I'm not letting a black eye or the vulgar posters hanging over on Zack's side of the room throw me off my game. How long do we have until he gets back? *Focus, Kaley!*

Also, shouldn't there be music at a time like this? There's only the sound of our heavy breathing and a few thumps as the headboard hits the wall. Someone bangs three times in response on the other side. Should I stop Blake and tell him to put on our playlist? Then I realize that *he* doesn't know my plan. To him, this is just our usual hot-and-heavy make-out session, amplified by the fact that our hormones are going wild since it's been so long.

I stop his wandering hands as they reach my feet. "What, you're not ready for me to blow your socks off?" he teases.

I am so not the seductress I want to be. "Um, I was thinking. Do you have, you know. Stuff?" This may be my first time, but I am not planning on becoming a statistic. Mom is a nurse, who was herself a young mom. She put me on the pill the moment

I turned fifteen. With zero dating experience and no prospect in sight, I almost tossed them in the trash, but she caught me.

"I don't need or want the details," she said. "But I promised myself my children would have the tools and knowledge I was denied. I need to protect your future." A bold statement, considering her decision-making about all our futures in the past twenty-four hours. But right now, I appreciate her foresight.

"Stuff?" Blake asks. Then comprehension dawns. "Oh! Wait, really? Are you sure?" He freezes, clearly wanting to leap off the bed but waiting for me to confirm. Maybe Zack has some condoms in his side drawer we can steal.

I nod. "Do you want to?" I ask, suddenly nervous. The thought that he might turn me down never occurred to me for this scenario. Maybe he has something else in mind for our first time together. A night away in a fancy hotel, maybe dinner beforehand, something that shows a little more planning than a quickie in a dorm room on a Monday afternoon while his roommate is gone for another fifty-three minutes. But hey, it's better than in the back of a car, like Leah.

He doesn't get up to pilfer through his roommate's sock drawer. Blake leans over to his own nightstand and pulls out a box of condoms. Why does he have his own box of condoms?

Seeing my panic, he says, "My dad made sure I had some here when I moved in. Look." He holds the box out to me. "Unopened."

My racing heart slows a little, but in all honesty the surprise box of condoms is the least of my insecurities. There are so many parts of Blake's life that I have no clue about now—what he eats at the dining hall, where his favorite coffee shop on campus is, which path he takes to get to the library, how many acquaintances he passes and fist-bumps along the way. I talk to him all the time on the phone, but I haven't lived this part of his life with him. I'm here, in his arms, and it's almost like the last year falling in love was just a practice round. I *don't* know this newer, more grown-up version of him, and it scares me. When Hannah put the thought of losing him into my brain a few days ago, I lost my mind getting here to him. The need to be close to him, to hold his heartbeat next to mine has me clawing at his back as I pull him in for a hug.

"I love you," I whisper.

"I love you too." His voice cracks a little, letting me see just how hard the past weeks away have been for him as well. Both of us are seeking comfort, and we are choosing right by choosing each other.

I always thought losing my virginity would be a serious occasion, where our souls would combine in a crescendo and it would signal the start of the first day of the rest of my life as a fully-fledged woman.

Turns out, there is sometimes laughter involved. And fun, as we try to figure out how to fit together in this new way. Some of it involved staring deeply into each other's eyes, and other parts were shocking new things I learned about my body and Blake's. Mostly, I just felt safe and happy we were on this adventure together because I couldn't imagine doing it with anyone else.

Afterward, I don't feel very different. I still feel like me. Blake is grinning at me like a goon and pulls me closer to his side as he tucks us in under the blankets. My hair is in his face, and he kisses my temple. "You're incredible, Kaley Marie Larssen."

I shrug. "You're okay yourself... whatever-your-name-is." That earns me a tickle to my side, and I screech at him to stop.

"I'm going to keep you here forever with me," he promises.

This is a fantasy I can get on board with. "Think Zack will mind if I move in?"

"I think he'll be *too* excited about it. Then he will have two people he can drag along to parties instead of mopey me. He hates it when I just sit in the corner and drink."

"What makes you think we're ever going to willingly leave the bed?"

He groans. "Right? Screw going to class too. I hate it, anyway. It's so much harder than Redson High. I thought..." He trails off. "It's going to be fine. The plan is going to work, and it's going to be so much better next year when you're here for real."

Warm tinglies spread throughout my body at his words. I don't want to tell him the truth right now, that he might have to wait a little longer than a year. My leg tangles with his, my anchor of certainty in the swirling hurricane that is my life. At some point I'll have to get up and out of his bed, walk the mile to my car, and have the strength to get in it and drive away. There's a sob threatening to bubble up as I think about it, and I can't open my mouth to contradict him.

Blake sighs. "My parents have really been riding me about my grades. I'm trying, I really am, but they think I'm too preoccupied with our relationship for my own good. What they don't understand is that you're the reason I'm doing all of this. You're the best motivation there is."

I know Elena and James aren't super affectionate people, but I have always assumed they somewhat liked me. "Ouch," I say. "But at least your parents want what's best for you." Unlike Jules and *her* children.

Blake sits up and turns to look at me fully. "What happened with your mom?" he asks. He knows me too well and hears my unspoken words. "Does she know you came all the way out here to visit me? How much trouble are you going to be in when she finds out where you are?" He shudders. "At least there's a nine-hour drive to cool her down if she decides to come out here and kick my butt."

Wincing, I admit, "It's only two. Ish."

"She came out here with you? Where's Zoey—" Then he stops himself. "Your dad. You guys came out here for him."

"Well, specifically for his kidney."

Blake's face fills with concern for me. "How was that? Did you see him?"

The moment he takes my hand, the last twenty-four hours spills out of me in a torrent of incoherent flashbacks. "And the worst part," I confess afterward, immediately unsure how he'll take the news, "is that Mom is looking into other care options for Zoey next year if navigating the medical stuff is too complicated on her own. I think—I think I might have to stay in Idaho a little longer. Defer enrollment until spring or something. Until we know for sure what life will look like post-surgery. I'm not saying it's what's going to happen," I rush to reassure him. "I'm hoping everything still goes as planned. I just didn't want to feel like I was keeping something from you. I wanted to tell you in person. You're so important to me, I didn't want you to think I was doubting us or the long distance."

Blake heaves a sigh and kisses my forehead. "It will all work out. It's temporary, right? You're worth waiting for, but I hope we'll know sooner rather than later."

"Yeah, me too. Mom even offered to let Dad terminate his guardianship of Zoey if he's able to quit smoking and give her the kidney ASAP. That's how far she's willing to go."

Blake rears back, dropping his hands to hang at his sides. "Back up," he says, incredulously. "Not about your dad's donation, but the paperwork."

I can still feel the thick stack of papers in my hands, as weighty as the contents. "Mom offered to terminate Dad's guardianship of Zoey if he gives her the kidney. To fully exit our lives scot-free, if that's what he wants." Blake's face is now turning red. "I get that it's a pretty extreme thing to do—"

"Don't you get it, Kaley?" Blake says.

Startling at his outburst, I ask, "Get what?" He's kind of scaring me.

Blake runs a frustrated hand down his face. "She's going to make you do it."

"Do what? I can't donate the kidney. Zoey needs it now, and I'm not an eligible donor."

"You're going to be the new co-guardian. The moment you turn eighteen, she's going to make you sign the papers."

His words turn around in my brain until they slot into place. There has always been a vague sort of general understanding that one day I would need to grow up and take on official responsibilities for Zoey, not just helping out as much as I can. That chapter in my life always seemed so far in the future, though, once I've had the chance to figure out who I am in the middle of my story. After college, career, maybe even a family of my own.

Blake is getting really worked up now. "This was probably her plan this whole time, having another child in the first place—"

Whoa. *That* is going too far. "What's your deal with this?" I snap. "It's not totally unexpected, even if it's years earlier than I thought." I can hear the falseness in my own words as I try to defend my mother. Maybe it's a good thing Dad will be off the paperwork, and I'll be co-guardian and have a say in everything. No more back and forth, caught between getting treated like an eavesdropping child and trusted only when it's convenient for Mom to lean on me without listening to my opinion.

But then again, so much of my future is already spoken for in every major decision I make, from Mom trying to influence where I go to school, to where I move to after graduation . . . how much control over my life do I actually have? Am I ready to take on a huge responsibility like that at eighteen? Do I even know what I'm doing? There's an elephant sitting on my chest and I can't breathe.

"This wasn't the plan!" Blake says. This is the second time he's mentioned a plan, and now I understand that it's not one he has shared with me.

"What is this mastermind plan you keep talking about? And *sorry* if I keep messing up something we've never even talked about together." I can hear myself getting snippy and defensive, and I hate it. I want to get back to basking in the afterglow of sex, but he's making it impossible.

Now his voice drops to a whisper, and that scares me more. "I was going to save you," he says, and my stomach drops. "You deserve so much more than to be trapped in Idaho for the rest of your life. Tied to someone who beats you, keeping you from really living and becoming who you're meant to be. This tether between you is going to get shorter and shorter until it eventually wraps around your neck. I just need to get you out so you can see it clearly. I love you so much, Kaley. I want what's best for you."

There's a roaring in my ears, and I can barely hear him. "That's really how you see me?" This isn't Blake, my kind boyfriend who spent weeks winning Zoey over and going above and beyond to support us both. Something happened. I bet his parents put him up to this. But as much as I want to blame someone else for this, it is still very *Blake* in a twisted way. He's always had a savior complex. My Prince Charming on horseback and his words when I fell off the horse bubble up in my memory—*It was my responsibility to keep you safe*. What seemed so sweet at the time now steals the breath from my lungs. And my autonomy.

I want to give him the benefit of the doubt. He doesn't realize the position he's putting me in by even suggesting that his "grand plan" is an option. Because for one teeny, tiny millisecond, I let myself consider what he's saying.

I wouldn't have to be strong when I didn't want to be, I wouldn't have to pretend to be fine all the time. For the first time in my life, I could prioritize myself. What does that even look like? What do I even want out of life?

To never step foot in a hospital again. To eat dinner without risk of a plate getting frisbeed at my head. To leave my house without notifying anyone. To not have to help change anyone else's menstrual pads. I don't need to treat myself with anything grand or flashy.

To believe this delusion, I'd have to be an only child, allowed to explore and dream with no limitations. Run off to Hawaii and work at a surf shop? Why not. Become a pilot and travel the world? Nothing is holding me back. No sense of responsibility beyond keeping myself alive for the next adventure. This is what Blake wants me to consider.

The thought is as tempting as it is terrifying. It is also ridiculous to taunt myself with a life I will never have. Furious guilt washes over me as I realize I've given this far too much consideration, betraying my sister by letting Blake plant seeds of doubt so easily. I am a terrible person for picturing my life without Zoey. I wouldn't be me without her. Everything that makes me *me* is because of what we've been through together, dinner plates and bruises and all. Blake is trying to plan a future with a Kaley that doesn't exist. She can't exist because there is no real Kaley without Zoey. The only way he's getting what he wants is if he changes me into a completely different person.

God, the *audacity* of Blake to suggest he could "save" me. Can he not see how messed-up it is to plan Zoey's abandonment? I used to admire him for trying to help people, but now he's gone off the rails. Trying to fix a problem with no real answer has corrupted that pure streak within him, twisted him into believing he is doing right by me. Altruism cannot fix fate that was decided at birth, and he's driven himself in circles trying to do just that.

By the look on my face, he realizes that he's gone too far and tries to backpedal. "Zoey is awesome in so many ways, Kaley. But you have to see how unfair some of it is to you."

"What do you know about sisters?" I snap. I'm up and out of bed, searching for my clothes. My limbs are moving independently of my brain as they yank on my shirt and pants. My sunglasses are nowhere to be found, but I don't care about covering up my face anymore. The walls are closing in on me; it's so stuffy in here I can barely breathe. I get to the door, but Blake blocks it.

"Babe. Please. I'm not explaining this right." He's pulling on a pair of sweatpants but gives up on finding a shirt.

"I think you're explaining it perfectly. But for your sake and mine, I need you to get away from the door." He folds his arms across his chest and doesn't budge.

He's determined to fight for me, but now I don't think I want him to. He doesn't love me, the *real* me; he loves the idea of me once he helps me find my "true potential." The realization shatters my heart. Me, Zoey, my parents . . . this situation is turning him into someone I no longer recognize. *I'm* not good for him. Even if I talk him down from this outrageous plan, I would be compromising part of myself to stay with him. He's confessed beliefs that I can never unhear. He's not good for me either.

This new realization must show on my face because Blake's expression transforms from contrite to panicked. There's a hardness in my eyes as I stare him down and wait for him to move. My iron spine straightens up—the one I inherited from my mother. I'm usually so worried about contorting myself into being the person everyone else needs in each situation that sometimes I forget it's there. But when my body feels like Jell-o and is threatening to collapse to the floor, it surprises me by holding me up. Immovable and unshakable.

Blake raises a trembling hand, as if to cup my face, but thinks better of it. He holds it out, shaking like his fingers weigh a hundred pounds. "But we just . . . you came out . . . I wanted to . . ." He's waiting for me to lean into his strong hands, to give him permission to touch me like he did mere minutes ago. How had we gone from making love to breaking up so fast? My soul aches.

There's a rattling outside the door and I peer around Blake's body to see the deadbolt turn. He doesn't look behind and continues to stare at me but finally drops his hopeful hand. The door opens into his back. "Hey, bro," Zack says. "Move, man." At first, I think Zack is holding a skateboard, but then I see it has a handle. And red wheels.

Blake takes a tiny step to the side, as if he's afraid that if I see a wide enough opening, I'll bolt like a bunny. Zack makes it into the room, smirking at Blake's shirtlessness. "Hope I gave you enough time—" His attention shoots to my face, and suddenly he drops his mode of transportation in the doorway. He's shoving Blake away from me and over to the desk.

"What the hell, man—"

Zack swears, cutting Blake off. "Did you do that to her?" he demands. His fist is cocked, like he's ready to unleash on Blake's stomach.

"No! Never!"

"Doll?" Zack turns.

Oh, I guess he means me. "No. Blake would never physically hurt me." Emotionally? The boy has wrecked me.

Zack has doubts, but aside from restraining me, there's nothing he can do as I turn and head for the door. "Zack, let me go!" Blake says, trying to shove his roommate off him. "Don't let her leave!"

"Dude. Lady wants to leave. Let her go." Who would have guessed my knight in shining armor isn't the guy who, you know, rides *actual* horses and is instead a man-child on a Razor scooter?

I slip out, nudge the scooter away with my foot, and gently close the door on Blake's stricken face because I don't have the energy to slam it. If I were angry, then this would be easier. I'm not angry, I'm resigned, and there's no passion in that.

My numb body carries me out of the dorm building and I take a shaky, free breath when I get outside. Somehow, I managed to lose my virginity and end my long-term relationship within one afternoon. Today is a *spectacular* failure. So comical I could laugh, but the person I want to laugh about it with is the same person I left upstairs. Choking back a half laugh, half sob, I walk away, hoping the campus will swallow me up and I can disappear for a while.

The anonymity soothes me as I meander with no goal but to keep moving. If I stop, then the thoughts take over, telling me to run back to Blake. But his phrases pop into my head in disjointed fragments when I try to turn around. *Having another child in the first place . . . She's going to make you sign the papers . . . Keeping you from really living and becoming who you're meant to be . . .*

Psh. What does he know? He's not going to override my brain and make me question my entire existence. I walk and walk and walk and can't escape his words, and now I'm starting to hate him for it.

My stomach rumbles, reminding me I barely ate breakfast and all my snacks are back at my car, wherever that is. Digging through my back pocket, I find a crumpled five-dollar bill. Perfect. The scent of coffee on the wind lures me to the right spot and I order a pumpkin scone. Blake hates pumpkin spice. He calls it pumpkin snot and detests that it has its own season now, like a virus that keeps spreading. Pumpkin-spice laundry detergent was the last straw before he snapped. I'm going to choke down this scone and relish every single freaking bite of it, just to spite him. There's not enough change leftover for a drink, but the barista hands me a tea with my food anyway.

"I was hit by a deer," I feel the need to explain, choking back emotion due to her kindness.

"It's not the bruise," she says. "It's your face."

My face? Wow, way to kick a girl when's she's down. I'm about to be offended, despite the free drink, but thankfully she continues: "You just really look like you've had a crappy day."

"You're not wrong," I concede.

There's a small, out-of-the-way spot in the corner and I settle in a comfy chair to make my treat last as long as possible. If I leave campus, then I admit it's truly over with Blake. Existing in limbo is how I'm surviving right now. Blake behind me, my family up ahead. How long can I bum around campus before someone realizes I haven't paid tuition and they kick me out?

Maybe I'll become a University of Oregon folklore legend. A cautionary tale to all incoming freshmen about the dangers of long-distance boyfriends and the tragedy of sex. If I stay long enough to become an adjunct professor, I'll teach my own class on how to blow up your life in the course of a single day. True to life, the lecture itself will take just a single day. I'll have the best teacher reviews—

The barista touches my shoulder and I jump. "Hey, just wanted to let you know we're closing soon." How long have I been here? Hours, maybe. The sun dips low on the horizon. I miss summer and endless days, but now having actually lived a truly never-ending day, I'm ready for the earth to call it for me. I surrender to the darkness.

"Um, okay . . ." the barista says.

Crap. Did I say that last sentence out loud? She's backing away slowly now. She'll be the one to spread my folklore legend. "Godspeed," I mutter.

She heads behind the counter to talk to her rather large and intimidating coworker now. That's my cue to leave before they decide to remove me.

I get up and stagger on shaky legs that have been deprived of circulation for too long. Weaving a bit, I push through the door and back outside. There's a pack of students heading down the sidewalk toward me, and they part for me like the Red Sea. One girl literally *jumps* off the sidewalk to get away.

Is this how Zoey feels sometimes? Being the one people stare at, just because she's a little bit different? Enough *otherness* to knock others off balance? I don't know if she notices, because it has always been her reality. Right now, though, I find it freeing to channel my sister. It's powerful. And after a whole lot of feeling powerless in my own life lately, I want some more of it.

When I pass the girl who jumped, I growl at her. She yelps

and hides behind her friend. Everyone else laughs and gives me curious looks. "Did she really just growl at you?" But I keep walking. I'm moving forward, and there's nothing they can do about it. I'll be a funny story at their study group tonight, but I'll never see these people again. Nothing I do matters—Everything is out of my hands—I have nothing planned for my future and yet everything decided for me at the same time—I'm going to be alone forever but never without my sister—Deer should be higher up on the food chain—I hate my parents—I'm going to get in my car and drive to the edge of the world—Boy, this scone isn't sitting well—I think my old scooter is still in the garage somewhere—Condoms really are just weird, greasy balloons—

"Hey! Parallel-parking queen!"

I look around in confusion. Despite my mental breakdown, I've made it back to my car. Huh. My sense of direction is notoriously terrible, but maybe now that my moral compass has failed, it's given way to an actual magnetic-north compass. This will be useful when I need to locate a cliff to drive off.

"You're coming in, right?" my new fraternity brother asks. "We're just getting started, but you're welcome to come pregame. Whoa. Did you already start or something?" He gestures to my face.

"Is it a pregame still when you all started hours ago?" I point out, dodging his question entirely. "When is the actual transition from pregame to game, and is there some sort of ceremony for it so everyone is aware?"

He laughs. "You're weird. But I like it." The glow from his compliment spreads through me. Yes, he thinks I'm weird, but he's also not shunning me for it.

My drive can wait. I follow him into the house, expecting filth on every surface, but it's surprisingly tidy. The recycle bin in the kitchen is overflowing with beer cans, but at least the guys *put* them there. There's a thumping bass resonating from down the hall, and I assume the DJ is set up in the living room. A few more paces behind my new friend and I confirm my theory, along with a beer-pong table in the center of the space. How fitting to end my relationship with the same event that snowballed me here in the first place. At least I know this is the last place on campus Blake will come looking for me.

Did he run out the door after me once Zack let him go? Or did his roommate get through Blake's thick head and force him to see reason? Maybe they're still up in the dorm room together while Blake tries to explain our convoluted history.

I'd give Zack a much better summary. *Blake's superhero complex ego broke my heart when he was going to force me to choose between him and my sister, with the belief he was doing me a freaking* favor. *After we had sex for the first time.* Bam. Conversation over. Somehow, I doubt this is the story that Blake is telling.

"You're welcome to chill or play pong or whatever until people start getting here," Frat Boy says.

"I'm sorry, I've been really rude. You've been so nice, and I don't even know your name."

"It's Dex. Well, Declan." I startle. Is the universe trying to hit me over the head with a very obvious reminder that I need to text my friends back? The thought of unpacking this all multiple times with multiple people makes me want to disappear.

"Thanks, Dex. I'm . . . Zoey." I'll be her for tonight, for my first college party. Then when I tell her the story, she'll get a huge kick out of it.

"Cool." He nods. "I gotta get the keg set up. See ya around."

By the time students start trickling in, I have a buzz going, I don't care at all what I look like, and the music starts to hit differently. There's a small group of people bumping and grinding out in the living room, scaring even the couches, which are pushed up against the walls in shock. Long legs spill over the faded cushions and armrests in a tangle of uninhibited bodies. Joyous laughter rings out in this celebration of student life. The pulsing heart of the party draws me in with a come-as-you-are attitude and I can forget how I got here. We are all united with the same goal—to not feel alone.

In a trance, I approach the dance floor. The collective ecstasy calls to me, showing me what I've been missing out on all these years. If I just let myself be truly free, I can look like them. My limbs freeze when I reach the center, stiff and unwilling to cooperate even though my brain and my heart are aching for this. Part of me wishes a pair of strong hands would wrap around my waist and pull me into a hard chest, to loosen me up and help me find the rhythm. Then, I would turn around and find Blake—nope. Not going to go there. Dex, maybe. Yeah. He's cute enough. He can help me dance.

Couples surround me in various states of awareness, and I'm alone. I'm alone. I'm alone. No one is watching me. No one cares. *No one cares.* I lift my arms over my head in surrender and tentatively shake my hips. I probably look like a puppet on strings, but I force myself to keep going. Kaleidoscope lights on the ceiling flash before my eyes when I throw my head back, bend my legs, and begin to move.

I lose count of how many songs I dance to. They all blend together, anyway, thanks to the skills of a mediocre DJ. Sweat beads at my forehead and I feel a drop trickle down under my shirt, but I don't stop. Lungs and limbs burn while I dance as my sister, for my sister. For me. For the girl I want to be and will fight to become. A little bit for my mother, even. For the free spirit she once was. To channel the intense strain on my body and release it to the universe, which has done a hell of a lot to try to break me lately.

I'm so lost to it all I don't even hear Dex when he's right in front of me, saying something to my face. "What?" I ask. I stop moving, and the lead in my limbs threatens to send me to the floor. My brain screams at me to ignore him, to keep going and refuse to return to earth. His hand shoots out to grab my shoulder when I stagger.

"The cops are outside," he says.

Even in my haze, I know the last thing I need is a minor-in-possession charge. "Should I run?" I ask. I have no idea where to go, but I have a feeling I'll weave a lot when I sprint to throw them off the track.

"They're just standing by your car. You got drugs in there or something?"

"No! Of course not."

"We really can't have them come in and shut down the party," Dex hints.

"All right," I grumble. I don't want them to get in trouble. He pulls my hand and leads me to the front door.

"Hopefully I'll see you around next year, Zoey," Dex says with a smirk, opening the door at the same time. "I'll let you drive my stick shift, and you can show me how it's done like a pro."

Standing on the front porch with a shocked expression is the person I last expect. "Dad?"

"Oh shit, see ya," Dex says, disappearing back inside the house.

"Kaley," Dad says, smoothing his emotions away until his infuriatingly neutral face stares back at me.

"How did you find me?"

"We have to go," he says.

"Did Mom send you to drag me back? I was going to come home eventually—"

"I called campus police to track down your car. You wouldn't answer your phone. We're not going home. We're going to the hospital."

"What? The hospital? Is Zoey okay?" My pace speeds up next to his and we are out on the street next to my car in no time.

Dad holds out his hand. "Keys."

I pull them from my pocket, and he hits the button to pop the trunk. Inside, nestled among the camping supplies and jackets and an extra running shoe is the dialysis machine.

CHAPTER TWELVE

MY HANDS BRACE ON MY KNEES AS I DOUBLE OVER, TRYING NOT TO throw up. I forgot. I forgot it was back there. How could I forget something that important? My lungs try to inhale but my guilt is squeezing them so I can't draw a full breath.

Dad doesn't run a hand in soothing circles on my back, trying to comfort me. He shifts his weight from foot to foot while he waits for me to recover. With my face mere inches from his shoes, his uneasiness is evident. When my stomach unleashes its contents onto the sidewalk, he jumps back, and the brown boots leave my periphery just in time to avoid the splash-back.

There's more room for my lungs with my newly empty stomach, and I'm finally able to stand back up. "You're not driving," Dad says. "My truck is over here." He points a block up the street. "Go get in it, I'll talk to the cops. We'll get your car some other time." It worries me that he doesn't say "tomorrow." Is he implying that we'll be in the hospital for longer?

Before I head for his car, I grab my phone from the dashboard. I press the power button so hard the tip of my finger turns white while I walk like a zombie toward the truck. I'm left to stew in my thoughts in the passenger seat while the freaking thing chooses this moment to run a software update. Dad finally appears on the driver's side, lifting the dialysis machine like it weighs nothing and sliding it into the small bench backseat with ease. He gets in behind the wheel and still doesn't explain himself.

The smooth motion of his expert steering is juxtaposed with the rumble of horsepower as this gigantic beast eases out onto the road. My right foot twitches, wanting to put the pedal to the metal and get to the hospital, but I have no idea where to go. I'm at the mercy of this man who insists on driving the speed limit. I kick a fancy purple thermal flask that's rolling around by my feet instead.

"Ow." When I examine it closer, I realize it's the same model as my newest acquisition, courtesy of Park Ranger Rachel. "Park Ranger Rachel such a catchy name, she should be on a kid's show." The words bubble out of my mouth, and I know it's my nerves taking over. My mind is bouncing all over the place, and there's no off switch for my anxiety. I latch onto the first thought that distracts me from Zoey.

"What?" Dad asks, his first word to me since we started driving.

I'm about to explain the events of this morning, but something in his tone makes me pause and connect the dots. "Your girlfriend, it's Rachel, isn't it?"

"How did you know that?" He tries to remain unruffled, emotionless like usual. But I can tell I got to him with my spooky revelation. Good. He should fear me.

"I know things," I say, with an air of nonchalance that I assume adds to the mystery.

Picking at the worn fabric of the seat, I try not to inhale too deeply. I've never been inside this truck, but I know it's his. It smells like him. Like his cabin, but more so, because I know he spends more time in here than at his home. And, judging by the thermos, he spends time in here with Rachel too. I really don't need additional details, and Dad offers nothing but silence. She's nice. Too good for him.

Finally, I can't take it anymore. I don't care what he does in his spare time, I don't need to get to know the new girlfriend he found to replace his family, I'm not waiting with bated breath for the story. None of this makes sense that Zoey had an emergency today. She just had treatment last night, she should have been fine until tomorrow night at the earliest. "What happened?" I demand.

He knows I'm not talking about Rachel. "Zoey got into the hundred calorie packs from your mom's purse."

I wince like I've been struck. Chock-full of chemicals, sodium, and other hard-to-process ingredients, they are worse for Zoey than sweets. "How many did she eat?"

"Five."

If we were at home, we would have driven straight to Doc Hayes. But in a cabin in the middle of nowhere, Zoey was fully reliant on the dialysis machine that I accidentally kidnapped. I'm going to be sick again.

As if reading my mind, Dad unrolls the window. Fresh, freezing air whips across my face, and I'm not sure if the tears that stream from my eyes are from the cold or my own devastation. Dad speaks, but he's so quiet I barely hear. "We were arguing," he says. I roll up the window to listen, but I can't look over at him. "I came back to the cabin at lunch to talk to your mom. She was livid you ran off. We got into it and didn't realize how long we had been fighting for."

"So Zoey found and fed herself a snack," I finish for him. If

I had been there, then I would have cooked her lunch, or seen her snatch the snack bags in the first place. Because I wasn't there, my sister is in the hospital.

"Then she wouldn't tell us where to find you."

My eyebrows shoot up my forehead. "What?" Zoey doesn't fully understand the concept of secrets. How did she withstand an interrogation from both our parents? She must have taken our conversation last night to heart. She came through for me today, even if I didn't come through for her.

"Yeah," Dad says. "All too soon, we realized that we were out of time and had to take her to the emergency room."

Zoey willingly picked hospital, her least favorite place, over betrayal. A sharp, painful laugh escapes me. Of all my secrets to finally decide to keep to herself, it had to be the one that hurt her in the long run?

"I can't believe she didn't tell you where I went. The last time I asked her to keep a secret, she spilled it *immediately* to Mom when we got home. No prompting, no interrogation, nothing. Just volunteered it, even though I specifically told her to keep a lid on it."

"You shouldn't keep stuff from your mother anyway," Dad mutters.

How can I make him understand my total shock? The full story tumbles out. "I had just gotten my driver's license and was itching to test out the car without a parent. Mom okayed it and Zoey called shotgun. Just me and my sister, taking a loop around town, until a torrential downpour hit. It felt like we were in a car wash."

Dad's only response is to hit the button on the steering wheel that releases some windshield wiper fluid. The wipers whip back and forth frantically, adding to both the realism and urgency of what I'm about to say.

"I couldn't remember how to turn the headlights on. The streets flooded and I made the first right turn I could, into St. Joseph's Chapel parking lot. I tried to ease the car into park but felt the tires hydroplane."

Dad runs a hand over his face, probably envisioning the worst. "I should have taught you how to drive." Was this actual regret at missing one of my childhood milestones?

"Anyway, Zoey yelled, 'Whee!' while I screamed and prayed for traction. I did everything I could have, the way *Mom* taught me. Not only were my prayers not answered in a church parking lot, but the butt of the car whipped around and took out the row of trash cans and recycle receptacles, domino-style. It even knocked down the clothing-donation bin." A tragic Christmas sweater had even floated in the current past the driver's-side window.

My mouth keeps babbling, and I can't stop talking. Why can't I shut up? Dad didn't ask to hear it, but I have a deep need to keep explaining and follow this through to the end, as though my admission means absolution. "As suddenly as it started, the rain stopped and we hightailed it out of there. So, then I told Zoey, 'You will tell no one of this day,' like a scary mob boss, and that if 'I go down, I'm taking you with me.'"

Dad's hands tighten on the wheel.

"Of course Zoey said, 'Kaley crash! Kaley crash!' as soon as we got home and saw Mom. She was smiling again after feeling so crappy the past few weeks on antibiotics, using her hands and some creative sound effects to give Mom the play-by-play." My breath hitches. I'm reaching an end to the story I've never told anyone out loud.

"I told Mom that we may have gotten into a teeny incident with the car. Just a scratch or two. She didn't even care."

Dad snorts in disbelief. "The Julie I knew once upon a time would have—"

"Then she told us that she just got a call from Zoey's primary care doctor. Apparently, we needed to go see a specialist about her kidneys . . ." I choke back a sob. This is all feeling full-circle, and not in a wholesome, teen-movie kind of way.

Dad realizes I've reached the climax of a story with no resolution, because he reaches over and I think he's going to hold my hand. He doesn't. But he does pull out some old napkins from the glove compartment and hands one to me so I can wipe my tears. The other he uses to blow his nose. I can't tell if it's tear-induced or if he just has some bad seasonal allergies.

"How far to the hospital?" I ask. My jaw is sore from clenching my teeth, but it matches the ache in my gut.

"Forty-five more minutes," Dad says. Is he blaming himself as much as I'm blaming myself? Or does he blame me too? I'm going with the latter. Considering there's no way he can be any more mad or disappointed with me, I may as well go for the gold.

"Did you smoke today?" He sighs but doesn't look at me. This isn't a good sign. "Seriously? She's gonna need that kidney sooner rather than later, especially after this little trip to the hospital." There's more caught in my throat, something along the lines of *You could just step up and, you know, be a father for once.* Habit, I suppose. But I'm not really in a place right now to throw stones. Plus, his appearance at a college frat house to drag me outside and stick me in his truck was very dadlike. Credit where credit is due.

We're both saved by the bell from continuing the conversation, or rather, by the buzz. The phone in my lap stops updating and starts buzzing with what seems like hundreds of notifications, texts, and missed calls. Knowing now what all of them are about, I brace myself to look through them. It's not like I have anything else to do for the next fifty miles. Dad and I don't have that much to talk about.

I scroll down to start at the beginning. The first calls and messages came from Mom, right after I took the car. The voicemails all start with the same tone. "Kaley—" Mom's voice is angry, struggling to maintain control. I hit Delete as soon as I hear it, going through the next three voicemails and doing the same thing.

The following voicemail is different though. Her voice cracks when she says my name, and my heart sinks. I make myself listen to this one, as punishment. "Kaley, please call me back. As soon as you can. Zoey just got into my snacks, and we don't have the dialysis machine. Dad and I are taking her to the closest hospital . . . William! Grab her, quick!" Mom's voice cuts out as she hangs up the phone.

The time stamp on that one says 2:08 p.m. About the time Blake and I were . . . occupied. I can't even think about what we did this afternoon, not when I'm thinking about what was happening to Zoey at the same time.

Then, 3:46 p.m.—"Kaley, it's Leah. I don't know where you

are, but your mom seems to think I do. All I know is that you have to call her back ASAP. Something happened with Zoey."

The next voicemail was at 5:22 p.m. "I just put two and two together and I called Blake," Mom's voice is clipped. "He said you showed up to his dorm, you guys fought, you ran out, and he doesn't know where you are. He's worried sick about you and Zoey. If you won't call me back, then call Blake." Like hell Blake was worried about Zoey. But if he really had been combing campus looking for me, I wish I had been less of a pro at hide-and-seek. I would already be at the hospital by now if he had found me.

Unsurprisingly, the next voicemail is Blake. "Babe, where did you go? I'm looking everywhere. Call me back, we have to talk." Really? Not one word about Zoey? If I thought better of him, like I had this morning, maybe I could give him the benefit of the doubt. With that voicemail, though—all about *us* instead—I'm ready to chuck my phone out the window. I settle on blocking him instead.

Thankfully there are no more voicemails. I side-eye Dad, noting the lack of missed calls or panicked messages from him. No paper trail. Is it on purpose, or does he naturally lean toward a witness-protection standard of living now?

He wasn't always a reclusive mountain man. There are glimpses from my childhood of him being, dare I say, *cool*. Dad was effortlessly stylish in his dark jeans, vintage band T-shirts, and steel-toed boots. My parents were younger than my friends' parents. What earned them begrudging acceptance among the PTA and church parents was that they were teenagers who "did the right thing" and got married. The timeline on this is a bit fuzzy.

The way Mom told it—she never tells the story anymore—Dad skidded into town one day in his brother's red Pontiac, took her for a drive, and never slowed down. Not even when Zoey was born. Even in her birth photos from the hospital, Dad is wearing a Nirvana shirt with ripped-off sleeves and cradling a snuggling, pink, wrinkly baby on his chest. He's looking down at her with such love in his gaze, and I wouldn't be surprised if he's humming "Come As You Are."

Ironic, really.

Later, it's like he slammed into a barricade after a lifetime of going a hundred miles per hour. I think it was right around the time Zoey was supposed to start kindergarten. Mom was fighting with the school, nobody had any resources for her, my sister was hitting us all the time, and her speech wasn't progressing.

My earliest memory is just after I turned three. I toddled into the office to look for Zoey and found her surrounded by shattered black plastic. She was screaming, a self-inflicted cut on her hand dripping blood onto the hardwood floor. Just as I was about to step barefoot into the room, Dad snatched me back and told me to stay in the hallway.

Then he stood in the doorway and just . . . stared. At the destruction. At his shrieking child. Like he couldn't force himself to take a step in and sweep up the last vestiges of the man he desperately held on to while the universe screamed the obvious at him that he would never, and could never, be that person again.

In my three-year-old brain, I knew I needed an adultier-adult to handle whatever was unfolding in front of me, because I knew sure as anything that Dad wasn't the one we could depend on to get a Band-Aid. With a pitter-patter of little feet, I ran to find Mom.

The changes in Dad were a slow flood after that day, wiping the man I knew away and leaving a blank slate in his place. One that dressed more like the other dads in cargo shorts and button-downs bought from Walmart the next town over. But the outside changes didn't make him as much of a stranger to me as the inside ones. He talked less and started disappearing in the evenings before bedtime. Mom said he was working late as she wrestled Zoey and me into the tub.

I would try to stay awake until he came home, but more often than not I would jolt from my dreams to the feel of a sandpapery kiss on my cheek and then he was gone. Eventually, he stopped coming in altogether, and I woke up well rested but with a lead weight in my chest.

"Where do you go?" I asked him one morning.

"Hiking, sometimes," he told me. Mom rolled her eyes but didn't correct him.

"Oh. Can you take me?"

"Maybe." He didn't sound excited, so I dropped it. I only ever received one-to-two-word answers anyway.

We never went hiking before he left. The closest I got was trailing around after him in the yard, until I guess even that was too much and he had to go live in the woods full-time. Without us.

CHAPTER THIRTEEN

"ARE WE ALMOST THERE?" I ASK, MY LEG BOUNCING IN ANTICIPATION. My phone is silent. Mom isn't going to call, not when she can yell at me in person soon enough. I'm dying for an update on Zoey's condition, but I don't deserve to have one.

"Ten minutes."

I need a distraction. Even though my head is still spinning a bit, I force myself to go through my text messages. Reading in the car always makes me sick, and the addition of nerves and booze and this headache that won't go away doesn't help, but anything is better than envisioning my sister lying helpless in a hospital bed. Plus, I should check the written record of the worst day of my life, for posterity's sake.

As anticipated, Mom sent the most texts. I open them but don't read them, just so the notification goes away. Blake tried to text me more times than he called me. I'm sure he waxed poetic, but if I start crying right now and have to explain to my *father* how I just had sex for the first time mere hours ago and ran out on my boyfriend, I might hurl myself out of the moving car.

Another text from Leah. One from Hannah too. I let them both know I'm on my way to Zo, promising to update them with more news when I've seen her. Then, I realize Declan has texted me back.

That earlier message could not have sent. Impossible. I hadn't clicked the Send button back at the cabin. I had been in a dead cell zone, for God's sake. I am being truly, deeply punished for sins past, present, and now future, because there is no way I'm coming back from today unless I get resurrected.

Silently cursing my network provider, the cellphone software update, and technology itself, I open the conversation thread, praying for a miracle.

Nope. It sent. It sent all the way.

My only hope now is that Declan doesn't show everybody he knows just how far off the rails Kaley Larssen has fallen. I reread the words I sent, mouthing them silently, picturing his face when that text was delivered. *Just on a crazed road trip to get my sister a kidney, visit my estranged father, avoid getting kicked by another deer, and maybe have sex with my boyfriend for the first time. NBD.*

His response—*Damn, girl, Thelma and Louise got nothing on you. Wishing you luck in all of your endeavors. Unfortunately, I don't have a kidney hookup anymore, but if you need help hiding a body (deer or otherwise) on your way back, you know who to call.*

What? I snort back a laugh that sneaks up on me out of nowhere. Declan has always been weird, but he took the unhinged I doled out and flung it right back, no questions, no judgments. Should I respond? Maybe I'll get around to replying to him once I know Zoey is okay; thank him for making quite possibly the worst day of my life a little better. Leah will kill me for inflating his ego even more, though.

The decision is out of my hands when he sends another text.

Declan, same-day texting? Has this ever happened before? It says, *I know you're there. Just heard from Leah. You okay?*

My fingers tap the screen rapid-fire. *Were you staring at your phone and waiting for the read receipt?*

I can picture his face as I read his response, eyebrow raised in mock disgust: *I have never done that in my life. Except for today. So, yes. I needed to hear from you if Zoey was okay. I don't trust those gossiping youths with secondhand information.*

Biting my lip, I think about telling him the truth, wondering if admitting it out loud will unburden me. *It's my fault Zoey is in the hospital.* After typing out my confession, I delete it before I can hit Send. Can I trust Declan with this? I can't even make myself tell Leah how the day unraveled. The only thing she knows, that anyone knows, really, is that Zoey got into some snacks she shouldn't have eaten, and salt hit the fan.

But maybe Declan is the perfect person for my confessional. I won't have to stare at Declan's face every day if he does judge me for my mistake. We don't talk nearly enough for it to matter. As an added bonus, juvenile delinquents happen to have far more experience acting first and thinking through consequences later, if at all, than the average person. Except as far as I know, he's never actually put anyone in life-or-death danger.

Leah would assure me it could have happened to anyone. Hannah would remind me that it could have been much worse. Charlie would just say to look on the bright side. What would Blake say? Probably that it was only a matter of time, and he was surprised it had taken this long for such a colossal Zoey screw-up.

Screw him.

What would Declan say? None of the above, that's for sure. He'd surprise me.

I decide to take a chance. *All that crazy stuff I mentioned doing on the road trip? Well, it turns out that a dialysis machine, much like a boyfriend, is easy to get lost in the shuffle. Both were huge mistakes that I need to take responsibility for.*

Three dots pop up, disappear, pop up again and stay for a while, then disappear. Have I done the impossible and rendered Declan speechless with my heinousness?

Dad finally pulls off the highway and follows the blue *H* signs. My stomach cramps with nerves. If Declan blames me for this, too, then how am I supposed to face Zoey?

In all the years I've known your family, I've never known a Larssen girl to run from a fight.

He's right. Take away all the drama of today and what's left? Me, needing to be there for my sister. "Just drop me off at the ER," I tell Dad, not expecting him to stay now that I'm here as Mom's backup. He doesn't answer me and drives to the visitors' lot instead.

When we finally park, he says, "They've been admitted overnight. They aren't in the ER anymore."

"Overnight?" Dialysis is only ever a few hours at a time.

"They want to keep a close eye on her," he explains. I hate that he knows more about what's going on than I do. I don't even know where the main entrance is, or which floor they're on. I just have to trust that Dad is leading the right way as we check in and make the trek to see my sister.

I've never been here in particular, but it is familiar. Bright lights, the smell of disinfectant, and hard edges surround me. Similar variations exist, but this experience is my childhood in a nutshell. Walking down the hospital halls, the transformation takes over my body, and I become Little Sister Kaley—as I once was introduced to all nurses, doctors, and assistants. "Hi, this is Zoey, your patient, and her little sister, Kaley." Dragged along to different specialists because I didn't have a sitter, always ready with a smile and a wave. Expected to be "so grown-up about everything" as they notice "Wow, what a great support system Zoey has!" Little Sister Kaley walks a thin line of being helpful in all situations while also getting left out of decisions involving Zoey's care because she's deemed "still a kid."

This is not my favorite version of myself, for obvious reasons. I hide so much of me when I become Little Sister Kaley, but I don't know how we would all get through it any other way. The behavior is so ingrained in me that it's automatic, and by the time Dad and I reach the correct room, I am *her*.

When Zoey sees me in the doorway, her mouth splits into a wide grin. "Kaley!" she says. Her excitement is worse than anger. I wish she would blame me, hate me, exhibit something other than pure joy at my presence to punish me for being a selfish brat.

Mom is more than happy to oblige me.

Before I can make it over to Zoey's bedside and give her a hug, Mom stops me. Her hand snaps out and her fingers grip my arm in a vise. "Was it worth it?" she asks.

The emotions of Blake's betrayal and Zoey's scare heat up underneath my skin until I want to scratch it all off. It's like I want to make the raw pain worse to punish myself. Regrets and apologies lie on the tip of my tongue, ready for me to release them. *No*, I'm dying to tell her. *It was horrible. I feel so lost. Help me.*

But Zoey is back in the hospital, and Mom looks ready to spit fire because it's all my fault. She wants to unleash her anger on me, and I'm inclined to let her use me like she needs to.

"Do you know how scared I was to realize we had no dialysis machine?" Mom hisses. "This could have ended in *tragedy*, Kaley Marie. I don't think you understand—"

Before I can snap back at her, Dad steps in. "She understands, Jules. Trust me. We can have this conversation later. Let her see Zoey first." Mom hesitates, like she is really going to keep Zoey from me.

"You don't want to upset the patient," I mutter.

Mom releases her grip and I muster a small smile for Dad. I ease myself down to sit on the edge of the hospital bed. Leaning forward and trying to avoid the seemingly endless mess of tubes and equipment and wires, I gingerly embrace my sister. She's fine.

In all these years, I've never cried at the hospital; but this time, the floodgates unleash. I'm sobbing like a baby, while Zoey pats my back and shushes me. "I'm so sorry," I blubber. She just hums a lullaby and relaxes back with me into the bed. We stay there while the rest of the world falls away, forgetting that our parents are in the audience, witnessing my heartbreak. I know I need to pull it together, but I can't. I'm not strong enough. I've been shattered and pieced back together too many times today.

"Next time, no matter what I say, you *have* to tell Mom things if it's a medical emergency." My voice is thick with emotion.

"Oh, we've already had a long talk about that," Mom says. "But I'm still hanging on to the apparently futile hope that my daughters won't want to keep secrets from me in the first place."

I wince, but Zoey laughs. Now that she's out of the woods, there's a slight shift in the hospital-room atmosphere and we collectively draw a deep breath. Mom is still pissed, though. Obviously.

She crosses her arms and stares us down until Zoey stops laughing. "I've never been this disappointed in you both. Not even when you were almost accused of a hate crime for defacing the church parking lot."

"Then why did you let Zoey cut out that newspaper article and put it on the fridge? 'Youths Deface Cornerstone of Redson Community.'" There was also a number to call the police station with any information about the godless hooligans running rampant in our small town, with possible gang affiliations.

"For knocking over some trash cans?" Dad asks. "Guess things have changed since our day, huh Jules?"

Mom sniffs. She darts her gaze back and forth from me to Dad, trying to figure out when he found out about that story. "Don't you dare say anything, William."

"Bad Mom? Bad Dad?" Zoey asks. The look on her face says Christmas has come early. I'm inclined to agree with her, mostly because everyone's ire is off us at the moment.

"We were smart enough not to get caught," Dad admits.

"William!"

"What? You remember how that lot was back in the day. Flat, new pavement, perfect for midnight drifts and donuts—none of it did any permanent damage."

"Donuts!" Zoey looks at Dad expectantly and holds out her hand.

"Now you've done it," I inform him.

"Nice try, young lady." Mom shakes her head at my sister.

"Donuts!" she insists.

Distraction!

"It's not like we had fond memories of that church anyway," I jump in, rationalizing our brush with the law. "Remember when we got invited to that Easter celebration all those years ago, Zo?"

"I can't even remember who invited us, or why I thought we should go," Mom mutters.

In her transition to single motherhood, Mom tried on a few new identity hats. The churchgoing mom was one that was short-lived, as were the arts-and-crafts mom (Zoey got into the glitter); the book-club mom; and the gardening mom—I fell into a blackberry bush, that one was on me. You know, identities that meshed so well with pre-marriage interests like midnight drifting, apparently. I guess she couldn't very well drag her children out of bed, buckle us up, and take a wild ride. I can't help but think maybe we'd have a better understanding of one another today if she had.

Looking back, she must have *really* been flailing, although I don't remember noticing that much. Filling the role of both Mom and Dad probably left such little time for anything else, much less a piece of her life that was purely for her. The label that stuck around long enough was the stationary-bike mom. Mostly, I think, because she could get out some rage and sweat while staying in one spot. It also did not involve other people, going anywhere, or needing a babysitter. This phase lasted right up until Zoey started dialysis, and since then, the bike has been gathering dust in the garage.

Zoey interrupts my musing and answers my original question. "Church play. Funny," she remembers.

That was an understatement. No one told us there was going to be a play, of all things, not just a sermon. A reenactment of the crucifixion. A few trigger warnings would have been appreciated. We were late. Mom snagged us seats near the back just as Millennial Jesus stumbled down the center aisle with a giant cross strapped to his back.

If there's one thing Zoey appreciates, it's physical humor. An unfortunate coincidence on this day.

Anyway, the guy started staggering and tripping his way to the pulpit, and people around us were actually shedding tears at this disturbing display. I tugged on my sherbet-colored lacy dress near my knees and tried not to listen to the moans of a small-town actor who just got his big break. Zoey, in a matching Easter dress that was butter yellow instead of dessert-colored, assumed that the reverence of the flock at this display was just because they didn't understand it was a joke.

She let out an encouraging laugh, calling, "More, more!" Turning to me, she said, "Fall down, Kaley. He fall down!" Heads whipped around to catch sight of the heathens in the back row who came to mock their savior on the most sacred of days. Zoey pointed a helpful finger toward the front, where pretend Jesus had fallen onto the stairs. "Look!" she told everyone. Then she cracked up some more.

Mom tried and failed to shush her. Eventually, she hauled Zoey to her feet and told me, "We're out of here." Our dramatic disturbance was much more entertaining than the subpar drama up on the pulpit, and while the adults steadfastly kept their eyes trained ahead, everyone younger than twelve—including quite a few of my classmates—had their necks craned around and stared back with open curiosity and glee.

"All the kids were smiling at you, Zo, remember? Like they were cheering you on for being brave enough to try and start a riot in the church."

She shrugged, as if to say, *Who wouldn't find me hilarious at all times?*

"At least we didn't get smited. Smoted? Smote? Not until after the trash-can incident, I guess." My eyes wander to the tubes still pushing the dialysate through my sister's veins. "Three strikes and we were out."

"That's not how the world works, Kaley," Mom says.

But how else did she explain my young, vibrant, funny sister hooked up to all this crap? Pure chance?

Zoey leans back on her inclined bed, looking like a peaceful angel, unbothered by the destruction the last few hours have wrought. Regardless, it is exhausting both wreaking havoc and witnessing it, as I've discovered. She lets out a yawn, and it's contagious.

I'm first, then Dad, then Mom, who slumps over in her chair in the corner of the room like a deflated balloon. The fragile truce that existed between all of us in the aftermath of relief evaporates. No more trip down memory lane. We're awkward strangers again. Zoey escapes the uncomfortable shift in the room by falling back asleep. Dad escapes by offering to go get food.

"What time do you think he'll be back?" I whisper to Mom.

"He looked like he needed a minute. He'll probably be gone for an hour."

Licking my lips, I taste the salt that's dried on my skin. I sit up and run my hands down sticky cheeks to pull myself together. Are Mom and I supposed to be on the same team again now that Dad's left; Larssen girls against the world? Or is she still mad at me? Wait, am I still mad at her or did I lose the right to hang on to a grudge when I took the dialysis machine?

"Is the doctor coming in to give an update?"

"Soon." Mom doesn't offer up any more information, but I think it's because she doesn't have the words, not because she doesn't want to tell me. However, she's had a lot of instances lately with things she doesn't want to tell me, and I'm sick of the lies by omission.

We sit in silence for a while.

To my surprise, Mom speaks first. "I'm sorry," she says. I want to ask, *Sorry for what? The road trip? My future?* I just decide to take it as a blanket apology.

"Me too," I say, and hope it encompasses everything on my end as well. There are too many apologies this weekend to count, one of them being the reason we're all in this hospital room. I do need to get one point of contention out on the table, though. "You've known for a while that I shouldn't go to Oregon next year, haven't you? You could have saved me a lot of heartache if you'd just admitted you needed my help earlier, rather than letting me believe you were going to be fine on your own when that's obviously not the case anymore."

Her swallow is so loud I hear it from across the room, followed by a whisper that barely reaches my ears. "I wanted you to have what you wanted. I was afraid you'd resent me if I told you outright I was looking into Fides."

"What I resent is the push and pull. Because you can't go and do stuff like investigate group homes behind my back while letting me hang on to hope that my college plan will work out. It makes me feel like I can't trust you."

"Look at this." She lifts a palm, gesturing between me and Zoey on the hospital bed. "It kills me to fail both you and her. I'm not enough."

"You're not failing anyone, Mom. We're in an impossible situation that nobody ever expected. And you don't have to shoulder things alone if you're honest with me."

She sucks in a haggard breath. "Fine. You want honesty? Today was one of the worst days of my life. I haven't been this scared since Zoey was six months."

"Six months ago? Yeah, that makes sense." That was when Zoey's kidney issues started to ramp up.

"No, Kaley. Since Zoey was six months old. I never thought I'd lose my mind like that again."

"Oh. Why?"

"I took her to a checkup appointment. The first one I'd been to by myself, because your dad had to work. I hated going by myself, because I felt like everyone just stared at me, looking at the poor, single teenaged mother." She gives a sad smile and looks past my shoulder at Zoey's sleeping form. "I talked really loudly, saying, 'Oh, Daddy is going to be so proud of you today!' just so the other moms in the waiting room wouldn't think I was some irresponsible screwup. The receptionist gave me a clipboard with paperwork I had to fill out. Milestones, and such. I read it, marking almost everything down as 'not yet.' I didn't think much of it, until I was supposed to tally up the 'score' at the end. I thought it was a joke. How do you score an infant? Reduce them to mere numbers on paperwork?"

"I take it the score was low," I say.

Mom cringes. "I threw a fit in the patient room. Ranting about how ridiculous this whole thing was, how there's no way they knew my precious baby girl based on a five-minute test." I'm inclined to agree with her. I nod, and Mom continues. "By the time I got done yelling at the doctor, they'd backed off. Told me they would check again at the nine-month appointment and fully assess at one year."

I already know where this is going. "But it didn't get any better. They were right."

She swallows hard. "Zoey fell further and further behind.

I can't help but wonder if I accepted what they were saying back then, if I intervened early enough—"

"I don't think it mattered, Mom. What was done, was done. Didn't she end up surpassing all their expectations anyway?"

Mom straightens up a bit with this reminder. "They told me she would never walk. Never communicate."

"Exactly. And look, she blew them out of the water."

"It's because she saw you walk. Then she decided to do it too. And when you started talking, she decided to respond."

Zoey used to scootch around on her bum. Not even crawl. Then there's a video stashed somewhere in a dusty family memory box of us holding hands and toddling around, both unsteady on new legs. Holding each other up, not dragging each other down.

"But I knew, back at that six-month appointment. I knew something wasn't right. And I've never been more scared of anything in my life, before or since. The night before we got her official diagnosis, that was the night I convinced your father that we should have another baby—"

I slap my hands over my ears. "La la la la la!" Like I really want to know about the night I was conceived. Gross. My moral support only extends so far.

Through my off-key singing, Blake's words haunt me—*It was probably her whole plan, to have another baby in the first place.* Considering how far down this rabbit hole we've traveled tonight, I can push to get some real answers or wait forty to fifty years and demand them on her deathbed.

This might be the bravest or the dumbest thing I've done all day. No, scratch that. The dumbest thing I did today, hands down, was accidentally abducting the dialysis machine. Wait, maybe it was losing my virginity. No, that's a tie. I can't be any dumber, so I decide to be braver and get the answers I deserve.

Acid churns in my stomach. Leftover beer, nerves, or lack of food? I take my hands off my ears. "Is that why you had me? Because you needed a backup?" I try to sound nonchalant, but my voice shakes, and I hate it.

Mom looks shocked. "No! Of course not."

"Then why?" I whisper, as my very reason for existence hangs in the balance. Will she just admit that maybe she had a mental breakdown? Or felt my dad pulling away and needed a "fix-it" baby? An easy armchair diagnosis would make sense, and I'm getting the feeling that she doesn't have it together as much as I always thought she did.

"Despite all the unexpected obstacles that were thrown our way during Zoey's first year, she grew, and I grew too. We were strong, both of us. Stronger than anyone else knew. The night before the appointment, I realized that the 'why' of all this was retrospect, and nothing could predict her future. I decided that if an official diagnosis wasn't going to dictate Zoey's life, it wasn't going to dictate mine either. I'd start right then, in fact. I always knew I wanted a second baby."

I stare at her in disbelief. "You had to have had *some* reservations about all of this."

"Was the world going to judge me, you mean? Assume I had another child to care for the first one, or to be a replacement? Every pregnancy in the world has risks, and no outcome is guaranteed. You may have ended up just like Zoey. But I also knew that I would love you no matter what, because I'd already proved I could do that with your sister. I was barely twenty years old, for God's sake, and I wasn't going to give up forever on the fearless girl I used to be. I found her again, underneath it all, when I decided to have you."

"So, my existence is basically just one big middle finger to the world?" That tracks.

"You are here because you were wanted." She leans across and takes my hand.

"I'm here because *you* wanted me. But what did Dad want?" My throat is so tight I can barely say the words.

Mom winces and releases me. "Your dad tried as long as he could—"

"Why are you defending him? This goes against every interaction between you that I've seen over the past few days. You hate Dad for leaving, and then swear that he tried, make him co-guardian, then offer to take him off—"

"What was I supposed to do? Babysit a man desperate for any way out while juggling everything else? Force him to stay? What good would that have done?" I feel her pulling away from me again, building back up her fortress to hide behind. "The writing was on the wall. At least this way, he's alive."

My thoughts screech to a halt. Mom realizes she's said too much, and her mouth snaps shut.

"Oh no, you don't get to just drop that on me and not explain," I say.

Shaking her head, she stands her ground. "It's not my story to tell. If you have any questions, you'll have to ask him." She puts her hand to her lips, pausing for a moment, as if weighing her next words. “No matter what, just know that he loved you. Loves you. So much.”

“You still didn’t answer my original question. What did Dad want?”

“Sometimes what we want and what we think we deserve are two different things.”

CHAPTER FOURTEEN

DAD'S BACK, MUCH EARLIER THAN WE'D ALL GUESSED HE'D BE. I HEAR the rumble of his low tones before my eyes fully open. He and Mom are whispering back and forth to each other, trying not to wake up me and Zoey. Keeping my body completely still, I let my breathing remain slow and steady, so they don't catch on that I'm eavesdropping.

"I already said yes, Jules." Dad's tone is barely above a whisper, but I can hear the irritation loud and clear.

The scent of greasy food tickles my nose and I hold back a sneeze. When I tense my stomach and face, though, the game is up, and they know I'm awake.

"Kaley," Mom says. "Food's here." Their conversation will be put on pause as long as they know I'm listening. I could fake it for a little longer, but I'm not going to learn anything new. My head is fuzzy, my previous discussion with Mom feels like a fever dream. I sigh and sit up, stretching the kinks out of my neck and snapping it side to side with some satisfying cracks.

"Ugh, Kaley. You know I hate that sound," Mom complains.

"I'm starving," I complain right back. Dad hands me a takeout bag covered in stains; the hangover cure for champions. Although at this point, my hangover has turned into an identity crisis, but the remedy for both headaches is the same. "Thanks."

"The doctor will stop by in a few minutes," Mom says.

"Great." I open my bag and pop a fry into my mouth.

"No," Mom says. "You need to go eat that down in the cafeteria."

"Then I'll miss what the doctor says!"

"I'll let you know the gist when you return," Mom says. "I've got this part, at least. Let me handle it." Yet again, she doesn't want me here for the important conversations. What happened to our bonding moment? It really felt like we'd made some progress, but I wonder if it has anything to do with Dad being back in the picture. Does she feel like she has to look like she's in charge, in some desperate need to prove to him that she's capable? I'm half-tempted to chuck the food bag in the trash and keep my butt planted in Zoey's room, but my stomach growls loud enough to make Zoey stir.

"Fine," I huff. Before stalking out of the room, I fix my parents with a pointed look. "I'll be back in half an hour." It's like they barely even register my threat, ready to get back to their secret whispers. Mom just waves me off, and I'm invisible.

The cafeteria is eerily quiet, not unusual for this time of night, but it isn't completely empty. A few tables are occupied by people with thousand-yard stares as they sip from coffee cups distributed by the vending machine in the corner. A few nurses in scrubs on their night-shift break scroll on their phones, trying to escape their surroundings for fifteen blissful minutes. Nobody talks. There's something about the bonds that tie late-night visitors together here. On the edge of their seats, waiting for updates, but dreading any news at the same time because it might be the moment that changes their family forever. I get it. Sometimes it's better not to know.

I slide into a seat next to one of the nurses and give her a half-smile, silently asking, *Okay if I sit here?* She doesn't look up from her phone, respecting the rules of the midnight cafeteria, so my vacant smile goes unacknowledged. I figure if I accidentally took someone's seat, she'd let me know.

I like nurses more than doctors, for the most part, the exception being Dr. Hayes. Nurses always give it to me straight if I ask them questions about Zo back home when Mom won't answer. They're the people who run the hospital. I'm pretty sure the doctors are just for show, or to jump in with a bit of heroic action to liven up the day-to-day. The nurses do the grind. They also know *everything*.

When I pull out an overflowing container of fries, I hold them out in offering to the nurse who didn't acknowledge me, putting them just inside her periphery to get her attention. Loose lips sink ships? Try french fry I spy, because I'm about to get the lowdown on the patient in Room 306.

I know she sees the fries at the same time she smells them, because she takes a deep inhale and her eyes go wide. She puts her phone facedown on the plastic table. Got her. "Would you like some?" I ask, the picture of innocence even though I know very well that there is no hot food here at this time of night and the only calories she's got access to are the kind from a stale package. Obviously, she wants some. I assuage her hesitation about taking food from a teenager when I add, "My dad always goes overboard on the food when he panics." A lie, but it softens her even more toward me.

"Are your folks upstairs?" she asks. Her gaze is full of sympathy, but I see a glint of hunger there too. I pop a fry in my mouth.

"Uh-huh. Ugh, I don't even feel like eating." I push them toward her. "Don't let them go to waste."

It's clear I've got her hooked when she hesitantly grabs one.

"So, do you work with my sister's doctor?" I ask as soon as her mouth is full. Her name tag reads Nicole. She looks young, possibly just out of school. It would make sense that she was assigned the crappy shifts.

Nicole chews and swallows before answering. "I don't know, hon. Who is your sister?"

"The girl with the kidney issues in 306."

"Oh!" Her eyes light up and she brushes her hands off before extending one to me. I take it and she gives it a firm shake. "You must be Kaley. I'm so glad to finally meet you. I wish we could have met under better circumstances, but I have to say, your sister is quite the spitfire!"

"She is," I agree. Did Zoey take a swing at her? The nurse doesn't seem too upset, so maybe not. Or she's ducked her fair share of violence from patients, which I would not expect given her age.

"She told me when your parents checked her in that 'her sister hates deer and is late but will be here soon.'"

I snort. "Zoey always knows what's up."

"She really wasn't exaggerating when she artfully described your animal encounter. I think I have something in here that will help you." Nicole reaches into her oversized purse and digs around for a while before pulling out a compact tube. "It's coverup for my tattoos, but it should work on your eye."

I take the makeup. "You have tattoos?"

"See? Told you it works."

"I can't take this."

"Sure you can! I go through it quick and have a ton lying around. Plus, you're kind of like a family friend already. I've been in contact with your mom for the last couple of months."

"How do you know my mom?" I ask, slipping the tube into my pocket.

"Dr. Hayes went to medical school with Dr. Jenks, the attending here. They've been in contact over your sister's case quite a few times, bouncing ideas and treatment options off one another." She takes a big sip of her drink. "It's why Dr. Hayes felt confident sending Zoey here when your mom called about the emergency." Nicole reaches for another fry, pausing when it reaches her mouth. "Where was I? Oh yeah. So, knowing my history, Doc Jenks asked me a few months ago if I would be willing to reach out to your mom about some stuff. Reassure her."

What history? And why? "Dr. Hayes always knows what to do," I say, leaving it open-ended for her to fill in the rest for me, skirting the technical definition of a HIPAA violation.

"Such frequent dialysis is so hard. It's even harder when the patient doesn't fully understand what's happening and why, or comprehend the severity of a simple slip-up."

I nod along numbly. There is danger all around now that I'm really looking. How am I going to keep Zoey safe amongst it all? The vending machine seems to leer at me from the corner.

Brightly-colored wrappers never looked so ominous. It was hard enough before, but after this accident it feels like we need eyes on her 24/7. I've been doing the best I can, but I'm not qualified for this. What if it happens again, but much worse? And it will be all my fault. Again.

"Hey, it's okay." Nicole reaches across the table to grab my hand, her touch grounding me. "It will all be over in a few months. It's so great your dad is a match. She'll get her quality of life back. It's not forever."

Yeah, if Dad holds up his end of the bargain. Nicole is assuming he doesn't live his life taking the path of least resistance. She must see the doubt on my face because she switches subjects. "You know, your sister reminds me a lot of my little brother."

I can tell she's trying to make me feel better, and a part of me wants to let her. "Your little brother?"

"Well, he's not so little anymore. He's twenty now and built like a linebacker." She chuckles. "We've had our health care scares with him—seizure disorder. Nothing we can fix with a transplant, unfortunately." I want to turn away because he sounds nothing like Zoey. But Nicole's gaze is locked onto mine and she still grips my hand, so I'm trapped. "He has pretty severe developmental delays too. And he's deaf."

Oh. Nicole knows *exactly* who I am. I've never met another sibling like me before.

Back home, there are a handful of kids who need extra help in school, or a bit of social support in the mainstream, but none are quite like Zoey. Those other special-needs kids will grow up and be able to grocery shop and navigate public transportation. They might be able to live by themselves in an apartment within walking distance of their childhood home. Maybe they'll fall in love.

These are the feel-good stories and types of people included with disability representation on TV or in the movies. A watered-down, safe narrative so people can pat themselves on the back for inclusion without having to recognize the really, really, *really* hard parts. I've never seen my story mirrored back to me the way Nicole is looking at me now.

Nicole looks so put-together, a successful career woman, doing important work and steadfast in her path. I want to be her. I need to know how she found her way to this point while navigating impossible waters, because right now I am drowning.

Might as well start with the obvious questions first. "Does he . . . does he live with your parents?" I ask.

"Nope," Nicole says.

"He lives with you," I fill in. "How do you make it all work? Life balance and everything. There's so much I want to do—"

Nicole holds up a hand. "Wait, I didn't say he lives with me."

"Oh, I thought he was more like Zoey. Unable to be on his own." My heart sinks. I really thought we had some bonding going on. She was going to be my prophet.

"He's at an assisted-living facility. He moved in just over a year ago."

I lean away from Nicole, my opinion of her in a steep nosedive. "I can't believe you would do that to your own brother!"

My new not-friend has the audacity to raise an eyebrow at me. Like she should be passing judgment. *I'm* not the one who banished my vulnerable sibling to a state-run hellhole just so they would be someone else's problem and I could skip around, responsibility-free. The voice of reason in my head whispers that Nicole isn't skipping around, she is helping people at work, but I tell it to shut up. She is not my mirror. I will not become her.

"Hold on," she says. "He loves it."

"Sure he does," I snarl. I push back my chair and stand up. "I need to go check on my sister. You know, because I actually care about her."

Nicole's eyebrows furrow and I can tell I've hit a nerve. Good. Her phone starts ringing, breaking the dramatic silence I've created. She turns her full attention to the device and answers it, propping it up against her water bottle on the table. I hate people who talk on speakerphone in public.

Like a switch is flipped, Nicole's face goes from pissed-off to a vibrant smile, and I realize she's on a video call. With a flurry of animated hand gestures and a series of expressions that flit faster than her fingers move, Nicole is deep in conversation without speaking a word out loud. I'm openly staring, mostly because the language looks so beautiful but also because this doesn't look like a sister who pawned off her brother to forget about him. From this one-dimensional view of their conversation, Nicole has deep love for the person on the other side of the call.

I'm about to sneak away more confused than ever when Nicole starts speaking her part of the conversation out loud. "And did you beat your bowling score today?" she asks. "You did! Way to go. I bet your team was so proud . . . Shakes at Miss Mabel's Café to celebrate? . . . Oh yeah, of course . . . And don't forget, your suit for the dinner dance will be ready on Thursday . . . Let Theresa and Lauren know to pick it up . . .

Okay, bubs, I'm at work, remember? And you should be in bed. You know you aren't supposed to call so late! But it's great to see your face. All right. Good night. . . I love you, too, Cade. I'll talk to you later . . . No, I'm picking you up this weekend, not next . . . Hugs to everyone at Fides. Tell them Cole sends love."

She hangs up and stares at me. I half expect her to chew me out for insinuating that she doesn't care about her brother, but she doesn't address it at all. "I can walk you back upstairs," she says. Her phone rings again. "Right on time." Nicole—Cole—sighs, but it's not exasperated. She shrugs her shoulders, like *What do you do?* then answers the video call again. "Yep, still here, bubs," she says out loud as she signs. "Good night."

"I can walk myself up, thanks," I tell her. "You stay and enjoy the fries." It's no mystery now where Mom found out about Fides. I'm a swirling mess of emotion and I need to find the nearest stairwell or supply closet to let out all these unnamable feelings, and I don't need a witness. I'll pull myself together before I get back to Zoey's room, I'm confident in that part. I've had lots of practice.

"Listen," Nicole says, waving a fry toward me like a pointer. "You're doing really great by her. Do great by you too. Sometimes it can be one and the same."

I turn and flee. On the surface, her message and Blake's sound similar, but in my gut I know it's completely different. Maybe it's because the words are coming from someone who has been where I am, but I'm not so quick to dismiss Nicole after watching her interact with her brother. I'm teetering on the brink of understanding, but I don't know which way to step.

So, I tread the familiar path back to my sister.

I burst into her room without knocking, hoping to catch the doctor and my parents off-guard to get some real information.

"You're back early," Mom says, unrattled by my presence. That must mean they're done talking about anything important.

"Can we go home yet?"

"I'll excuse myself," Dr. Jenks says. "I'll send Hayes the update." He steps out, followed by Dad, who doesn't glance at me. I'm left staring at Mom, who isn't looking at me anymore, but over at Zoey.

"Your dad is coming out to Idaho in six weeks," she finally says. "He swears he won't smoke, and that we can get the surgery scheduled." This news should have her jumping for joy, but the look on her face says she's handed him her heart to break all over again.

Then I recall how he couldn't make eye contact with me on the way out. "He's going to sign those papers, though, isn't he?"

Mom tears her gaze away from the hospital bed. "We didn't discuss it any more in-depth. So I honestly don't know."

"Where's he running off to now?"

"His colleague is picking him up outside. They are driving back to the university to pick up our car so we can head out in the morning when Zoey gets discharged."

"Oh. That's nice of her."

"How do you know it's a her?"

"It's Dad's girlfriend." I don't tiptoe around Mom's feelings now. The big reveal had already played out this morning, and we are all too tired for any additional drama. "She stopped me on the way out of the park when I was lost. She's a good person."

"You're making it very hard for me to hate her," Mom grumbles.

"You don't hate her. She hasn't done anything wrong. I'm not sure she even knows we exist. You really think Dad told her the whole story? They're . . ." I struggle to think of the word. "Companions, I think. That's the vibe I get." Not epic love. Not like how my parents were back then, before life changed them into people they no longer recognized.

I used to think Blake and I had epic love. Our high-school-sweetheart story would be told at our wedding, all about how we beat the odds and made a beautiful life together because we fought for it. Despite distance and money and whatever other obstacles were thrown our way, love could conquer all.

But now I know that Blake never fully accepted me and who I am from the very beginning. He never understood that the core of who I am—what he claimed to love—was molded from Zoey. One cannot exist without the other. When he confessed his plan in the dorm room, he did not simply betray my sister but essentially said that only certain parts of me were worth keeping.

Did Mom and Dad's epic love shatter in one day? Or did it slowly chip away over time? I also question if it ever really went away. Mom hasn't been on a date since Dad left, a fact I'm totally sure of now that the question of the mysterious Cole has been answered. Dad seems to have moved on, but only in the most basic sense. I only have to be in the same room to feel that connection still stretched between them, an eternal one thanks to their choice to have children together.

But Mom offered to sever the link between them with the guardianship paperwork. I thought it was just an incentive to get Dad to follow through, but maybe she needs to in order to give herself a chance to move on. Why couldn't they have just decided to live happily ever after, instead? It would have saved everyone a lot of heartache. In the end, they weren't good together, but they aren't good apart either, and there's nothing I can do to fix it.

While I space out and mull that over, I have a great view of the parking lot through the giant window. Rachel's truck pulls up, and I see Dad's tall figure stride across from the hospital entrance to meet the vehicle. At first, I think he's just going to hop in and drive away with her, pretending that getting picked up in the middle of the night at a hospital is completely normal.

But Rachel surprises me when she climbs out of the driver's seat and heads Dad off before he can get inside. I can't see her face from here, but based on how stiff her posture is, I guess she's reading him the riot act. She's handling it all pretty well from where I'm sitting, better than I would be if I found out my boyfriend had a family he never talked about and a daughter with serious health conditions that he just . . . never mentioned.

Maybe I'm being too hard on him. Maybe she knew about us, but just not the full extent of what's at stake. Either way, knowing Dad's modus operandi is enough to assume Rachel has been left in the dark about a lot of this.

She's listening now while he speaks, arms folded across her chest. Dang, how are we going to get the car if she drives off without him? I'm convinced I'm witnessing my father's breakup, but then, Rachel reaches out with both arms and wraps him in a hug. He folds into her and his shoulders shake.

They stand clutched together for a good two minutes. Maybe I don't understand their relationship at all. As I'm reassessing, Mom leans her head next to mine to see what I'm staring at.

Before I can slap my hand over her eyes to protect her from the sight below, she witnesses Rachel holding Dad together. She swallows audibly but says nothing. I should have resorted to the less-painful technique of headbutting her away in the first place, and I curse my slow reflexes.

Mom spins back around in her chair to face Zoey again. "I'm going to get some sleep," she says, speaking to me but not able to look at me. "You should too. We're doing a straight shot home in the morning. I already scheduled Zoey an appointment with Doc Hayes late in the afternoon, so we have to get there by then."

"That will be fun." I do as she says, settling in next to Zoey on the narrow bed and closing my eyes. Sleep calls to me with desperation, but it's a long time before I give in to it. Flashes of the day appear like a horror movie behind my closed eyelids, along with the faces of the people I love wearing expressions I'll never forget. But eventually, the familiar beeping of the monitors lulls me to sleep.

CHAPTER FIFTEEN

OUR CAR KEYS ARE AT THE NURSES' STATION, WAITING FOR US WHEN Zoey is discharged. When the charge nurse hands Mom the clipboard to sign, I glance at the paperwork listing the insurance information. Mom swears my first full sentence at two years old was "What do you mean, out-of-network?" because I liked to eavesdrop while she yelled at people over the phone. Apparently, I did it with my head cocked to the side and my pointer finger waving around, the picture of a mother on the edge.

Looking at the paperwork, I'm about to summon my inner toddler again. My pointer finger is ready, along with its buddy for backup in case this gets ugly, prepared to throw down. The total cost is blocked by Mom's hand as she signs the bottom, but I read enough of the per-item breakdown to know this is not going to be pretty. I'm skimming as fast as I can, and I already know the final number is astronomical.

"You can work some magic, right?" I ask while she scribbles her signature.

"I don't know, Kaley," she says, sounding resigned instead of defeated. "But to leave and go home I have to sign this. I'll fight with insurance later."

The nurse, to her credit, at least looks sympathetic to our plight. With a genuine smile, she says, "I'm glad that Zoey's stay wasn't too long with us, but it was a pleasure having her here." The rest of us, aka Mom, are not included in that statement. When I went to find a bathroom a few minutes ago, I heard some of the floor nurses gossiping around the corner about the overbearing mom in 306 who came running into the hospital yesterday like her hair was on fire, barking out orders to the entire staff. "I swear I thought I was going to have to sedate her!" one of them said with a chuckle. "Dr. Jenks had us give them the VIP treatment. They must have friends in high places."

Zoey, on the other hand, had been a model patient up until thirty minutes ago. She even said please and thank you to everyone who came to check on her. I don't know if it was because her body went through so much that she needed to conserve energy, but she didn't fight the long dialysis process at all. Except now she's back to her usual feisty self.

Breakfast earlier was unacceptable, but I caught the tray before she chucked it. Mom and I had to tag-team getting her dressed, because she insisted that a hospital gown was a fashion-forward outfit to wear home. I will admit, I was kind of on her side about that one. A comfy, wearable blanket, no bra, and plenty of ventilation? Sign me up, because that sounds perfect for a long car ride. Eventually, we wrestled her into her clothes and stood back, sweaty and triumphant, only for her to decide she was *starving* now and would go get a cafeteria snack on her own, thankyouverymuch. I had to chase her down. When Zoey and I got back to the room, we found it vacant and hustled to catch up with Mom. Which brings us to the not-at-all-surprising cluster that is the American healthcare system.

In what I consider a stroke of brilliance, I realize I'm about to save the day. "Is this hospital in Dad's network? Can't he just come sign the papers?"

Mom shakes her head. "It doesn't work like that."

We're talking a five-figure number, here. It's not insignificant. "Can't you at least ask?"

"I just told you, that won't work," Mom says, voice raising in frustration.

"Stop talking to me like I know nothing," I snap back. The night of broken, uncomfortable sleep might be getting to us. "Just *call him*!" *And ignore the fact that he dropped the keys off at the front of the hospital rather than see our faces again.*

Zoey starts to shift next to me in agitation. The rumble and squeak of her teeth grinding together sends me over the edge into a sensory meltdown of my own. "Jesus Christ! Stop grinding!" I don't know why I say it, taking out my frustration on her while knowing it's one of her self-soothing techniques. It's a mistake as soon as the words leave my mouth.

There's no doubt that Zoey is back at full strength now, because two sharp blows rain down on the top of my head, quicker than I can block them. *Pow! Pow!* A little dazed, I come to my senses in time to dodge the next hit. Mom drops the clipboard with a bang onto the linoleum floor and grabs Zoey's wrists to restrain her. She pins Zoey's arms to her sides while my sister struggles against the unwanted contact.

Pressing my hand against the tender part of my skull, I curse. Then, I take a deep breath to calm down. "That was *not* nice, Zo." She shakes her head and refuses to look at me. Perfect.

"Um, should I call someone?" the nurse asks. She's relatively calm about the display of violence. Based on Mom's own stories,

I know they see a lot of wild stuff in their line of work, so this shouldn't be anything new. But the way she's looking at me with wide, shocked eyes tells me she was not prepared for Zoey to snap like that. Nobody ever is.

"No, it's under control," Mom says. "Kaley, grab the clipboard and hand it back to her."

I reach down and get the paperwork, locating the pen that rolled halfway across the hallway. Gathering it all up, I hand it back over to the nurse. She hesitates, as if she doesn't want to take it. "It's fine," I urge her. Although if the forms end up in the shredder and the bill never reaches us, I won't complain.

"Come on girls, let's get in the car," Mom says. She frog-marches Zoey down the hallway, keeping her from hurting herself or anyone else. We draw a few curious stares from people, but it's still early and the hospital is mostly quiet. One old man in the waiting room gasps. "Oh dear, is she all right?" Zoey picks that moment to throw her head back in an attempt to crack Mom's nose. It's only eight a.m., and it has already been a *day*.

I'm a few paces behind Mom and Zoey, and I slow down to answer him. Cupping my hand by my cheek, I whisper, "Too many videogames."

The old man shakes his head. "I keep warning my grandsons. Violent videogames are ruining this nation. I'll pray she lets the Lord into her heart, and He heals her."

Great, thanks. I should have just kept my mouth shut and ignored him. Can he pray for a windfall to pay our bill instead? Or ask the angels for a winning Lotto number? Something at least a little useful?

By the time we make it outside and the fresh air hits our

faces, Zoey has calmed down. She's still tired from her ordeal, so the rage fit is already over. The car is waiting for us right at the front of the parking lot. Perks of middle-of-the-night delivery.

As we get closer, I can see inside the windows. All of the snack packs and wrappers have mysteriously disappeared. Did someone vacuum? And is that a ticket on the windshield? There's a white piece of paper all right, but it's inside on the dashboard.

Mom's getting Zoey buckled in the back, so I open the passenger door and snatch the note. There's no name on the outside of the folded paper, so I take a chance and open it.

Kaley, it reads. *I looked for you all night and finally found your car, but I still can't find you. Please, call me back. Text me. Anything. I can't believe the afternoon of my dreams turned into a nightmare so quickly. I love you. I can't lose you. Not like this. I'm sorry I'm such an idiot. Yours always, Blake.*

I hold the letter to my chest, feeling the words pierce my heart. Maybe it really was just a misunderstanding. Maybe I really did overreact. He looked all night for me, missing out on cramming for his tests. If I had called him, I'm sure he would have driven out to the hospital to be with me this morning.

And missed his classes. Yeah, his parents would've loved that. But I'm already to blame for him not living up to his potential, so what else is new?

If he had appeared last night like my knight in shining armor, would I have collapsed into him and let him hold me up? No. Not anymore. I would have spent the whole night wondering what was going through his mind every time he spoke to Zoey. Would he be concerned for real, or just for my benefit? I can't live forever with this question hanging over my head, no matter how good it feels in his arms. Yesterday afternoon took me through the looking glass, and I can never see Blake the same way again. I just wish the price hadn't been so high.

I sigh. Better to know now than realize twenty years from now we were never meant to be in the first place.

"What's that?" Mom asks.

"It's, uh, a letter."

"From your dad? Is it for you or for me?"

"It's for me. From Blake."

Mom huffs, still blaming Blake for being the reason behind all of this in the first place. She and Elena would get along great if they ever decided to hang out. They have a lot of opinions in common, namely that their kids shouldn't date anymore. Well, problem solved as of eighteen hours ago.

I open my mouth to summarize, but there's an invisible hand squeezing my throat. I try to swallow the lump, but it's stuck, along with the words I need to say. Giving voice to it will make it real, and I can't bring myself to say it yet. It's too hard and embarrassing. Oh God, I still have to tell Leah and Hannah and everyone else back at school that we broke up. After spending all summer swearing up and down that we were staying together, I'll have to admit that we broke up by *October.* We couldn't even hack it until Thanksgiving break, when most "forever couples" post–high school decide to end it.

People are going to want a reason. I'll have to come up with a believable story, because there's no way I'm repeating what really happened over and over again. I'll have to make it vague enough that it won't conflict with whatever story Blake tries to tell. Should I call him and make sure we have our story straight? No. I can't call him. I blocked him. Do I delete all my social media pictures of him? Can I just do that, and not have to explain? No, that would be worse and cause everyone to speculate, and I'll be the lead story in the rumor mill. Why did Blake and I break up? *We wanted different things for our futures.* Yeah, that'll work. That's kind of what celebrities do to "consciously uncouple," right? No blame game.

I could also just delete my profiles and go dark. *I'm just living in the present, right now. Focusing on my mental health. Social media isn't serving me anymore.* Zoey would have a field day if I gave up my phone altogether. She'd know I went off the deep end.

Oddly enough, the only person who knows about the breakup (besides Declan, thanks to my meltdown) is Dad. He read enough of the letter to leave it on my side of the car. He knows, and Mom doesn't. I don't think that's ever happened before.

I shove the letter into my back pocket and slide into my seat. Mom's gaze bores into the side of my head, but I don't elaborate on the hidden contents. We've got a nine-hour drive ahead of us, I'm sure I'll find time to spill the story, or she'll drag it out of me. I might as well confess instead of facing the Inquisition, because then at least I control the narrative with some strategy. Game plan: I'll start the story when we're close enough to a scheduled stop to create a physical end to the conversation if I need to escape the car. However, if she starts in on my sex life—do I have a sex life now? Does "one and done" qualify?—I am not against throwing myself out of a moving vehicle.

"So, Zo," I say casually. "How does this hospital rate compared to your other stays?"

"*None*," she declares, voice cutting from the backseat.

"Really? Not even four stars for saving your life?"

She shakes her head. "Maybe. One," she concedes, holding up a finger. Her hospital bracelet is still on.

"One star? Tough crowd. It was the food, yeah? Can't say I blame you for that."

"No stars for Zoey." That's something new. What's she talking about?

"What do you mean? It wasn't your fault you were at the hospital. Well, it was sort of your fault for eating the snacks. My fault for running off."

"Hurt Kaley," she admits, looking down at her lap. "Sorry."

My first instinct is to jump to her defense. Tell her it didn't even hurt; despite the goose egg I feel rising under my unwashed hair. She's been through a lot the last few days. But she's also handled it with a lot fewer meltdowns than I expected, and me downplaying the severity of my injury is only lying to both of us and not helping long term.

My tentative fingers prod my most recent Oregonian souvenir. "It hurts," I tell her, and she nods sadly. "It will probably be sore for a few days. I'd appreciate it if you could use your words next time when you're mad. I know it's hard, but I also know you can do it. Let's make it a five-star Zoey next time."

"Five stars," she agrees, holding up a splayed hand. Then she frowns. "Five stars for Kaley too."

"Hey, I'm not the one who—" I cut myself off, remembering how quickly I snapped at her at the desk. My reaction had also been uncalled-for. "You're right. Five stars for me next time too."

I know we're in accord when she changes the subject. "Music, now."

I smile. "Okay, sweets. What do you want?"

She hums the melody and I have to guess. "Um . . .'You Can't Always Get What You Want'?"

"Nooo." She drawls it out gleefully.

" 'Dani California'?"

"No."

" 'Come As You Are'? Sing it again!" I order.

She does.

"Are you *sure* it's not 'You Can't Always Get What You Want'?" I swear it sounds exactly like it.

"It is!" she exclaims.

"Zo! That was my first guess!" She just cackles. "I think you want to drive me nuts more than you want to listen to music." Her silence is telling. "Yep, I'm so right about this." Still, I put on her request and turn it up.

"Kaley," she reminds me. "DJ."

"Oh, right." I deepen my voice and continue. "This one goes out to all those listeners feeling extra resilient today. I hope you know, you're not alone. Sit back, relax, and let the sounds take you away."

I look back over my shoulder as Zoey does what DJ Kaley suggests, grateful not to sit in the tense silence anymore while the music washes over us. The trees zip by in a green blur and we are on our way home. Mom seems relieved to be back on the road, her shoulders relaxed with hands loose on the wheel. No surprise visit to her ex-husband on her mind, no question of kidney donation hanging in the air. Just the return to our regularly scheduled life. I wonder if she's tempted to floor it and race home. I bet she could get us there in under seven hours, if not for those pesky police holding her back.

Thank God it's a straight shot. My bed is calling me, and I need to curl up and forget this trip ever happened. Maybe I'll wake up tomorrow morning to Blake's texts and respond like, *I had the weirdest dream! I went out to visit you and we broke up. Can you believe it?* He won't see it coming, my outrageous claim throwing him off so much he begins to doubt his memory, and we can just erase the whole thing and move past it. Gaslighting—the key to a healthy relationship.

"Who's gaslighting you?" Mom asks.

I have to stop doing that.

"No one," I say quickly. "You."

"Kaley Marie," Mom warns.

"Fine." Might as well get this over with. So much for strategy. "Blake and I broke up," I whisper, not wanting to upset Zoey. "And I don't want to talk about it right now."

I hope that she'll take my words at face value, see my stoicism, and respond in kind. Because there is no room for me to be anything other than fine while we still have miles to go before home.

What I secretly want is for her to see past my words. To pull the car over and pull me into her arms and hold me while I sob out my first heartbreak. To hear and understand the ache behind my words and know what really happened in his dorm room. To swear and rage on my behalf and promise to egg his parents' house with me in the dead of night.

"Oh honey. Let's talk about it when we get home," she suggests. "We can go out for coffee. Just you and me."

"I'd like that."

Kicking my feet up on the dash, I accidentally pop open the glovebox underneath. I already know what the stack of papers is—quite a few of them are a bit ragged around the edges and I think there's some mud smeared on the side of one. I am surprised, though, to see a package of peanut butter cups stashed in there. We *never* have peanut butter in the vicinity anymore because of Zoey's diet, even though it's my absolute favorite. Those should definitely not be in there.

I reach in and tilt the package toward me, keeping the candy hidden in the cubby so there's no chance Zoey will see it. There's a sticky note on top that reads *I hear chocolate helps.* It's been a long time since I've seen that handwriting, but I know it's Dad's.

I promise myself that later, when I'm behind the wheel and everyone else in the car is asleep, I'll take out my treasure and savor every bite, and let the tears silently roll down my face.

CHAPTER SIXTEEN

WE'RE LESS THAN TWO HOURS DOWN THE ROAD WHEN ZOEY INFORMS us that she needs a snack. There's nothing in the car anymore, so a detour is inevitable. "You should have eaten your breakfast earlier," Mom chastises.

Zoey shakes her head. "Gross."

I'm on my sister's side for this one. "Yeah, it didn't look great. I don't blame you for trying to chuck it." Mom grumbles about never getting home and I check out the highway sign as the car whizzes past. "Don't take the next exit!" I burst out. "Take the one in four miles. Inglewood."

"Was there even a sign for food?" she asks.

"Something about a diner," I say. Miss Mabel's Diner, the one Nicole and her brother talked about. That must mean Fides is around there somewhere, and if I'm right, I can prove that Fides and everything like it is out of the question for Zoey. Sure, Nicole seems to think it was right for her family, but that doesn't mean it's right for mine. I don't want the question of Fides to haunt me through the transplant process, so I'd rather settle any doubts now as long as I'm here.

I'm not sure if Mom even puts two and two together after so little sleep, because she takes the Inglewood exit without an ounce of recognition or suspicion. "Hopefully they will have something suitable for you to eat, Zoey. I'm going to be ticked if we have to go too far out of the way."

Mom drives us down an adorable main street with shops lining both sides of the quiet road. The tires bump over a set of train tracks. Kids play at a park up ahead, and mothers push strollers down the street with cups of to-go coffee, sipping them like they contain lifeblood. It's a Stars Hollow multiverse, but with sleep-deprived parents to add to the realism. We'll fit right in, which is *not* the goal.

I can't look at how perfect it all is anymore. Instead, I flip down the visor to test out Cole's miracle makeup in the mirror. Dammit. I hate it when people I don't like are right. Minus some puffiness that looks like I've either been crying or had a minor allergic reaction, I look almost back to normal, all traces of purple and blue gone. As if this weekend never happened.

"Food!" Zoey yells, pointing to a building that Mom drives past. I almost poke myself in the eye and bring myself back to square one.

"Oh shoot." Mom flips a U-turn and parallel parks out front like a boss. Even the babies stare from their strollers, drooling with envy at her skills.

"Think this place was called Luke's once upon a time?" I ask, distracted from my mission to hate this place by the startling similarities to my favorite show.

"It's apparently Miss Mabel's now," Mom says. "Although, I'd like to hold on to the possibility of a surly-yet-handsome man behind the counter who both feeds me and falls in love with me."

A broad-shouldered man in a backwards baseball cap would work wonders for getting her mind off Dad. Considering we are still in Oregon, there's a great chance he'll be in flannel too.

"You know, we're due for our annual rewatch," I tell her. The reminder of our fall tradition has Zoey humming the theme song as we exit the car.

A bell chimes when we enter Miss Mabel's diner, and a sign by the hostess stand instructs us to wait to be seated. Craning my neck, I spot an empty booth near the back. This place is popping for a Tuesday morning.

"Sorry!" A woman sees us and hustles over. When she gets close enough, I startle.

"Kaley," Mom warns.

I think she has Down syndrome! I'm excited. I want to ask her without being totally inappropriate and invasive. Instead, I grab Zoey's arm and drag her around to stand in front of me, so she'll be the first person the hostess greets.

"Hi!" she says, a big smile on her face. "Welcome to the diner," she continues, slowly but clearly. "Three today?" She holds up three fingers in front of her name tag, which says Gracie.

"Yes, three," Mom confirms.

Gracie leads us to that back booth and seats us. "Are you here . . . for Fides?" she asks, eyeing Zoey.

"Fides!" I burst out. "You know Fides?" *Ha.* I was right. Time to get the true lowdown on that sketchy place. Mom looks across the table at me like I've grown three heads, but she also winces, realizing her mistake in bringing us here before she's had more time to feed me propaganda.

Gracie nods. "Family day camp started . . . yesterday." She makes a sweeping gesture with her arm around the diner at the other customers, and I look a little closer. There's a boy rocking and stimming on a counter seat next to a man who looks enough like him to be his dad, making sure he doesn't fall off while engaged in laughing conversation. There's a woman in a wheelchair being fed oatmeal lovingly by a lady with graying hair. Someone near the front window knocks a cup off the table. It falls with a crash, but no one bats an eye. A man appears with a broom to calmly sweep it up. Zoey is more interested in stacking jam packets than taking in our surroundings, but I'm wide-eyed. All these people are affiliated with Fides?

"Menus," Gracie says, handing us slightly sticky tagboard. "Oliver is coming. Enjoy!" She scurries off to help the next people waiting at the hostess stand.

Mom opens her mouth to interrogate me, but our waiter appears. Oliver. "Hello, guys! Welcome to Miss Mabel's. What can I get you started with?"

"How about some information," I ask, leaning toward him. He leans away, so maybe I come off as too much of a mob boss. Or an assassin.

"Do you have questions about the menu?" he asks.

"Fides," I say. "What's the deal?"

He looks a bit confused, like we should already know because of Zoey, but probably humors me because he wants a big tip. "Fides is the special-needs community here. We employ a few of the core members here at the diner, as do many of the other local stores. Their neighborhood is just outside of town, a cluster of five houses, and a produce farm."

Aha! I was right not to believe how great Nicole made it seem. I stare straight at Mom when I say, "So, it's a cult."

"What?" Oliver asks. "No. Wait, aren't you here for family camp?"

"Just passing through today," Mom says, shooting me a glare. "Once upon a time Fides may have been a passing thought. It's on the backburner for now." I wonder if she had planned to sign us up for family camp in the future, once Zoey had recovered from her transplant. I guess I wrecked the surprise. Sorry, not sorry.

"Oh wow, that's kind of an odd coincidence." Oliver says. "Family camp is twice a year, if you want to come back in the spring." Mom nods along because she already knows. Oliver takes it as a sign to continue his explanation. "It's for prospective members—a tour of how they do things, a chance to meet the aides in the houses, that sort of thing. But family camp also provides free resources and support for families with special needs, even young kids who have a while before they grow up and get on the waitlist to move out here. There's also a sibling workshop," Oliver says, eyeing me.

I stare back at him without blinking. There has to be a catch. And I'm still not convinced that it isn't a cult. "So, people just . . . ditch their family members there. Kick 'em to the curb like, 'Good luck!'"

Oliver shakes his head. "Not even close. You'll have to go by and see it for yourself. The whole point is giving core members appropriate care, but it's more than that too. It gives them community and as much independence as possible. The goal is to let people with varying disabilities have as much control over their lives as they can safely handle, usually far more than their families do—" He cuts himself off and blushes, probably afraid he just offended us. "Anyway, what can I get you?" He asks the last question like the last two minutes didn't just shake our very foundation as a family.

Well. That wasn't what I expected. Mom rattles off our usual breakfast order because I'm incapable of finding my words at the moment. One part keeps repeating in my head—*as much control over their lives as they can safely handle, usually far more than their families do.* I try to dismiss it. Zoey has independence with us, right? I'm not going to consider ripping Zoey away from everything she has ever known just because she was nineteen before anyone thought to teach her how to do laundry.

I turn to watch the other families like ours and begrudgingly admit that there is nothing like this where we live, no special-needs community. Has Zoey felt like she missed out on anything? She's still focusing on her mini jam tower instead of looking around. *See?* I prove to myself. *She has us. And all your friends love her, and Bla*—Whoops, almost thought the forbidden B-word. *We aren't holding her back.*

But Nicole's conversation with her brother pops into my head. Bowling? Dances? He probably works somewhere in town too. I try to imagine Zoey doing all these things by herself and just can't. She needs us, all the time. Everyone is too starry-eyed over promises of the impossible to see the truth. Once Zoey gets her new kidney, our lives will all go back to normal.

I have to push down the feeling that "normal" isn't necessarily as good as I'm remembering. Normal is surviving. It's better than being in constant crisis mode over Zoey's health, but a part of me thinks that we should be striving for more than a return to normal. But it's not like we have a ton of options, so I should just be grateful for what we get.

Oliver delivers our food. Zoey receives her plain oatmeal and sighs. I wait for her to pick up the bowl and chuck it, like she did back at the hospital. Instead, she looks around the diner, picks up her spoon without complaint, and starts eating. The pancakes and bacon in front of me lose all their appeal, and more than anything I want to offer them to her, but I can't.

"Kaley, eat," Zoey says, mouth full.

Why do I have so many options and she doesn't?

It's a long drive home and I know I need fuel for it, but as I nibble the bacon, it turns to ash in my mouth. We eat in silence for a while, the three of us caught in our own heads, people watching a whole different community than we're used to.

The dad over at the counter checks his watch and suddenly stands up. He helps his young son off the stool next to him and turns to a teenager on his other side and speaks a few words to him. Oh, they're related too. The dark-haired woman must be their mom. The happy family stands up and gathers their things, then they walk toward us. And past us, to the restrooms.

I'm still trying to force food into my face when they come back out, and I hear the mom say, "Ask her. Go on."

The shy teenage boy gets nudged toward our table just as I take my first full bite of pancakes. He's around fourteen, wearing glasses, and has a few pimples on his face. "Mymomwantstoknowifyou'redoingtheworkshop," he mutters.

"Wha?" I ask, a mouthful shoved in my cheeks.

"My mom. She wants to know if you're doing the sib workshop today. There's not a lot of kids around my age this week." He's blushing furiously at this point and turns around to stare daggers back at his mom, who is waiting by the bathroom doors, presumably for her husband and other son to reappear. "They think it will be good for us to talk."

He looks so embarrassed I want to throw him a bone. "You're here for your little brother?"

"Yeah," he says. "Mom and Dad are very into planning for our future. And joining all the groups. Even though he's only ten." He rolls his eyes. As if on cue, the ten-year-old walks up to our table, led carefully with a hand on his back by his dad.

"Just wanted to come say hello, and that we hope we'll see you later today!" the mom says with a big smile.

Zoey bats Mom's hand away from where she's holding out a napkin for her and finally looks over at our guests. Her gaze flits from Glasses Boy to the mom and then to the special-needs brother, where it stays for a little longer than usual. When our hostess, Gracie, walks up to check on us, Zoey's attention fixates. She looks from Gracie to the brother and back again. The gears are turning in her brain as she tries to figure out what she's missing. The concept is there, and she's reaching for it.

"Sorry for the staring," Mom interjects. "Zoey hasn't met many other special-needs kids."

The little brother steps into Zoey's space, where she sits on the edge of the bench. He lifts a hand and places it gently on her cheek. Zoey doesn't move a muscle, and when the boy drops his hand to return to his mom, I see that the woman has tears in her eyes.

"Kenny doesn't usually take to strangers," she explains, sniffling. "He's in his own world a lot of the time. He must see something unique in your daughter."

My grinning sister digs back into her food with gusto, and I almost believe the oatmeal has been transformed into an ice-cream sundae with how much she's beaming. I always wondered if Zoey realized she was different but couldn't express it. Have we failed her by not letting her explore this side of herself? I always thought that my friends were her friends, and that would be enough. Now I'm not so sure. Whether she can articulate it or not, that boy is a kindred spirit.

"We're on our way out, actually," Mom says, motioning to Oliver across the diner for the check.

"Oh," the dad says, visibly disappointed. "Maybe next year, then."

"That depends," Mom says, staring right at me. "We live quite a ways away."

I'm not ready to think about if we'll ever come back here or not. But the other mom nudges Glasses Boy, still trying to salvage the situation. "Go on, Ian."

Ian blushes and pulls out his phone. "I have a girlfriend," he prefaces.

"Um, okay. Good job?"

"But I was wondering if you'd like to exchange numbers. We

have a sib group chat going from the Fides meetups. I can add you to it if you want. It's mostly memes and some dumb jokes, but it's nice to have other kids who get it, you know? On the rough days."

I want to smack the phone out of his hands for insinuating I want anything to do with this cult, but my earlier conversation with Nicole stops me—how amazing it felt for just a moment to be truly seen. I sigh. "Sure. I'll try it out." Mom's eyebrows fly up. "What? If it's weird, I'll block them. No offense," I say to Ian, who is standing there, ready to punch in my phone number.

"We are all a little weird," he admits. His honesty is refreshing. "But at least you'll know going into it."

"Ian!" his mother says. "You're all perfectly lovely." She looks like she regrets encouraging him to talk to us, but the damage is done and I'm part of the sib chat, as evidenced by my phone buzzing nonstop. Someone just welcomed me with a spicy pepper emoji, plus a punching fist emoji, and a lit bomb emoji. I respond with a unicorn and tornado emoji. "Safe travels," the mother wishes us. "Come on, boys."

"Bye," Zoey says, watching them leave. Is that a wistful look on her face? I've never seen her make that expression before. "I like it here," she states, clear as a bell.

The strength and certainty in her statement jolts me. Maybe we should just go with them to check it out real quick. I mean, we're already here. My initial doubts about Fides haven't changed, but maybe I should confirm that it's really a terrible place. Proof that Kenny and his family really are all a bunch of cultists in disguise. It could be how Fides recruits—send out the young, cute ones as bait. Nicole at the hospital also has a modus operandi—targeting families in crisis mode when they're weak, luring them to the compound. Although, she never told me directly where Fides was located. It seems that would be a key part of the luring process.

Mom seems to read my mind. "It's been a long trip; we need to get back home in time for Zoey's appointment with Dr. Hayes, remember? There's no time for any more detours."

Zoey leans back in the booth and crosses her arms. "No more Doc. Home."

"We're on our way, sweets," I tell her. "Back to regularly scheduled programming soon enough."

Her face lights up. "*My Little Pony*?"

It's my turn to drive when we get back to the car. When we get to the roundabout, I'm so preoccupied thinking about the directions Oliver gave to get to Fides that I miss the exit. The car keeps going around the loop and Mom says, "Oh, you missed it."

"I know." The exit to head back the way we came is next, but I can't bring myself to take that one, either. That way leads past the parks, over the train tracks, past the diner, all the way to the edge of town where the Fides neighborhood is located. I chicken out and drive past it.

We've now done a full 360. Zoey starts to laugh, thinking I'm messing with her on purpose. I'm taking the correct exit this time. I hope.

The car is driving itself at this point, because I miss the exit again. "Are you having a stroke?" Mom asks. "Pull over. I'll drive."

"I can't," I answer through gritted teeth. I swear I'm trying, I really am. But I'm stuck in this moment of indecision where choosing the right direction is literally impossible, so the wheel keeps turning in an eternal loop. Fides. Home. Fides. Home. I feel like I've been taking the wrong medication. What do the sides of pill bottles always say, again? *Use caution when operating heavy machinery.* I know the labels mean cars, but I always feel like they're talking about, like, an excavator. Or a bulldozer. If I pick a path right now, I'm going to leave destruction in my wake, and it will be impossible to return if I choose wrong.

It's easier not to choose, and we go around again.

This time, Mom waits like a predator, ready to spring into action. She waits until the exit back to the highway comes around, and she yanks the wheel over. The decision is physically out of my hands. I breathe a sigh of relief and we are on the straight and narrow again. The direction Mom chose.

"Are you good?" Mom asks. "Want me to take over?"

I'm a little dizzy from the self-induced spiral and my stomach bubbles in discomfort. "No, I got it. Just a momentary lapse."

"It's been a long weekend," Mom agrees. Placing the blame on seeing Dad, Blake's breakup, and Zoey's hospitalization. Yeah, the Fides thing is just the cherry on top, not the real cause for my crisis of confidence. This morning was the extra drop in the bucket that made it overflow, not the earthquake shaking the foundation *under* the bucket that sloshed it all over the place and made a huge mess.

When we get home, I'll have to pick up a mop—metaphorically

speaking. The actual floors should still be fine from the last time I mopped, when Zoey tried to do laundry. Was that really only a few days ago? A lifetime has passed since then. I remember how she lit up when I decided to teach her how to do it safely and wonder which exit Zoey would have pushed me to take on the roundabout if she had been riding shotgun instead.

CHAPTER SEVENTEEN

HOME SWEET HOSPITAL. AS MUCH AS I WOULD LOVE TO COLLAPSE face-first into my bed and not move until my alarm goes off for school tomorrow, we barely make it in time for Zoey's checkup before the clinic closes for the day.

"How's my favorite patient?" Dr. Hayes asks. "I hear you've had quite the adventure. And you got to see an old colleague of mine, Dr. Jenks!" He's talking only to Zo and barely glances at me or Mom.

Mom clears her throat. "I brought the portable dialysis machine back and it's all checked in." That was our first stop upon arrival. I'm not proud to admit I almost dropped it outside the elevator. Mom, holding up the other side, narrowly missed getting a toe crushed. I told her I knew it was cursed when she brought it home in the first place. However, she did not agree it needed an exorcism before we stuck it back in the closet.

Dr. Hayes nods once. "Thank you." He's stiff and weirdly formal. "I wish it had been of better service on your trip." Reading between the lines is easy on that one. He's furious at us, but he refuses to crack his professional mask. This is as heated as I've ever seen him, but he'll stay calm for Zoey's sake.

"The trip was worth it, actually," Mom declares. "William is a match and is going to donate." *Only if he can quit his addiction,*

I want to add, in case Mom's version makes Dad seem too magnanimous. If he had quit when Zoey's trouble started instead of expecting Mom to be the match, Zoey could have had the new kidney by tomorrow.

Dr. Hayes's eyebrows shoot up. "That's excellent news!" He glances back and forth between me and Mom, waiting for the full explanation.

"Yeah, then once it's done, he'll be off the hook forever," I mutter, thinking of the guardianship paperwork that's still in the glove compartment.

"Kaley doesn't know what she's talking about," Mom assures him.

"Well, financially—" I start to point out.

"If the donation has been coerced, you know where the ethics stand on that, Nurse Larssen," Doc Hayes says sharply. He pinches the bridge of his nose and closes his eyes. "If I'm suspicious that there is *any* money exchanging hands, I'll have to report it immediately or I'll lose my license—"

"There's not," Mom says. "I swear."

Dr. Hayes opens his eyes and fixes Mom with a stare. She doesn't back down or flinch, as if willing him to see the sincerity. "I know you will do anything for your child, Jules. But don't cross this line," he says.

"I am not paying William for a kidney," Mom declares. "In fact, he said he would help cover the medical bills from our trip to Oregon."

He did? I don't remember that conversation. That must've been who she was texting in the car. I thought she was updating Cole on our brush with Fides. I tried to send Leah a text on our way back describing it all, but I wrote and deleted it three times before I gave up. It's impossible to put how I'm feeling into words right now, so I just told her that Zoey was okay and we were on the way back. Plus, every version made the town sound amazing, which is *so* not what I'm going for. I'll just have to tell her how awful and wrong it is for Zoey in person once I process the trip and focus on the negatives. It's far away, for one. And two, it isn't with her family. And three . . . three . . .

Doc Hayes sighs. "Moving forward." He pulls up Zoey's files on his computer and scrolls through them. "I am relieved that Zoey will be getting a transplant sooner rather than later. This latest . . ." Screw up? Misadventure? Trip from hell? I shift my weight back and forth on each leg, waiting to see what a professional has to say on the matter of our road trip. He's surprisingly tame with his choice: "*Emergency* has me concerned about the toll on her body long-term. She's fine for now," he rushes to reassure us, "but I know we are all eager to put dialysis behind us."

I look over at Zoey to confirm, who is staring up at the ceiling, looking bored out of her mind. Everything seems like business as usual on her end, but she'll actually be getting a kidney a few weeks from now. The realization slams into me. It's hard to recall a time when her kidneys weren't the center that all our lives revolved around. God, we're going to have *so* much free time. I do a little booty shake to celebrate.

"Kaley, do you have to go to the restroom?" Mom asks like I'm a four-year-old.

"No."

"Dr. Jenks just sent over the patient summary from your

visit. I see the note that William agreed to quit smoking for six weeks so he can undergo the surgery. So, if we're going with the best-case scenario timeline," Doc Hayes says, "Zoey could have her new kidney by Thanksgiving. Wouldn't that be something to be thankful for?" He has a smile on his face now, like it's not often he gets to give such great news to worried families. How much of his day is spent giving bad news? I've seen his bad-news face—a perfect mixture of sympathy and reassurance. We've been on the receiving end of it many times. This is the first time I've seen his good-news face, and I gotta say, it's a bit uncanny valley–ish.

Mom smiles back at him, their fight from minutes ago already forgotten as they grin like besties at each other. Should I excuse myself?

I slip out of the room unnoticed, lean back against the hallway wall, and let out a huge exhale. My fingers come up to chew my nails, but I stop myself.

I never want to repeat the last three days. Did the ends justify the means? Yes. We got what we came for. Will anything be the same ever again? No.

But I'm pretty sure that's for the better.

The Larssen girls are different people now. Not just in the way we see one another, but in how we navigate through the world. Mom's more willing to let the cracks show, Zoey is done being underestimated, and I'm taking off my rose-tinted glasses. It's still Larssen girls versus the world, but we're showing off our battle scars now instead of keeping them hidden.

When Mom's done talking to Doc Hayes and finds my hiding spot a few minutes later, she's buzzing with excitement.

A complete contrast to me and Zoey, who are the walking dead at this point. I don't think Mom has really slept in days, so it is pure adrenaline that's propping her upright.

Mom rides the high from all her hard work paying off until we walk through the front door to our home. Once inside, it looks like someone pulls her plug. She collapses onto the couch in an unruly pile of limbs and greasy hair. Leaning her head back and closing her eyes, she mutters, "Just give me a second before we unpack the car." Surrendering completely with palms up and heart open à la YouTube yoga, she's out like a light.

The house has a smell. It must usually smell like this, but I've become nose-blind to it day-to-day. I don't think I've ever been away longer than two days. This must be the smell visitors are hit with when they come over. Am I detecting undertones of soup? Overlaid with Mom's perfume. Dawn dish soap. General mustiness from throw blankets and old couches. Does this mean *I* smell like this delightful combination? Maybe we need some essential oils up in here. Too bad I don't have Mary-Langston's number.

Glancing over at the kitchen, I notice there are still dishes on the table. I'm afraid to look too closely and see if they are contributing to the aroma. A vision flashes through my tired brain of the four of us—me, Zoey, Mom, and Dad—sitting around the ancient rectangular table, just like we used to, my thoughts misfiring and confusing past, present, and future. But Doc promised a kidney by Thanksgiving. Does that mean Dad will stay here through the process and we'll spend the holiday together as a family? What a weird concept. Will he think the house still smells the same, or will it be completely different from when he lived here? He hasn't stepped foot inside in years. What if he walks in, gets a big ol' whiff, and books a hotel?

I realize I've been standing in the kitchen for far too long, breathing heavily through my nose, and now I'm a bit lightheaded. There's no time to hyperventilate right now, there's still too much to do.

"Come on, Zo." I drag Zoey upstairs and help her put on her pajamas. She could use a shower, but I don't have it in me right now. She lies in my lap and is half-asleep while I floss and brush her teeth with a spare toothbrush, going through the motions like a zombie. When that's done, I tuck her into bed, turn on her nightlight, and sing her a song. Surrounded by familiarity, she's down without a fuss.

Her sleeping form rests easy, chest rising and falling with gentle breaths, one arm tight around Moosh. God, she's had that raggedy stuffy forever. For Zoey's sixth birthday, Mom took me to the store and told me to pick out a toy that I thought my sister would like. Something about the joy of gift-giving and the importance of sibling thoughtfulness. I picked out the most realistic, colorful stuffed animal I'd ever seen. "Mama, look at that beautiful bird!"

"That's a chicken, Kaley."

"It's perfect."

Mom tried to talk me out of it, directing me over to the horses and unicorns Zoey had already started obsessing over. I would not be deterred. My sister *had* to have this fantastic fowl. I didn't even want it for myself, a fact I'm sure of because Mom even offered to buy it for me for my birthday instead and get Zoey something different. This chicken brought me joy, but it would bring my big sister even more happiness.

I was bouncing up and down when I helped her unwrap it. She and I have watched the home video many times. "It's a chicken!" I screamed, before the paper was all the way off. Zoey pulled it to her chest and squeezed, hard.

"Don't smoosh it!" I yanked on her arm, but her grip was too strong.

Smoosh turned to Moosh, christened forevermore.

Zoey's room has pretty much stayed the same over the years. Same nightlight. Same stuffies. Same posters. Frozen in time. Does she see it that way? Or is it comforting, like being snuggled in bed? Most of my stuffed animals are bagged up in the closet. I put them there after Blake and I started dating. I felt weird making out with him in my room in front of so many watchful eyes.

Gathering all the willpower I possess, I force myself out of Zoey's room and into the hallway. I'm at the top of the stairs. I could force my legs to walk all the way down to the first floor, out to the car, haul the suitcase inside, remove all the dirty clothes, start a load of laundry, finish the dishes, and get back upstairs to take a shower. Or I could do none of those things.

"Screw it," I mutter, and head into my bedroom instead. Before I collapse onto my mattress, I hunt around in my closet first. Locating the black garbage bag, I tear it open and free my little friends. Gallop. Sparkle. Unicorn Princess. Definitely *not* Strawberry Shortcake. Birthday presents from years gone by. I curl up with the biggest one, Neigh Neigh, and bury my face into her mane. I hate horses.

"Kaley, up, up, up! You're late for school!"

I'm in the middle of a rather terrifying dream, trying to outrun a giant pumpkin that's bearing down on me like the boulder from *Indiana Jones*, so the interruption is not entirely unwelcome. What is unwelcome, however, besides Mom's shrill tone, is my rancid morning breath, the horsehair in my mouth, and the stench of cold nightmare sweat.

Fine, I can't blame it all on the nightmare. The culprit is most definitely the fact that I haven't showered in an embarrassing number of days. There's hospital all over me, frat house, and . . . oh God. That's the last thing I want to think about. I bolt upright in bed like a resurrected mummy, and Mom jumps away from me with a warranted scream.

"Hey, you don't look much better!" I tell her. She's already backing away, not trusting my lunge and grasp capacity.

"You've already missed the bus! Just take the car and go, I don't have a shift until later this afternoon."

Throwing the covers off, I'm up and moving in record time. Neigh Neigh flies into the wall like a Pegasus without wings. When I reach the bathroom, I pee with firehose force while brushing my teeth with my finger and waiting for the shower water to heat up. It's still cold by the time I jump under the spray, teeth chattering while I soap off as best I can, paying particular attention to the areas last touched by He Who Should Not Be Named. Ugh. I'm going to burn my sheets. I can't believe I fell asleep pre-sanitized last night.

I'm clean, but pale and shivering, when I yank on some sweatpants and throw on a hoodie. My sopping-wet hair leaves drops behind me as I race downstairs, but there's no time to dry it. Shoes, shoes, where are my shoes? Dang, forgot socks. Too late. I shove my feet into an old pair of slippers and grab my backpack from the hall closet.

Keys in hand, I dash out the front door and into the car. I'm backing out of the driveway, 99 percent certain that the trunk has not been unpacked yet and I'm hauling all my dirty laundry to school with me. At least my toothbrush is probably still in there. Know what's not in here anymore? Snacks.

My stomach protests all the way to the student parking lot. There's a single spot left in the back, and I snag it with minutes to spare. The center console still holds the magic makeup, and I glob it onto my finger and swipe it around my eye without looking as I throw my body out of the car. I can't run very fast in slippers, so I shuffle my way inside the building and all the way to first period. The halls are empty, and sneaking into AP bio unnoticed is impossible now. I don't know why I still care so much about being on time. My college plans have already imploded. I spent the last few days dealing with medical emergencies. I saw my *dad*. I broke up with my boyfriend. Missing the Wednesday Wakeup assignment should not rank high on my priority list.

But right now, that assignment is my lifeline. A tether to lead me back to normalcy, and if I miss it, I might as well surrender to the ether. If I can't make this work, it's admitting that this trip changed me past the point of no return, and that's too scary to contemplate.

I turn the handle and jerk open the door to Room 12 harder than I need to, and sure enough, everyone's heads pop up and look over at the familiar girl who reminds them of a long-lost fellow student . . . Kaley was her name? No, that couldn't be right. Kaley was not a pale, bedraggled, half-drowned rat of a girl. At least, not one who dressed in oversized clothes, wandering in wide-eyed and unhinged. Aw crap, this is Blake's hoodie. Any second now someone is going to offer to escort me to the school counselor's office.

"Oh. My. Lanta." Leah's voice carries from her spot at the back corner desk.

"Here's your quiz, Kaley," Ms. Maxwell says. "Good to have you back. Find your desk and get to work."

I slide into my usual seat, and I can feel Leah's gaze wander over sporadically as I finish the paperwork with gusto. I'm sure of exactly 10 percent of my answers. Really knocking it out of the park today, but at least I'm here.

Once the five minutes are up, we all pass our papers to the front of the room to be collected. Leah immediately pounces. "What the hell happened to you? You said Zoey was fine. Did something else come up?" I turn to fully face her, giving her a long stare, and she gasps. "Oh God, you and Blake broke up, didn't you?"

Don't make me say it out loud. Don't make me say it out loud. Wait, how did she know? Did Declan tell her? Were they talking about me behind my back?

"Partner up," Ms. Maxwell says. "You'll start the lab today and finish tomorrow. Take your time and don't rush, the steps are precise." She looks around the room, and I swear her stare lingers on me. I can't afford to screw anything up. I should probably pick a partner who won't distract me, but Leah is like a dog with a bone now. The last thing I need is her shouting questions at me from across the room.

Leah gathers her stuff and plops down next to me.

"Did Declan tell you?" I blurt out.

Leah rears back, offended. "No, I just know you. Hold up. Did you tell my cousin about your breakup *before me*? As your best friend, I should be privy to all important information first!" Crossing her arms, she thinks for a second. "When I asked if he'd heard from you yesterday, he told me to kick rocks! But then he also told me to bring you these." She reaches into her backpack and pulls out a handful of Hershey Kisses.

"He told you to bring me chocolate?" The breakfast of champions.

"Hershey Kisses, specifically." Leah narrows her gaze. "Does that mean something to you?"

Does it? Maybe it's just, like, the equivalent of a peck on the cheek from afar. Affection from a friend after the longest weekend of my life. I don't have time to confirm or deny because Leah is onto the next shocking revelation.

She takes in my clothes, my expression, and the utter madness in my eyes after scrubbing all evidence of him from my skin this morning and whispers, "You had sex with Blake?" The tone filled with disbelief is gone, and in its place is something far worse. It sounds an awful lot like pity for the high school girlfriend who thought she could make long distance work by offering up her v-card.

I jump to my own defense. "Well, *I* dumped *him* when

I realized he was both bad in bed and a bad boyfriend." How's that for controlling the narrative? "I mean," I start again, getting a firmer grip on my emotions, "we wanted different things for our futures." The smile I try to sell it with comes out as a grimace. Plus, this is Leah we're talking about. She sees right through it in a second, and I'm laid bare. Awkward, because I'm just now realizing I never put on a bra this morning.

"Girl, you are not okay."

"Definitely not. But I think I might be by Thanksgiving."

"Isn't that when Blake is coming back? Do you think you'll get back together?"

"No." That's for sure not happening, but I don't have the energy to explain all of his secret biases right now. "Zoey is getting her kidney by then."

Leah claps a hand over her mouth and lets out a small shriek. Then she drops her hand to reveal her wide-open mouth filled with perfect teeth. Those braces really were worth it, even if she had to have them twice and cost her parents a small fortune. "No freaking way! That's fantastic!"

"As long as Dad holds up and doesn't smoke for six weeks, it's a go."

Leah snorts. "As he should. Sucks that it's even a question."

I can't tell her the rest, feeling the need to protect his already-tarnished reputation in this town. I also don't tell her that even though we got the end result, it doesn't feel resolved. He's donating the kidney. He'll help with the Oregon medical bills. But he also wouldn't look at me on the way out the door. What is really going on?

"Get to work, girls!" Ms. Maxwell orders.

"Kaley has an important announcement!" Leah shouts to the whole class.

What if Dad doesn't follow through? What if everything goes wrong? A small voice whispers in my head, *But what if everything goes right?* As much as I always prepare for the worst, shouldn't I be allowed to hope for the best? A smile breaks out across my face. "My sister is getting a kidney in six weeks." Everyone claps and cheers.

A warm glow spreads through my chest, warming me up from my sorry state moments before. My head is still frozen with wet hair, but at least I can feel my toes again. I wiggle them in my slippers, basking in the reality of the words. This is a much better story to tell than my breakup one. I think I've found another Zoey card to play this week. *Yes, Blake and I are no longer together but it's not important because my sister gets her life back!* Who's gonna be like, *Actually, we need to circle back around to the "why" of your breakup . . .*

I unwrap a chocolate and pop it into my mouth, savoring the taste of victory.

CHAPTER EIGHTEEN

IF I GUZZLE ANY MORE OF THIS PUMPKIN-SNOT LATTE, I'M GOING TO BE sick. I've drunk an embarrassing number of these coffees over the last two weeks trying to prove a point, but now I think I've crossed the line into self-punishment. But it's Halloween today and I'm determined to get into the spirit, even if the smell makes me gag.

It started out innocently enough. A quick treat to comfort myself before or after school, a cup to warm my hands around as icy wind whipped up around my face, caffeine to keep me stable and sugar to keep me smiling. Something to hold while looking busy. The ability to sip it if I needed to pause and collect my thoughts during conversation while still holding myself together. The taste on my tongue is a reminder of the confusion and rage that day Blake and I broke up, the words he said brought to the surface of my memory with every swallow.

I should start a support group called Coping with Coffee. There should be a subgroup called PSA—Pumpkin Spice Anonymous, where we all promise to take it one day at a time until peppermint mocha season. That is, if I can hold on until then. Our flyers might be confusing, though—PSA about PSA!

Thankfully, I'd been successful in my public-relations spin to keep people's focus on Zoey's kidney and off my breakup. It was hardly a blip in the rumor mill around school, but that might have been due to the fact that Leah was out for blood if any speculation happened to drift her way. I staved off questions mostly because I was vibrating on a different plane of existence thanks to my new, expensive habit.

Apparently, I "won" our breakup because Blake had dropped off the face of all social media. He didn't even have the decency to let me get a good stalk in at the end of the day, which frankly was inconsiderate. Even if he had blocked me, Leah would have kept me updated, but going scorched earth on the entire town seemed like overkill.

I know I'm reading too much into it. He probably deleted his socials to focus on school and avoid the drama. Did he realize that by doing that he put me in charge of the story? If he did know, was it a gift to me? A way to apologize?

Walking home, I pull out my phone to text him and ask. *No! Bad Kaley.* I text Leah instead: *Pick me up at nine tonight?*

Her response is immediate, raising my suspicions that she must have an alert tone set especially for me. A blaring alarm, maybe. One that clearly communicates *Fragile best friend is trying to text her ex!* I truly don't deserve such an amazing friend, especially after prioritizing Blake for so long. Her text reads, *Do you want to get ready together before the party?*

Teeth gnaw the inside of my cheek while I prepare to be a not-so-great friend once again. *Can't,* I text. *I'm taking Zoey trick-or-treating around the neighborhood first. I'll already be in costume.*

Three dots pop up while I wait for her to type. *You're not making Zoey coordinate with you, right?*

A snort escapes me. *I'm Princess Buttercup with or without my Westley*, I write back. *I'm gonna look freaking fantastic in that dress*. By "that dress," I mean my thrift-shop score from back in August. Mom promised I could borrow her pearl necklace, and I crafted a gold crown to complete the look that should hold up for at least a few hours tonight.

Hell yeah, girl! Leah cheers me on. *Your chariot will be outside your house at nine.*

So what if I'm only half of my perfect couples' costume? People might think I'm Elsa or something, but it will still be iconic on its own. Zoey clapped when I showed it to her for the first time, so at least I have her approval. She's going as a rainbow unicorn, same as last year. I offered to go costume shopping with her, but she turned it down. She likes anticipating the known entities. Her costume was a hit previously, so this year she looked forward to wearing it again for the past fifty-one weeks and six days. Why fix what isn't broken? The costume-to-candy ratio definitely worked in her favor. Not that she can eat much of it, this year. But next year will be different!

My sneaky sister is waiting by the front door when I enter the house, letting out a slightly-delayed *Boo!* when I cross the threshold. "Jesus!" I yell and stumble back, the dregs of my latte flying to land on the porch behind me. No great loss there. She cackles like a witch when I ask, "Why aren't you at dialysis? I thought Mom said you wouldn't be home until four."

"Early," Zoey explains. "Trick-or-treat."

"It won't be dark for a while longer," I say, trying to unravel the truth from her. "Why did Doc have you end so early?" Since the emergency, dialysis protocol makes me a little shifty.

"Not end," Mom interrupted, appearing at the top of the stairs. "He started us early today. Wanted to get home to his kids in time to take them around his neighborhood."

Wait, Doc Hayes has kids? By the look on Mom's face, that's news to her as well. I always kind of thought his work was his life, and we were way up high on his pedestal of importance. He always brings his A-game into appointments, so it's wild how saving lives is still just a job to him at the end of the day. I guess Mom is the same way. I've never seen her in action at work, but it's clear her heart and her focus are on Zoey when it comes down to it.

"He also gave us a strict warning that all candy is to be locked away until well after the transplant," Mom says.

Zoey shakes her head. "No, no, no."

"Yes, yes, yes," Mom counters. "No more emergencies, young lady. Not when we are this close to putting dialysis behind us."

"How about one lollipop?" I argue for my sister's sake.

"No." Mom stands firm.

"Just one. And think about it, if she's busy eating that for a good chunk of time, she'll be less likely to sneak anything else."

Mom holds up a finger. "One. *One* lollipop."

I pump my fist in victory. "Give us candy or give us . . . hopefully not more dialysis." Oof, maybe not that rallying cry.

Too late. Zoey also pumps her fist and says, "Huzzah!" just like I taught her to a while back. Her eyes are sparkling, but her movements are sluggish. Taking a closer look at her face, I see the bags under her baby blues, the puffiness of her face and neck accentuated by the pallor of her skin. Her body is working overtime right now to keep running. Is trick-or-treating a good idea tonight? What if something happens? What if she collapses and we're too far from the house? What if—

My hands tremble as I try to get myself under control. *Snap out of it!* Zoey has been through too much lately; she deserves to have a bit of fun. We'll just hit a couple of houses, just to say we did, then come home, Zoey will go to bed, and Leah will pick me up for Halloween shenanigans.

Shenanigans. Who even says that anymore?

"What are you doing with your friends tonight?" Mom asks, as if reading my mind.

"Definitely no shenanigans. There's a pumpkin-carving contest in the woods later."

"Uh-huh. Sure. Don't forget, you still have curfew tonight, or I'll turn *you* into a pumpkin," Mom warns.

With a flourish, I sprinkle the final dash of glitter on top of Zoey's head. She gives a spin, her dramatic rainbow tutu on display along with her sparkling tights underneath. On top, she has a cotton candy pink fuzzy sweater with white feathered angel wings looped over her shoulders, and for the pièce de résistance, a headband with a golden unicorn horn. Flowers weave through the band into her hair, which I curled softly around her face.

"You look incredible," I tell her. "Even better than last year."

"You too," she says, reaching out to touch the beading on the bodice of my dress.

"I certainly hope I look better than last year." Last year, I went for funny instead of fancy and showed up to the cool kids' party as a giant gumball machine. It was Blake's and my first big party together. His face when I tried to squeeze into his car and not pop all the balloons stuffed into the clear plastic garbage bag around my torso . . . Really no mystery why I decided to go with a classic couple this year. But now Princess Buttercup is going to make the best of it solo and rage. Hard.

Zoey and I exit the bathroom and make our way downstairs. "Mom!" I call when we're halfway down. "Come see!"

She appears, wiping her hands on a kitchen towel. "Oh wow," she gushes. "Look at my beautiful girls!"

Zoey lets out a realistic neigh and paws the air with her "hooves." I ham it up and throw in a few dramatic poses, swooning against the banister and managing to almost trip the rest of the way down the stairs.

Mom pulls her phone out from her pocket and snaps a few candids. "You'd better hurry," she says, checking the time. "Neighborhood sundown trick-or-treat starts in five minutes."

"Wait," I say, handing her my phone. "Get some on mine." There's a costume contest on the sib chat group, and based on what I've already seen, Zoey and I will come in at least top five. Ian also posted a hilarious bingo game, with squares like, "Aren't you too old to trick-or-treat?'" and "Ringing the doorbell before all the kids" and, my favorite, "Punching anything too spooky." He and a few other sibs have already started, and I don't want to lose. "Come on, Zo. Let's go show off your look." I hold her arm as she makes her way to the door where her black patent-leather flats await. She slides her feet in and we're ready to leave.

Outside is chaos. Kids in costume overrun the neighborhood

streets, screaming with excitement. The main roads in and out are blocked off for the next hour, keeping everyone safe and the sugar high going.

At nearly every house, parents gush over Zoey's costume and congratulate me on my sister's upcoming surgery, heaping handfuls of candy into her bucket in a well-meaning gesture. Zoey has a glint in her eye that tells me she isn't going to refuse the candy Mom won't let her eat yet, so I settle on being extra vigilant instead.

By the time we've completed our street, Zoey is dragging both her feet and her bucket. "Want to head home?" I ask.

She shakes her head. "More."

"You look pretty tired—" The stare she fixes me with shuts me right up. "All right, it's your night. A couple more houses over on the next cul-de-sac and then we're done. Deal?"

"Deal." Zoey finds her hustle again, and we round the corner to the next street over.

"Not that house, Zo. See, it's on the market." She points at a dinosaur and a witch who are leaving the porch, comparing king-sized candy bars with amazement. "Oh, maybe someone just moved in." Whoever they are, they are looking to make an impression. King-sized? That'll be the talk of the next neighborhood potluck.

Zoey rings the doorbell, and I can practically hear her heart pounding in excitement. A balding man with glasses pulls open the door. "Happy Halloween!" he says. His smile fades a little as he looks past us, craning his neck as if looking for someone else. "Where are the kids?"

"Just us," I say. He's definitely new to the neighborhood.

He stares at us over his glasses, mouth now a thin line. "Aren't you a little old to be trick-or-treating?"

And that's bingo!

"I'm not trick-or-treating," I correct him, holding up my empty hands. "Just my sister."

"Candy," Zoey prompts.

The man steps farther over the threshold and blocks the doorway. I can envision him calling his realtor right after we leave and cussing him out for selling him a home in a neighborhood filled with juvenile delinquents. Does he think we're going to bum-rush his precious new house for some candy? "And no manners?"

As tempting as it is to reveal my actual predilection for property damage, my need to complete this interaction is greater than my desire to watch this guy dig himself a further hole. "She just wants a candy bar." My sister is unraveling as we speak, reaching the end of her rope as this stranger refuses to play by the rules of Halloween. Wear a costume. Ring the doorbell. Receive candy. It's not rocket science. I knew we should have called it a night when we reached the end of our street.

"Trick-or-treat," Zoey insists.

"I don't think so," he says, narrowing his eyebrows. "I won't be pushed over by a couple of high school kids. I'll be posting about you on the neighborhood watch page. Stop stealing the fun from all the little kids. It's entirely inappropriate."

Sliding in front of Zoey in case she decides to start swinging her plastic bucket, I slap on a falsely apologetic smile. "You know what? You *should* report us. Make sure to let everyone know you denied Zoey Larssen your precious king-size candy bars."

And have fun getting absolutely torn to shreds for it. "C'mon, Zo. Let's get out of here."

I turn to grab Zoey's arm and help her down the steps, bracing myself the entire way in case she takes a swing at me or runs back and teaches our soon-to-be-ostracized neighbor a lesson for not playing by the rules of Halloween.

"Candy?" she asks. I hear the front door slam behind us.

"Not from this house," I tell her. "You already have a lot, what do you think about going home?" The interaction left a bad taste in my mouth. I hate for it to be the last experience of the night, but I'm not in the mood to hit up any more houses. Exhaustion sets in as the confrontational adrenaline wears off. Zoey is going to throw a fit, insisting that I told her a few more houses, most likely confused that she received only prejudice at the last stop, and she couldn't fit that into her pumpkin bucket.

Much to my surprise, Zoey looks me up and down and simply says, "Okay." That's it. No fighting me on it, no forcing me to drag her home, no knockout punches.

She's grown up so much in the past two years, and I haven't stopped to really take in how much she has changed. The medical issues have aged us all, but I think we've been underestimating her. Old patterns of behavior still pop up, but she's proved that I shouldn't expect the worst all the time. Mom and I are caught in the same patterns, too, because it's what worked over the years. Are we preventing Zoey from reaching her full potential simply by not wanting to rock the boat with her routine? Maybe she is more independent and flexible than we give her credit for, and *we* are the obstacle.

"Well, awesome. Thanks, sweets. Let's go show Mom your haul this year."

Zoey holds the bucket up to her face and digs around with her free hand. "Lollipop," she insists.

"You totally deserve it," I tell her.

She pulls out a rainbow swirly one that matches her outfit. It's totally going to turn her mouth blue. Handing it to me, she dives back in.

"Hold on, I said only one treat."

Reemerging triumphant, she holds up a peanut-butter cup. "You can't have those," I remind her.

"For Kaley," she instructs.

Well, I can't say no to that. Each with our treats, we take our time strolling back home, nudged by the swirling tide of children around us. "Did you have a good Halloween?"

"Yes," Zoey confirms.

"Good, I'm glad."

"Kaley party?"

"Yeah, but it isn't until after we get this candy locked in the safe and you're in bed." Nobody is taking any chances tonight. I check my phone for the game stats. "Guess what? We tied with Ian and Kenny for bingo. Leni, Gwen, and Sophie won, though." As I say it, my phone buzzes again with more bragging on the group chat. There's also a separate message from Ian: *You'll crush bingo next year when big sis can sprint from house to house! Hang in there. Just a few more weeks.*

Zoey leans her head on my shoulder and waits for me to open the front door. "Have fun," she tells me. "Thank you. Love you."

I kiss the top of her unicorn head. "Love you too."

Leah doesn't honk in the driveway when she picks me up. Nope, she rings the doorbell just as Mom is getting Zoey into bed, meaning that now Zoey is no longer in bed. My irritation melts away, though, when I see my best friend standing on the front porch in her all-black costume, complete with an eye mask and knee-high boots.

My mouth falls open in shock. "You didn't."

"I did," she says, cracking up. "I couldn't let you experience another Halloween-party disaster, especially after last year's debacle. It's your senior year, and you are not going to be remembered as the bubblegum screamer."

"In my defense, I didn't realize getting too close to the bonfire would make the balloons pop like that." I'd jumped like a cat and also peed my pants a little. Not that anyone knew that part, but having let out a shriek that a panther would have been proud of, I'm sure some people suspected. No one except Blake got very close to me the rest of the night. The party also got shut down early, probably due to noise complaints.

Leah sweeps her arm over to her ancient minivan. "Princess Buttercup, your chariot awaits."

Before I follow her, I lean back on the doorframe and call upstairs. "Bye, Mom! Bye, Zo!"

"Curfew!" Mom reminds me. I'd planned on trying to come home early, still not in the party mood, but seeing the effort Leah put in marginally lifts my spirits.

The front passenger seat of the van is unoccupied, for once.

Everyone else is crammed in the back. I clamber in and spin around in my seat to get a peek at everyone's costumes. I guess my gumball machine from last year caught on, because all the soccer girls, minus Leah, are all dressed as various junk food. Little Amy looks cute as a button in a French-fry outfit, and Melanie is yet again encroaching on her space with the crust of her pizza outfit poking Amy in the face. Bekah and her sister, Ingrid, match as ketchup and mustard bottles, and are currently trying to swordfight with their pointy hats. I can't make out the rest of the crew, because blocking my view are a zombie cheerleader and a zombie football player.

Hannah, wearing a torn, bloodstained jersey and full pads, is sitting in Charlie's skirted lap. He has two tiny pigtails in his hair and fake blood smeared around his mouth. Realistic stitches also mar their faces. "Charlie lost the bet," Hannah explains.

Charlie loops his arms around Hannah and pulls her more securely to his chest. He doesn't look the slightest bit upset at his current uniform situation. "Yep," he admits happily. She's not just wearing any jersey, I notice. Seventy-seven is Charlie's number.

"Everyone all set?" Leah asks, grinding the shift into reverse to back out of my driveway. A chorus of "Yeah!" from eight people resonates as Leah shifts again and hits the gas.

A song comes on the scratchy radio that reminds me of Blake. "Can I change it?" I ask Leah.

"As you wish," she says. "You can plug in your phone too."

I realize I left it at home again. Except this time, instead of pure panic and guilt, I just feel free. "Actually, this song is fine."

It stings a little, but it's almost easier to feel the pain alongside my joy tonight. I'm not trying to forget; I'm just remembering that it happened. It happened, and now it's over, and as the song lyrics remind me, I'm still here.

"How was trick-or-treating with Zoey?" Hannah asks.

"Pretty good! Only one jerk, and Zoey didn't punch anyone. We also lost the sib-group Halloween bingo, but I promised her we'd try again next year."

"It will be more fun anyway when she can actually eat the candy," Charlie agrees. "Man, that would suck so bad to get a bucket full of treats I couldn't even eat. Props to her for standing strong. She's handling it better than I would have."

"Same," I agree. "As many times as I wished we could trade places, I don't know if I would have been able to withstand what Zoey has over the past year. It was hard enough bearing witness to it, but to physically endure it all?" I'm proud that my voice doesn't waver and that I can talk more openly about this now. Having an end in sight has definitely changed my attitude about everything. When surgery day comes, I'll have a whole community pulling for my family.

Hannah leans forward at the same time Leah reaches over, and they both grab my hand. Charlie puts his hand on top and then says, "And, break!" before throwing his arm over his head. "Team Zo!" Charlie evaporates the tension, and I pull out of my serious thoughts. This party was the catalyst for all the recent changes in my life, and I want to be 100 percent present for it tonight. And this time, I'll get to party guilt-free!

The first thing I notice when we get to the woods is another shadowy figure, all in black, backlit against the roaring bonfire. "Did you coordinate costumes with someone else too?" I ask Leah as we exit the car.

She looks just as confused as I am. "Nope. But damn, do my pants make my butt look as good as his?"

"You know it," I say, without taking my eyes off the mystery man.

"Come on, let's go see who it is." Leah grabs my arm and drags me to him.

The guy's face breaks into a smile when we get close, but the top half of his face is masked. I try to come up with something to say, but all that comes out of my mouth is "Looking for your bride?"

"No, but I *was* actually looking for you." I know that voice. It's Declan. I should throw myself into the bonfire and be done with it, because I can see this conversation going down in flames. I hadn't known what to say after the Hershey Kisses thing, so I just ignored it, and he hadn't brought it up. Our last communication was him texting for a kidney update, me telling him the new timeline, and him responding with a thumbs-up. Where on earth do we stand?

Leah looks equally horrified at his presence. "This is why you popped by my house earlier? To drop off pumpkin bread from Aunt Rose and to *steal a pair of my yoga pants*?"

"I didn't know we'd be dressed the same. You told me last week you were going as a hot dog, and Kaley kept her costume plan top-secret. I'm actually supposed to be Zorro."

"Keep the pants. I'll never be able to wear them again after tonight."

Declan pops his legs out into an exaggerated stretch. "Thanks, cousin. They're more comfortable than I thought they'd be."

"That's because they're expensive," Leah growls, watching him sink into a deep squat before shuddering.

"Aren't you supposed to be partying on campus?" I ask him, trying to head off their fight. "I thought Boise State Halloween was legendary."

Declan puffs out his chest. "I'm trying to take things more seriously these days. Keeping it low-key."

Well, Redson is definitely low-key, especially compared to just about everywhere else.

But Leah is staring at him, head cocked. "No, tell us why you really came."

If I could see under the mask, I would swear Declan is blushing. "Came to see how you were, Kaley," he admits. "Also wanted to tell you congrats on Zoey's kidney, in person."

"Thank you," I respond, beaming. "No black market required."

He shoots me a wink, and I feel the energy between us shift. Leah must feel it, too, because she excuses herself to go grab us drinks. Yes, Declan is still a goofball and a flirt, but I've also seen such a different side of him lately. "You know, your texts really talked me off the ledge on the road trip. Thank you."

"It was nothing you didn't already know," he assures me.

How do I explain that it wasn't just him holding up a mirror to me? It's his humor. His acceptance. His belief in my abilities. "Sometimes it's nice to just have people be there in the way you didn't know you needed."

He takes a step closer, and my breath hitches. Out of the

corner of my eye, I see Leah returning, drinkless. *Go away, Leah!* But she doesn't slow down. Heaving a sigh, I turn. "What happened to the drinks?"

Only, it's not Leah standing there. It's Blake. Also dressed as Westley and looking pissed, standing with his arms crossed and glaring back and forth between me and Declan. Before he says a word, Leah returns with three red Solo cups, and I'm surrounded by three versions of the other half of my couple's costume. "Well, I look very popular."

"*You*—" Leah starts, moving toward Blake. I intercept her before she can dump the drinks over his head.

"I got this," I tell her, arm barred across her torso.

"Would be a waste of beer anyway," she mutters, backing down but not breaking eye contact with him. She moves over to stand next to Hannah and Charlie. Close enough for her to intervene if I need backup, but far enough away to let me handle this mess.

Now I'm down to two.

My eyes are begging Blake to calm down, but he's fixated on Declan instead of me. "I can't believe you already roped another guy into this," he says.

Declan holds up both palms in front of his chest. "No, dude. I'm not who you think I am. Pure coincidence."

Blake scoffs. "Sure. Whatever. I need a minute alone with my girlfriend."

Ex-girlfriend. But I don't correct him out loud. I'm too stunned that he's here, in the flesh. Declan is backing away to a safe distance while I whack Blake on the arm. "Are you kidding me? You think you can just show up and accost me in public?"

"I'm here to undo the last three weeks," Blake declares. "This was the argument that started this entire sequence of events in the first place, so now I'm here like you wanted."

"And you're *oh so* happy about it." My initial shock has given way to rage. The audacity of him, appearing out of thin air and being mad at me for living my life when *we broke up*.

"Well, I wasn't expecting you to be here with my replacement so soon," he snarks. Then he takes a deep breath, collecting himself. "This wasn't the plan. I'm sorry. Look, I'm here. I missed you. Let's start again."

I stare at him in disbelief. "I'm not just going to forget our conversation at your dorm. That's what broke us. Not disagreeing about this stupid Halloween party." Can he really not see that?

"I gave you space like you wanted. Just tell me you're still coming to U of O next year," he begs. "We can get back on track."

I stare at him like he has three heads. Then I realize he has no idea what happened since I left campus, what with his social-media blackout and all. "Zoey is getting a kidney in a couple weeks. I'm going to be here for her, however long the recovery takes. We're entering a new chapter, and I realize I don't want to be nine hours away. Thanks for your concern, by the way. I'll be sure to send along your well-wishes."

Blake's face pales. "Your mom really did this to you?"

"Well, *I'm* not donating the kidney, remember? My dad is."

He puts both hands on my shoulders, like he wants to shake me. "She took your future. You're stuck here," he says slowly, like he's talking to a moron.

I step back out of his hold. "You're just as tied to your family as I am, you're just in denial about it," I tell him. "Your parents are never going to release your tether to them and their expectations. At least I'm brave enough to admit mine and deal with it. But I can tell you one thing, there's nothing binding us together anymore. You're free. As much as you can be."

Blake shakes his head sadly, and for a minute I actually believe I got through to him. Then he says, "I guess you can't help anyone who won't help themselves."

Of course he still thinks he's right.

I expect hot frustration and anger to bubble up from my stomach, but I feel empty. Then I realize I don't have to care what he thinks anymore. I turn and walk away, over to where Leah, Hannah, and Charlie are standing, trying not to look too much like they're eavesdropping. They all startle when I approach.

"All good?" Leah asks.

"Yeah," I say, sighing.

"Know your worth, girl," Hannah says. "He couldn't see that before, and that's on him. Too late to the party."

Blake is already gone when I turn to look over my shoulder. Probably had to get some beauty sleep in before driving the long trip back tomorrow. Wasting everyone's time and energy has got to be exhausting.

"It's okay to be a little sad, though," Leah murmurs, putting a comforting hand on my shoulder.

I shake my head, unable to trust my voice right now. Hannah jumps in and saves me. "So, no University of Oregon, huh?"

"Your grades are amazing! You could get accepted anywhere you want," Leah emphasizes. "I can even look over your applications."

"Or you can go to BSU like the rest of us!" Charlie says.

I groan. "Let me get through the next few weeks, first. I can't decide yet." And as unsettling as it is to have no plan this far into senior year, at least I'm not deferring to Blake's plan and coming along for the ride as a side character in my own life. Whatever I decide to do next, it will be because I *choose* to.

"Are you really that desperate to avoid me?" Declan says, coming up behind me. "I know my texting is out of control, but I kind of thought you were into that. If not, BSU is still a big campus."

"What?" Charlie interrupts. He's completely lost, but Hannah sends an elbow to his ribs as a hint.

"Charlie, Leah, flip cup. Now," Hannah orders.

Leah doesn't need to be told twice as she beelines it across the party. Charlie looks at me and Declan, a bit baffled at the turn of events. Then he shrugs at us, like, *What can you do*? before saying, "I love it when she's bossy. The woman knows what she wants."

I watch their retreating backs. "Twenty bucks they're still together at the ten-year reunion."

"Yeah," Declan agrees, "but they'll have married and divorced each other twice by that point."

"Third time will be the charm."

Declan laughs, and I relax a fraction. I know he's not going to make me talk about the breakup, or the upcoming surgery, so there's an easy lull while he waits for me to speak again. "I just realized; I never asked you what you're majoring in, or are you still undecided?" Oh God, could I be more boring?

He doesn't seem to mind boring, though, because his eyes

light up. “I’m pre-law. They have a joint school, the ‘three and three’ program there now. Three years at BSU, and three years at University of Idaho Law School. I have to submit my forms by this spring to show intent, then take the LSAT during junior year. Then if I get accepted, I’ll be up in Moscow, Idaho.”

“You’ll be a lawyer after only six years?”

“Yeah,” he says. “And it’s not super expensive.” The immature, party-boy image falls away, and I’m staring at an eager, driven guy who can’t wait for the next big thing.

“I can’t believe you gave up on your artistic passions.” It takes him a minute to catch on, then he remembers.

“I know, it’s tragic. I had such a promising career as a muralist when I was young.” He holds my gaze and the grin fades. “I’m not that kid anymore, Kaley.”

He’s not, and I think I’ve known it for a while. “What are you going to do with your newfound maturity?” I tease.

He shrugs, trademark Declan nonchalance. “Try to change the world, I guess.”

“Oh, is that all?” But honestly, that might be a great place to start.

CHAPTER NINETEEN

IT'S K-DAY. ALL THE ANXIETY AND PLANNING OF D-DAY, BUT WITH scalpels instead of tanks. Dr. Hayes has walked us all through the procedure at least ten times over in an attempt to assuage our worries. He talked to Zoey, calmly explaining it again and again to his patient, but I know he really did it for Mom's and my benefit.

"And the risks, again?" Mom asks in the hallway outside Zoey's preop room.

It's not even seven a.m., and I rub the sleep from my eyes and brace myself for the audible reminder of terrible outcomes I've had on repeat all night long. The final time I looked at the clock last night, it read 1:46. I still tossed and turned for probably another half an hour after that, letting my thoughts spiral to a dangerous place. Every time I closed my eyes, my body jerked like I was falling. I kept thinking, *If I get to sleep now, I'll have six hours of sleep. If I get to sleep now, I'll get five hours. Four hours.* The clock kept ticking down and I just stared at the ceiling.

At some point, I must have drifted off, because I'd hit fast-forward and my alarm was going off. It dragged me out of bed to face either the worst or the best day of my life, and I had zero control over any of it.

"We've been over this, Jules," Dr. Hayes reminds her. "The surgery is happening today. It has to, so please try to take your mind off the risks. Worrying about them is not going to change the outcome. You'll just put yourself through it twice."

"So you *do* think there will be complications," Mom accuses.

"That's not what I'm saying," Dr. Hayes explains. The man really does have endless patience.

I reach out and grab Mom's hand. "We'll know in a few hours."

Mom gives my hand a quick squeeze before dropping it. She's so far in her head, nothing can reach her there. "Let me go in one more time," she begs the doctor.

Dr. Hayes moves aside and lets her through. I follow to stand at the foot of Zoey's bed. From the doorway, he says, "I'll meet you in the OR, Zoey. The nurses will be here in a minute to wheel you in."

Mom is murmuring into Zoey's ear, unable to keep the emotion from her voice. If she's not careful, she's going to cry, and that's going to set Zoey off.

Swallowing the lump in my own throat, I plaster a huge smile on my face. "Today's the day, sweets!" I tell her from my spot near her feet. "What you've been training all year for. Are you about to kick some butt and boot those slacker kidneys to the curb?" I hold my hand out and lean over her for a high five, and she hesitantly lifts her own to return it. "That's what I'm talking about. You're gonna crush it, girl."

Some of the color comes back to Zoey's face, and Mom looks at me gratefully. I keep going, rambling while we wait for the nurses to come in and wheel Zoey to the operating room. "We gotta plan your first great post-op meal! I know Thanksgiving is the obvious choice, but what do you say about having an unsupervised visit to the 7-Eleven with a hundred bucks? That would be a great start."

Four nurses file in and start fiddling with the monitors. "Don't watch them, sweets. Eyes on me!" I jump away from the bed and start doing an energetic dance like I'm Cotton-Eyed Joe. My moves are so legendary I come inches from elbowing Nurse Paul in the face. Man has reflexes like a cat, though, because he dodges it no problem.

Zoey is laughing, and that's all that matters. "I'll still be dancing when you get back," I promise her. "Yee-haw!" I'm a sweaty, rambling mess but keep going while they take her from the room, all the way down the hall, and push her through the double doors. When she's out of sight, my limbs fall still and I shout, "I love you!" as the doors swing shut.

"Hush, Kaley," Mom says, appearing by my side. "You're going to get us kicked out."

"What, like I'm concerned about my dignity right now? Plus, there's not a sign saying 'No Yelling' posted here. I'd get a warning at best."

"It's just common sense." I let her lecture me. She's grasping at anything to take her mind off the OR. "And why did you tell her she could run amok in the candy store? You know she has a long road of anti-rejection meds. Her diet will need to be similar to how it is now . . ."

I tune her out. She's not expecting a response anyway. When she finally slows down to take a breath, I give her a hug and ask, "Should we stop by Dad's room too?"

"Oh," Mom gasps. She relaxes a fraction in my arms. We've

been so focused on Zoey, I don't think the idea occurred to her. Besides a few phone calls confirming dates and times, we have had the normal amount of contact with Dad. That is, next to none.

Well, that's not true. He did send me a magazine article he thought I'd find interesting. Sent it in the *mail.* Who does that? But he did throw in a few stickers for Zo. When I opened the letter, neither one of us knew how to react. The look on Zoey's face mirrored my own, the prevailing question being *Why?* But it's not nothing, at least for him, and his desire that I know about the environmental impacts on big-game migration in Eastern Oregon. I'm not sure what I'm supposed to do with it, but for now I'm keeping the envelope and its contents on my dresser. Zoey put the stickers on top of her dresser, too, but in a more permanent fashion.

"How about you go and I'll meet you in the waiting room. I doubt he wants my face to be the last one he sees," Mom says.

She's afraid of running into Rachel and having to make awkward chitchat in front of Dad. I have no such qualms. If Rachel wasn't here, then Dad would probably try to get in his truck and attempt to drive back to Oregon hours after surgery. The choice is clear for me between awkward chitchat versus the headline *Post-Op Patient Drives Wrong Way Down Highway, Causes Catastrophic Pileup.*

I thought I heard Doc Hayes say Dad was in Room 3. Mom veers left toward the exit, and I'm on my own. Until I'm not. Rachel comes out of Room 3, wiping her eyes with a tissue. "Is he still in there?" I ask.

She startles, not expecting me. "Oh, hi." Sniffling, she pulls it together a fraction. "No, they took him about ten minutes ago. I was just having a moment in there." Ah, she's avoiding us too. "I'm being silly," she says, waving a hand in front of her face. "It's all going to be fine."

Considering I just attempted to line dance alone, I'm not one to judge people's coping mechanisms. "I know this is a super weird day," I tell her. "But we're really glad you're here."

Her tear-filled eyes are hopeful but also guarded. "You didn't want to see him this morning?"

Fair question. Dad probably told her some of our history, but not all of it. "It's complicated," I say, explaining nothing but being truthful at the same time. "I actually was coming to see him just now. I didn't know they would take him back there before Zo." Fingers come to my mouth, and I gnaw at my nails, gathering the courage to ask my next question. "How was he?" I mumble.

"He seemed fine," Rachel admits. "Stoic. You know how he is."

"You mean treating life-altering surgery like a trip to the grocery store?" With the look on her face, I try to backpedal. "Was he waiting to see me?"

I'm not sure whose court the ball is in right now. Mostly because I'm terrible at sports, but also because I have no freaking clue about Dad's motivations like, ever, so hopefully Rachel has a better time with it.

"I think he was just trying to keep the demons at bay. He wouldn't admit it, but all the memories from his last hospital stay reemerged over the past few weeks, and he didn't know if he would be able to get through it." Rachel shakes her head sadly. "He's been really brave."

I understand most of what she's saying, except . . . "What hospital stay?"

Rachel's eyes get huge. "You mean—your parents never . . . I should just—ah, I think you need to talk to your mom."

"You mean to tell me you're going to drop a big secret on me, not explain yourself, and make me stew over it for the next four hours?"

She winces. "Yes?"

"No way, lady. Start talking."

"I really can't," she says, backing away.

"Did Dad have some kind of accident?" I ask, pressing forward. "Mom said something a few weeks ago about being grateful he was alive." The pieces of the puzzle are starting to come together, but I'm afraid to step back and see the whole picture.

"When the time is right, ask your dad," Rachel begs. She looks like she's about to burst into tears again, but I don't care. She has answers, and I need them. Now.

Then I remember how nice she was to me upon our coincidental meeting. Her words stuck with me. She's not trying to give me a hard time; right now she's having a hard time. And here I am, looking around and wondering what medical instruments I could use to extract information. I should at least try to make her feel better. Honesty is a good place to start. People love confessions, they are very distracting. "You know, I was driving a stolen car when we met."

She nods, undeterred by my whiplash-inducing conversational skills. "I know. I didn't know who you were that first time we met, but I could tell you needed to run." Emotional meltdown this morning aside, I'm impressed with Rachel's stoic calm. From helping a girl with a black eye on the side of the road to dropping off a car at two a.m. in a hospital parking lot to watching her sort-of boyfriend—whatever kind of relationship they have—get wheeled off to have an organ removed. Something in life had prepared her for this, and I want to know about it. More specifically, how to get where she's at. A place of inner acceptance.

"I think I'm done running now," I say.

She gives me a small smile. "Are you sure? Some people never reach that point."

I can read between the lines. "People like Dad."

Rachel sighs. "And me. I've gotten better, though."

"But you seem so brave about it all." Dad certainly does seem to have a type. He's so freaking lucky to have Rachel, and I wonder if he fully appreciates it. I really hope he doesn't end up running away from her one day too.

I'd like to think he won't bolt. This kidney donation seems to be giving him greater perspective and the opportunity to start righting his wrongs. He can't fix the past in our family, but there is a slim possibility he won't let Rachel be a repeat.

"I'm trying. I'm a work in progress, as are we all. However, I find it's often easier to have courage for other people than it is for yourself."

Speaking of courage, the clock on the wall lets me know that there are three hours and twenty-six minutes of surgery left. Can I hang on until then? "Want to come down to the cafeteria with me and grab some coffee?"

Rachel's face brightens at the invitation. "Are you sure? Is your mom going to mind?"

"Nah, I'll bring her back a cup. Decaf. To be honest, I don't think her heart can take any caffeine this morning. She hates decaf, though, so don't tell her. Apparently, it tastes like lies, but I don't think she'll notice this morning."

She makes a sympathetic noise, a little hum of understanding. "How is she doing?"

"As well as Eisenhower." I can see Rachel trying to connect the dots, but I jump in before she gets too far down the rabbit hole. "Never mind. You can ask her when we get back to the waiting room."

"Oh, I was just going to wait in the car until the surgery is done. I don't think she wants me there."

"Well, I do," I inform her. "You're a part of this too." I know how she's feeling, because I hate it when I get left out of stuff involving Zoey.

Rachel bites her lip, weighing her options. "All right. Lead the way," she decides. I'm not sure if she agrees for her or for me, but I'm glad she does.

Despite a giant cup of coffee, I manage to fall asleep in the waiting room during the final half hour of the surgery. I blame it on navigating the tightrope between Rachel and Mom for the last three hours, even if they coexisted mostly in silence. Other than a terse "Hello, I'm Julie, thanks for driving Will," Mom didn't have much to say to Rachel. We were all in agony while we waited out the clock, unable to read, chat, or even look at our phones. Mine buzzed a few times, Leah, Hannah, Declan, even Charlie asking for an update. My eyes could hardly focus enough to get the gist of the messages.

In contrast, my sib group chat has been quiet today. Messages were flying last night—random, hilarious video clips and story snippets shared back and forth. Nobody said it directly, but I knew they were all doing it for my benefit, to try to keep my mind off the next day. It was sweet that they were thinking about me without asking me for anything—no explanations for my feelings, updates on my family's mental state, or Zoey's projected outcome. Words that they instinctively know would cost me too much to put into a message, because they've all been where I'm at. And on the day of the surgery, they're waiting with respectful silence because they know I'm not capable of anything more than getting from one breath to the next.

Mom, Rachel, and I stayed frozen in time in the aptly-named waiting room, mostly staring at the wall, lost in our own thoughts, as if by worrying and anticipating every possible way things could go wrong, we could deter them from happening with our mental powers alone.

I was so emotionally drained; I couldn't keep my head up anymore. There was also the distinct possibility that Mom anticipated my decaf trick and switched our cups early on when I was too busy pacing the same track on the carpet that hundreds of other family members must have worn in before me. My money is on a switcheroo, because she's shaking me awake now with wide-eyed mania written all over her face.

"You stole my caffeine," I accuse her, slurring my words a bit while I orient myself.

"It's over, Kaley." I have a mini moment of panic before she continues, the adrenaline like an EpiPen to my heart. "The nurse just came out and told us everything went fine. It went fine. It's all fine. Fine!"

"Break the loop, Mom," I say automatically, but my brain is stuck too. *Fine. It's all fine!* Lurching from my chair, I stumble a bit on my tingly, numb foot before jumping up. "She's fine!" I yell.

I throw my arms around Mom and squeeze. I'm staring down at the top of her head, realizing that not only do I have more than a few good inches on her now, but she's also got more gray streaks in her hair than I remember seeing. She's so thin and frail, and she feels almost like Zoey in my arms.

Zoey will live and thrive long enough to have gray hair one day too. The enormity of today hits me like a tidal wave, and I sag onto Mom. She props me up while wave after wave batters me, washing away the last year like a baptism. It slows to a trickle, and I'm able to stand up straight. "When can we see her?"

"The nurse said she's in recovery now, and we can go back one at a time for a quick visit in a few minutes." She exhales and slumps back down in her chair while the weight of the world leaves her shoulders. All except for 117 pounds, which won't lift until she witnesses her daughter in one piece with her own eyes.

Still standing, I turn to look across the room at Rachel, who moved to give us a little privacy to celebrate. I motion for her to come over, and she does. "We did it." Caught up in the moment, I pull her in for a hug as well. Her arms hang stiff at her sides for a second before they wrap around me.

"I'm so happy for you and Zoey," she says.

I pull back slightly, giving enough space to ask, "How's Dad?" I'm assuming they reported his condition to her.

"They said he did as well as can be expected. There was apparently a small hiccup, but because I'm not a family member they can't tell me much more than that. I hope it wasn't anything major."

The muted celebration makes more sense, now. I'm also a little put out to discover a slight dampening of my own excitement. Six weeks of no smoking is the minimum to give patients better outcomes for withstanding the surgery and the recovery after. The minimum. Did we push for the transplant too soon?

Rachel sees the change in my face. "Hey now! They said he's okay. We'll get the full story in a bit."

All the talk about Zoey needing a kidney, and I never fully considered the ramifications for the other person going under the knife. The healthy person. The person who has enough kidney to spare. A "hiccup" is a sobering reminder that surgery is still slicing and dicing a living person, and there is always a risk under general anesthesia. My hands shake with the realization that I might have carelessly missed my last conversation with Dad.

Deep breaths. I didn't miss it. I'm caught up in the dramatics of today. Rachel's hands run down my arms to clutch my fingers and keep them still. She gives them a tight squeeze, and the pressure calms me. "How about you go in and see him first?" she offers.

"Oh, I think he'd rather see you," I say, trying to brush off her generosity because I don't deserve it.

"Your mom is going to see Zoey first, anyway," Rachel points out. "You'll just be sitting here in the waiting room all alone. You need to go talk to him. Make sure he's all right too. Then, you'll be worry-free when you see Zoey and truly celebrate with her."

Rachel makes a compelling argument. "Are you sure?"

"I'm just fine here, Kaley. I'll wait. I'm not going anywhere."

I go with the nurse when she calls us back, walking side by side with Mom into the recovery hallway. "Remember, it's one at a time in there," Mom says as we get to Zoey's room. "I'll be out to get you in a bit."

"I'm going to see Dad first," I admit. Her eyebrows shoot up in surprise, but she doesn't try to deter me. I kind of wish she would. Once I walk in there, I won't exit as the same person. As I approach Dad's room, I hear Mom behind me. "Hi baby," she says gently, already halfway into Zoey's room. I want to cry.

Instead, I straighten my spine and give a quick courtesy knock on the open door of the next room. There's no response, but I walk in anyway. Dad is lying on the bed, propped up in a slight incline. His face is pale and clammy, eyes closed. He feels a presence in the room, because he finally asks, "Rach?"

Clearing my throat, I say, "Actually, it's me."

It's a struggle for him to crack an eyelid open, but he does. "Kaley?"

This is a mistake. "I can go get Rachel for you. Hold on, one sec—"

"No, stay." He's looking more alert now, and for the first time since he left after Zoey's stint at the Oregon hospital, he looks me in the eye. There are multiple IV's hooked up in his arms, as well as a blood bag. I wonder if the "hiccup" was some unexpected blood loss. That would certainly explain him looking like he just saw a ghost.

"Hi," I say. It's lame, but it's a start.

"Hi," he says back.

I hover in the doorway, wondering if I should close the door or not. He's silent, leaving the choice up to me. I gently swing it shut and cross the room to his bedside.

"Thank you," I tell him, perching on the edge of the nearest chair. He gives a noncommittal grunt, already uncomfortable with the direction I'm taking the conversation. "No, truly. I don't know what Zoey would have done without you. I know you didn't think you'd ever have to . . . so thanks." Should I leave now? I said what I came to say, and he looks like he could use some more rest.

"Don't thank me," he rasps. "I don't deserve it." He turns away from me to stare up at the ceiling, as though looking at me is painful. "I'm not a good man. I am a coward."

"I mean, I'm not going to lie to you. You're not perfect, as a dad or a former husband." Wow, this is going great. I bet Rachel will be so glad she sent me in here first. I take a deep breath and continue. "But I don't think cowards undergo major surgery for their children."

I'm waiting for him to turn back to me, but he doesn't. Instead, a single tear slips from his eye and runs down his cheek, onto his jaw, and then his neck. I follow the slide, transfixed. I've never seen my father cry.

"I signed the papers," he says. No further explanation needed. I know exactly which papers he is talking about. I knew it. I knew he wasn't this altruistic.

"It was a trade, after all. A kidney for your freedom. Mom didn't tell me," I say. Now she's the only guardian, with no backup.

"I think she was waiting until the dust settled."

Or she was waiting to tell me when I turned eighteen. *Happy birthday to me! Thanks for the present, but you are about nine months early. Nine months of leaving Zoey vulnerable in case something happens to Mom.*

He's quiet for so long I assume he has fallen back asleep. I stand up to leave, but he gathers more of his strength and starts talking again. "I signed it to save you all."

"What *is* it with the men in my life trying to freaking *save me*?" It all just seems like an excuse to do what they want and pretend it goes toward the greater good.

I should cut him some slack.

He just gave up his kidney.

Summoning all my YouTube yoga training that mostly consists of Savasana and napping, I take a few deep breaths. *Inner peace. Inner pissed-off. Inner peace.* As I inhale and exhale through my nose, I remind myself that I always knew this scenario was coming. I should reach acceptance quickly. But I also came here for answers, and after today, now that he's signed the papers, does that mean he's washed his hands of us? I'm not sure where we stand.

A nurse pops her head in to check on us. "Oops, our patient is looking a little tired. I think the visit is over, dear."

"Just five more minutes," I beg. Dad turns his head to look at me, as if surprised I'm willing to hear him out.

The nurse asks, "William? Are you sure?"

Dad sighs. "Yes. I can rest later."

"All right. Five minutes, no more." She looks at me. "Your sister has been asking for you too."

The urge to run to Zoey almost pulls me from Dad's bedside, but I've waited years for this truth. When we're alone again, Dad spends his first minute in silence, presumably gathering his thoughts, but I'm getting more apprehensive by the second. We're down to four minutes left. I stare at him while he looks at the ceiling. Finally, he speaks.

"I loved being a dad. But I was not a good one."

Not going to argue the second part, but that first sentence throws me. Most of what I can remember points to him resenting us, his life, his choices. His departure happened years before he physically left.

"I'd always struggled with depression," he confesses. "And I believed for a while I could just white-knuckle through it. I was gripping on a cliff's edge for so long, eventually it just became the norm." He pauses, struggling to go on. I can see how much effort and energy this is costing him. I don't think I've ever heard Dad say this many sentences in a row, much less ones about his feelings.

"We've all been there." Hello, does he not remember the sacrifices Mom made during our early childhoods? "We could have all helped each other hang on, if you had stayed."

"I was pulling you all down with me. You're too young to remember—"

"Nobody thought that."

He gives me a level stare, and I know I'm about to find out what everyone is keeping from me. "Intrusive thoughts started to take over. How it would all just be silent if I turned the car head-on into traffic. If I happened to leave the gas on after cooking. Ghosts and ideas haunting me, berating me, never letting me rest. I could not trust myself around my family anymore."

My voice is surprisingly steady when I ask, "Why didn't you ask for help? Going nuclear and leaving—"

"Help came too late." Dad's voice cracks, and I hear how weak he is after the surgery. "I wanted to end it, and I couldn't risk hurting you girls, so I tried to take matters into my own hands."

My heart pounds and my palms sweat, but I force myself to ask, "What did you do?"

He shakes his head, even though the movement can't be comfortable. He isn't able to trust his voice right now. After swallowing audibly, he says, "Your mother found me. Saved my life. Told me to leave and never come back. She couldn't carry us all on her own."

Lips parted in shock, I try to reconcile my own memories of this time with this new, disturbing information. I picture my mother stumbling upon a scene from a nightmare, thinking her one true love would rather say goodbye forever than live another day in our house. "She told me you left, not that she kicked you out."

"I may as well have left. I tried to die. But now I know why I didn't—for this. For today. To try to make it up to you girls as much as I can, even if it will never be enough." His voice is stronger now. Either it's the morphine kicking in, or he's digging down deep to get through our conversation.

I guess everyone had to put on their own oxygen mask first. Mom couldn't do it all, she had to prioritize the greater good of the family. And it sounds like Dad's oxygen mask will always be a little wonky, through no fault of his own. But at what point do we choose others over ourselves? There's a huge part of this saga that doesn't make sense. "If you're trying to make it up to us, then why did you give up guardianship?"

"Because you love Zoey enough to do right by her, and you'll do a far better job of it than I was ever able to."

Tears prick my eyes. "But what if I can't? You know what you're signing me up for. I'm seventeen years old. It wasn't supposed to be me for a long time." Goose bumps prick my arms, and my shoulders curve in.

"You're strong. Stronger than me or your mother."

"That doesn't mean I'm ready for this!"

"This responsibility is going to turn you into something more extraordinary than you already are, because all this pressure will set your soul on fire. You're going to use it to remake the world for Zoey. Burn it all down."

My brain rewinds. The awful neighbor on Halloween. Blake's plan. Blake's parents. Those dumb kids at the gas station. That bigoted transplant list. Back even further. Bullying on the playground. Side-eyes in the grocery store. Lack of services and family support. People constantly underestimating her.

Me included on that last one. Mom too.

"I don't know where to start or what to do." He thinks I can just overhaul everything in one fell swoop if given the chance? Why does he have that amount of faith in me? "It's not fair!" My voice cracks, hoarse from the overwhelming emotions I can't keep down anymore.

"It's not fair," he agrees. "None of this is fair to you, and it hasn't been for your whole life. But you aren't going to carry it around as baggage, you are going to embrace it and *use* it. You're already doing it. How you care—that is innate, that is your strength, and there is no one stronger to fight in your sister's corner." There is a fierce certainty in his voice that makes me think this second brush with death might have changed his perspective on a few things. He picked a hell of a day to be a father again.

My head is spinning. What Dad is saying makes both perfect sense and none at all. I can't tell if I want to laugh or sob. He sees me teetering on the knife's edge and pulls me back. "You won't have to sign anything until you're ready. You can't, anyway, until you're eighteen. Your mom will still be in charge of her. Nothing has to change right away."

The vacancy on the page will still be there, though. Haunting me.

"What's going to happen to you?" I ask.

"I'll head back to Oregon with Rachel once they discharge me. Go about life as usual, I guess." Now that his earlier intensity is gone, his face softens into a fraction of a smile. "I'm feeling better after the surgery than I thought I would."

Before I can respond, the nurse comes back in. "Out, out!" she ushers. "William, you're overextending yourself," she chastises her patient. "I'm ordering a mandatory hour rest before sending in your next visitor."

Whoops! Sorry, Rachel.

"Does Zoey need more recovery too?" I ask.

"She will probably fall asleep again pretty quick," the nurse says. "But you can pop your head in for a minute. Just one minute!"

I go to hightail it out of Dad's room, but when I get to the doorway, I stop. Turning around, I look back to see Dad with his eyes closed, leaning gratefully against the pillows. He looks younger than I ever remember him being. Like a weight has been lifted. "You're more than just a kidney, you know," I tell him. "I hope that one day you can believe it." His eyes pop open, but I'm gone before he can respond.

Crossing the hall, I run into Mom, who looks like she's been hit by a truck but is still smiling. "I'm going to see Zo real quick, then we should go home for a bit while she rests," I tell her. She doesn't fight me on it like I expect, like she actually trusts me and my judgment.

"Okay," she agrees. She sways on her feet. I'll be the one behind the wheel this afternoon. "We did it," she says in a dreamy tone.

"We did." I hold back my next question: *Now what?* The crisis is over, but Dad's words are still fresh in my mind. Now that Zoey's future is more secure, what is it going to look like? Will our family keep on keeping on like we have been? Or will we ever sit down and talk about what we saw at Fides? The truth is staring me in the face, but it hurts to look at it. Zoey deserves more out of life.

When we get out of here, I know who I need to call. I'll sneak Cole's phone number first chance I get.

I push it aside and forget everything except pure joy when I step into Zoey's recovery room. The nurse was wrong; she's not awake but already out like a light. It doesn't matter to me.

I want to climb into bed with her and listen to the sound of her breathing, but I'm too scared to jostle her torso. I lean over and kiss her forehead instead. She knows it's me, even asleep and drugged up, because her mouth lifts into a grin.

Nine months left and some very big decisions to make.

CHAPTER TWENTY

IT ISN'T UNTIL A FEW DAYS LATER THAT THE REALITY OF ZOEY'S FUTURE hits her. "Hookup? Next time?" she asks, looking at Doc Hayes from her hospital bed. Is she asking if next time her dialysis will be back at the regular clinic? I know she's for sure sick of her hospital recovery room, despite the fact that it's filled with bouquets and balloons. The soccer team even sent her a team jersey with "get well soon" messages. Her favorite gift, though, is a Tootsie Roll–shaped squishy from Charlie with a note that just said, *Soon.* It was less menacing than it sounds.

Dr. Hayes is removing Zoey's IV and monitoring equipment in preparation for her discharge. "No, Zoey. We're all done. All done with dialysis, all done with treatments."

Zoey's mouth drops open. "*All done?*" Incredulity is written all over her face. Despite Doc Hayes's earlier explanations of the surgery itself and expectations for the future, I think part of Zoey always assumed the hookups would never fully go away. Now, instead of scheduling the next appointment, there is no dialysis appointment. Instead, there is *freedom.*

"A lot to be thankful for, right?" he says.

She's processing his words, the upload bar creeping forward in her eyes. I know the second my sister fully accepts the truth because her eyebrows fly up to her hairline and she yells, "Ahhh!" To be honest, I think she's handling it better than me and Mom.

Zoey's getting discharged on Thanksgiving with strict instructions to rest as much as possible for the next few weeks and continue taking her cocktail of medications and painkillers. Dr. Hayes needs to prescribe this treatment to all the Larssen women; we deserve a little medication vacation.

"Can I get my own prescription in writing?" I ask him as he's going over the paperwork.

He raises an eyebrow at me, but the pull of his mouth to one side tells me he's trying not to laugh. We have witnessed such a different side to him these post-op days. I think he's relieved beyond belief that the surgery was successful, and that Zoey is going to be okay; he just won't admit how nervous he was. She has this way of worming her way into people's hearts and never leaving, and I think Doc Hayes is really going to miss us now that we won't see him multiple times per week.

"I can prescribe you a multivitamin," he offers.

"The gummy kind?"

"You know it." He pulls a pad out from his white coat and scribbles on it.

"Make it really illegible," I tell him. "I'll show it to my teachers and make them give me an extension on my assignments."

His pen stops moving. "Do you need a doctor's note? A real one?"

Every minute I can spare, I've been at the hospital by Zoey's side. Mom, too, but since she works at the hospital no one has questioned why she took a few personal days. If anything, the whole staff has worked extra hard to give us the royal treatment.

I've never had so many extra treats slipped onto my cafeteria tray. With all the focus on Zoey's recovery, I haven't been honest with how far behind I've fallen.

"It's wonderful how you've been here for your sister," Doc says. "But you need to look after yourself too." He gives Mom a look, as if urging her to jump in. She's fussing over Zoey's pillow placement, even though we're about to leave. He clears his throat. "Jules?"

"Huh?" she glances up. Why is it that Dr. Hayes calls her Jules instead of Julie? Everyone else this week has called her Nurse Julie. Nobody else here calls her Jules. I wonder if Mom realizes that. She's fluffing the pillow with enough ferocity that Zoey flinches.

"I was just telling Kaley that you both need to be taking care of yourselves as well. Caregiver burnout is real."

Mom's hands still and she takes a shaky breath. "I don't know if it feels real yet," she confesses quietly. "But you're right, no more tunnel vision and no more sprinting. Especially you, Kaley." She reaches over and tears off the multivitamin prescription that Dr. Hayes was writing and crumples it up.

"Hey! I need that," I protest.

"Write my daughter an actual excusal note for her school," she says to him.

Doc raises an eyebrow. "Yes, ma'am."

Turning to me, she wraps me up in a hug. "You've been an integral part of this process and Zoey's recovery, but that doesn't mean it has to be at your own expense. You've missed a lot of days, haven't you?"

More than last year, which is saying something. "Not too

many," I lie. "I can still get back on track." That part is not a lie. I can do it, and I have more meaningful motivation now other than wanting to go to college with my boyfriend. Since my conversation with Dad, I've started cultivating a plan. It's in the baby stages, one I haven't voiced out loud to anyone else because I'm not sure how to explain it yet. But it's there, a tiny ember that has started to burn, waiting for the right conditions to alight.

These conditions include applying to Boise State in the coming months, then seeing what happens from there. I don't hate the idea anymore. I'm actually getting excited about it. I know I'll get in, even with my recent poor attendance. My admissions essay is going to kick butt.

There's a new feeling of acceptance in my soul with this plan I'm about to put into motion. A lot of it is thanks to the conversations with my sib group chat and knowing what to do to best help my sister long-term. Mom is going to be thrilled with my college plans whenever I get around to telling her, and I'll even let her believe my decision was because of her influence—something that would have irritated me to no end earlier this fall. I'll let her get her wins in while she can.

She and I may fight for control many steps of the way in the coming years. There are going to be huge changes for all of us, but it's to be expected when we burn down former versions of ourselves and rise from the ashes. Our identities have been defined by being Zoey's family. Fierce protectors. Advocates. Caregivers. When we start to change it, to be brave enough to grow, we might all freak out. I know I'm going to feel raw and exposed, and the urge to rebuild those self-preservation walls around myself and Zoey and get back to the survival-mode routine is going to be overwhelming.

I can't let myself. And it's quite possible Mom and Zoey will hate me some days for it. But too bad, my name will be in ink on the dotted line right next to Mom's, and not like how Dad was involved. We'll be equal partners. Equal guardians. If I'm going to do this, I'm going to do it right.

"Kalcy, phone!" Zoey says, interrupting my train of thought. She pulls Mom off me with surprising strength for someone bedbound, and hands me my cell.

"Nobody texted me," I tell her.

"Picture."

"Sweets, that's the best idea. We should get a family photo before we leave," I announce. My sib chat group will want to see proof of Zoey's "graduation," and so will Leah, Declan, Hannah, Charlie, even Cole. I'll need to send hers with my long list of questions, including but not limited to "Where do you buy your makeup?" and "Can you give me all the details you know about Fides, including the things I don't know enough to ask, and also explain to me the step-by-step development of your life and career and how will I make this all work?"

"Come on, everyone gather around Zoey," I say. "You too, Doc. Scootch in. You're just as much a part of this as we are." Is that a blush I see in his usually calm face? I make a mental note to get his number from Mom's phone and send the photo to him, as well. I'll add her on the thread, too, then get them chatting before I remove myself from the group. Kaley Larssen, queen of subtlety.

Mom and Doc Hayes are on either side of Zoey's bed. I'm

leaning back into her carefully from my perch near her legs. I hold my phone up high. Our faces squish, smiling, into frame while I line up the selfie shot. “Everyone say what, Zo?”

“Peanut butter!”

We’re sitting around the table, about to carve the store-bought turkey, when the doorbell rings. “Got it!” I announce, standing up out of my chair.

Ignoring the doorbell is not an option when Zoey is present, unless I want to be pestered with reminders that someone is, was, and might still be at the door for the next three hours. I smile, even though I had just gotten comfortable in my seat. It’s great to be home with all of us for the first time since the surgery.

Sprinting down the hallway in my fuzzy socks, I almost faceplant on the hard wood. With a surprising amount of agility, I manage to right myself and stay on my feet. I’m not about to let my dinner go cold if I knock myself out. Whoever this is, they’d better have a good reason for interrupting Thanksgiving.

I open the door and find two of the last people I’d expect. Channeling my inner Zoey, I simply ask, “Why?”

Dad had been discharged before Zoey. When Mom and I had gotten to the hospital, we’d simply been informed that he’d left with Rachel early that morning. It’s not like I’d spent a lot of time in there with him after our last conversation, but I did wave at him going in and out of Zoey’s room. I’d even seen him give Mom a smile, which she actually returned. It might have been reflex or relief, but she'd done it just the same. I had expected to at least say goodbye to him before he went back to Oregon, but I wasn't surprised to find he had snuck out. Some habits are hard to break.

Except maybe he did, if him standing next to Rachel on the front porch is any indication. I look down at their entwined hands and wonder if maybe she dragged him here. Her fingers are gripping a bit too tightly. Wait, it's the other way around. I think he's gripping her hand.

"Room for two more?" Rachel chirps.

I stare at them some more. Dad is equally at a loss for words, so I stand aside and let them in. His presence alone fills the room with bittersweet nostalgia. I'm acutely aware of how much time has passed since he last stood in that same spot on his way out. His hair is longer, streaked with gray. Despite the stress of the surgery, his body isn't as thin as it was the night he moved out. It's like there are two versions of him overlapping right now, two photographs of past and present, stacked so the lines are blurred. I can't tell which one I should be looking at.

He's staring at me like he's thinking the same thing.

"Mm! Smells great in here," Rachel says.

I whirl to face her, grateful to break this uncomfortable spell. "Too much like dish soap? Maybe like soup?"

"It smells like turkey," Rachel assures me.

Dad finds his manners. "Yes, delicious," he says. He shifts from foot to foot. Do I detect a wince? Pain from the surgery, or the memories? "We don't have to stay; we were just stopping by on our way out."

Rachel opens her mouth but shuts it a second later. I fill

in what she was about to say. "You got discharged before Zo. I thought you'd be home by now."

"We were partway through the drive and I was eating these terrible protein bars because we didn't want to stop," Rachel rambles. "After a few bites of those I started daydreaming about Thanksgiving and Will said your mom used to make the most amazing pecan pie and then I talked him into turning around so I could maybe try some." She's out of breath and takes a deep inhale to continue the stream of consciousness but is interrupted.

Zoey wanders over to see what the disturbance is about. "Happy Turkey Day!" she announces.

"Hey, Zo, you're up and back in action," Rachel says.

"Dinner?" Zoey asks, staring at Dad.

He holds her gaze a moment before looking down at his shoes. When he puts his hand on the back of his neck, I know he's going to tell her no. But after a breath, he straightens up. "Sure, kid."

His response knocks the wind out of me, like I've already consumed my tryptophan for the night. Somehow, I've manifested the Thanksgiving of my post–parent divorce dreams. It's what every kid longs for in elementary school before they wise up and realize a happy holiday with everyone is just a fantasy, right? As an almost adult, I know this might be a terrible idea.

Mom looks resigned as I bring our unexpected guests over to the table. "I thought you'd left town," she says to Dad.

"Rach pointed out that I didn't say a proper goodbye."

Mom raises an eyebrow. “Can’t make that a habit now, can we?”

“I’m trying not to.”

Mom stands up, goes to the lower cabinet in the kitchen, and pulls out two more plates. She sets them on the table and then grabs a stool from under the bar counter. Trading out her chair for the stool, she rearranges the place settings to cram us all in around the table. “Sit,” she instructs. “There’s always enough room.”

It’s late by the time Dad and Rachel put their shoes and coats back on. “Well, this was nice,” Mom says, and I can tell she’s sincere. She looks so different since Zoey got her transplant. Her face is softer, the sharp edges of her body smoothing out, her shoulders lighter. I haven’t seen her this rested in years. I’m sure it will take her more than a few days to recover—alongside Zoey, who is currently passed out on the couch—but it seems like she’s getting there.

We all have a lot to be thankful for this year. Who’d have thought our family would end up here? Today might also mark the start of a new tradition.

“Well,” Dad says, shrugging.

“Well,” I say. God, somebody better break this loop of awkwardness. Do we hug? No. I need to say something else. “See you in the spring, maybe.”

Dad looks over at Rachel, as if confirming that they might have missed a conversation. She looks as confused as he is.

"I signed up for a Fides family day," I clarify. "Me, Mom, and Zoey. You guys can come if you want. If not, no worries. We don't have to get into it now but look for my email."

"You can stay at the cabin," Dad blurts out at the same time Mom says, "You signed us up?"

Whoops. I had been planning on telling her and Zoey over dinner, but Zoey kept interrupting with her favorite memories of past holidays, including the origin story of Zoey Baloney and the insistence of wrapping up the processed meat to gift on Father's Day instead of a card. She had Rachel rolling, and it was hard to get a word in edgewise. Dad was also laughing. It's like he's a different person. I wonder if it's because he's starting to forgive himself for not being the person he needed to be while we were growing up but is realizing he can still show up in his own way. Not as a dad, not as a guardian, but to the extent of his capabilities. It's enough right now to see him try. We'll see what the next few years bring.

"Yep! I coordinated with the sib group. I think it's time we have real community for Zoey, and us. Maybe it will be her next step, one day, if she chooses, but there's no rush."

Mom's eyes get misty. "I'm so proud of you," she says. "I didn't want to push, not when there's been so much going on." She waves a hand in front of her face, too choked up to continue.

I answer Dad instead. "That's . . . that is a very generous offer, Dad. Thank you. Cole mentioned she'd be happy to have us, but I think we'd rather stay with you. And Rachel."

"Anytime," he says, and it sounds like he really means it.

Rachel is nodding and beaming next to him. I hope everyone stays on board, because if the first family day goes well, we might be back and forth a lot more. But I'm getting ahead of myself.

I usher our guests off the porch and out to their truck. "Okay, bye Dad! Bye, Rachel! Drive safe."

"Drive safe!" Zoey shouts behind me, right into my ear.

"Gah!" I yell, jumping a mile high. "Where did you come from? I thought you were sleeping!"

She laughs at me, like *Obviously I'm not anymore*. Then she asks, "Road trip?"

"Did you hear me talking about Fides, sweets?" She nods. "Yep. We'll take another road trip soon." This time without hauling a dialysis machine.

"It's a big step," Mom reminds me. "Do you think we're ready?" Her soft gaze, almost begging, encompasses both me and Zoey, as if she's trying to freeze this moment in her memory before life changes.

"No one will love her more than us," I assure Mom. "But that doesn't mean we should keep her to ourselves forever. Zoey deserves to have all the doors opened, with her choice to walk through them or not. You don't get to decide for her. *We* don't get to decide for her." I turn back to Zoey. "What do you say, Zo? You've got a whole new kidney and a whole new lease on life. How do you want to spend it?"

EPILOGUE

NEXT FALL

"BURNING THE MIDNIGHT OIL AGAIN?" DECLAN ASKS AS HE POPS HIS head into my dorm.

I startle at my desk. "How did you even get in here?"

He rolls his eyes at me. "Your roommate, obviously. Caught her as she was heading out."

Huh. I hadn't even noticed Leah had left. What time is it? How long have I been staring at the screen? I vaguely remember her saying something and me agreeing, but I don't know what I agreed to. Maybe not to wait up?

I yawn and rub my eyes, trying to clear the words from the computer screen that are seared into my brain and riddled with stuff I still need to fix. "Yeah, this project is nowhere near perfect, and I have to present *either* the pro or the con side at the end of the week. I won't know until the day of."

"You'll get it right," Declan says, coming over to stand behind my chair and read over my shoulder.

I reach back and poke him in his ribs. "We should just switch. Gimme your essay for that mock trial environmental violations case you have to argue on Thursday, the one about the nature preserve. I need to channel my rage right now."

Declan barely notices that I'm mid-rant. I see his lips moving as he reads my work to himself. "Mm-hmm," he says.

At least he's here to provide a little distraction. "I'm so lucky to have such a handsome boyfriend."

"Mm-hmm."

"He's so smart."

"Mm-hmm."

"I bet he wishes he was as smart as his girlfriend."

"*Mm-hmm.*"

"At least he's strong. Strong enough to help construct new garden beds."

He finally breaks his gaze from the screen and fixes me with a stare. "Did you happen to sign me up for something at Fides, babe?"

"I volunteered *us*," I clarify. "We are going to be there, anyway. It's family camp weekend, remember?" Zoey and Mom are picking us both up on their drive over, our third visit to hang out, see some friends, and attend the workshops. It's a long way to travel, but the community is worth it.

Now, if only I can convince Fides to expand into Idaho and form a sister organization, that would be ideal. It's on my to-do list after I graduate BSU, go to law school, and also convince Idaho to have its own state disability program. It will be a long fight, but when you break it down, it's really just three things. Four, if I include the long, long-term plan to set Zoey up to live at the second Fides location one day because she loves it so much. Four steps to accomplish my life's purpose. How many other college freshmen already know what they're meant to do in life? I figure I'm ahead.

"I never forget," Declan says. "I have twenty video calls from Zoey so far to remind me."

Zoey with her own phone is a terrifying sight to behold. I suppose it's my fault; I was a terrible example. "Only twenty? She must be preoccupied this week."

"Yeah, probably calling all her Fides friends. She's excited about the fundraising auction on Saturday night."

"Mom and I took her to get a dress last weekend! Oh, Dad said he'd drive out to help too. Just for the garden part, not the auction."

"So will I be elbow-deep in manure on the compound before or after I'm in a suit?"

"I thought you wannabe eco lawyers liked it that way."

Declan laughs, then kisses the top of my head. "As far as I can see, your assignment looks fine so far. You're overthinking it, but that's a good thing. The ethics portion is really strong. If you want to keep working on it tonight, though, I'll read over it as many times as you need." He spins my chair around to face him.

My phone rings. I glance back at the clock on my computer, and it's almost eleven. Of course I'm still going to answer it.

I swipe up and the camera turns on. "Hey, Zo! Why are you still awake?"

"Declan, phone!" she orders. Of course she knew he'd be here with me.

He leans over so we are cheek to cheek on the screen. "What's up, Zoey?"

She stares us down. "See you soon?" she asks.

"Of course. We'll all be there this weekend," I tell her. "Wouldn't miss it for the world." *This new one I'm working toward, word by word behind this keyboard, just for you.*

ACKNOWLEDGMENTS

I'll be honest, this book would not exist without some very important people.

Firstly, my husband, who is the "planner" to my "dreamer" and has always believed I would get here someday. My children, whose arrivals unlocked a deeper creativity (and need for efficiency) than I could have ever imagined. My parents, who have always wanted the world for me. And obviously, my sisters, who taught me to laugh our way through the journey.

My agent, Michaela Whatnall, who saw right through to the heart of this story in the earliest editions. My editor, Kristin Allard, and the entire team at Norton—Rebecca Munro, Delaney Adams, Hana Anouk Nakamura, and Naomi Duttweiler—who embraced Kaley's chaos and brought her voice to life.

The L'Arche Organization, for inspiring the concept of Fides. The Pen Parentis Organization for motivating me to write the short story that turned into this novel. The Night Owls accountability group for keeping me on track.

Carly for her legal advice and Dr. Adri for her medical expertise. Annie B, for reading every single thing I've ever written.

Thank you.

And to my readers, who have hopefully enjoyed this story despite my self-indulgence in crafting the book I craved but could never find while growing up. As a middle child with an older sister who has severe disabilities, I needed a book that showed me I was not alone in asking the hard questions about the future while appreciating the hilarity of our day-to-day "normal." This story truly is the book of my heart and the one I became a writer to tell.

How lucky am I to say "my" a ridiculous number of times in these acknowledgments and feel impossible gratitude with each? But in the end, the point of all this is for me to let go, hand it to you, and make Kaley and Zoey yours.